Behind the Golden Mask

William G. Collins

Copyright © 2015 William G. Collins
All rights reserved.

ISBN: 1507672209
ISBN 13: 9781507672204

*"May your ka [spirit] live
and may you spend
millions of years,
you who love Thebes,
sitting with your face
to the north wind,
Your two eyes
beholding happiness."*

inscription carved on a white
lotus goblet in Tutankhamun's tomb.

Valley of the Kings.

DEDICATION

For my beloved wife Evangeline Rose, who has always encouraged me to write about Egypt and its glorious past.

CONTENTS

Acknowledgments		ix
Preface		xi
Chapter One	Nen-nesu	1
Chapter Two	Thutmose	9
Chapter Tthree	Ugarit	17
Chapter Four	Gold of Valor	27
Chapter Five	White-water Rapids	37
Chapter Six	Ikhey	47
Chapter Seven	Abar	57
Chapter Eight	Into the Battle	67
Chapter Nine	Intrigue	77
Chapter Ten	Caught	87
Chapter Eleven	Unexpected Choices	97
Chapter Twelve	Love and Marriage	107
Chapter Thirteen	Mysterious Journey	117
Chapter Fourteen	The Valley of the Wind	127
Chapter Fifteen	Tutankhaten	135
Chapter Sixteen	Imperfections	143
Chapter Seventeen	Dangerous Decree	153
Chapter Eighteen	"City of the Horizon"	161
Chapter Nineteen	Family	171

Chapter Twenty	War in the North	181
Chapter Twenty-One	Pharaoh Tutankhamun	191
Chapter Twenty-Two	Victory in the South	201
Chapter Twenty-Three	Ay's Shadow	211
Chapter Twenty-Four	The Hunt	221
Chapter Twenty-Five	The Mask	229
Chapter Twenty-Six	Man of the Spear	237
Afterword	Horemheb with the falcon god Horus	245

ACKNOWLEDGMENTS

I am deeply indebted to the Florida Writers Association's Daytona Beach Group, under the leadership of Veronica H. Hart: Chris Holmes, Bill Dempsey, David Archard, Amanda Alexander, Ethel Wilson, Joyce Senatro, Walter Doherty, Kimberly Park, Mike Berry, Judith Lawrence, Angelo Dalpiaz, Sam Hossler and Virigina Gawthorpe. Without their support and encouragement, and fantastic patience with all the Egyptian names and words, this book would not have been possible.

PREFACE

Just who is the man behind the mask now on display in the Cairo Museum of Ancient Egyptian Antiquities? This golden work of art depicting Tutankhamun's face, known around the world, has come to symbolize Egypt's glorious age. This book is an attempt to peer behind all of the gold, ivory and lapis lazuli, to find the real young man.

Countless books have been written concerning the boy-king's death as a possible murder, but with the scientific tools of the twenty-first century, such ideas have mostly been rejected. Science has provided these instruments for the archeologist's study of ancient ruins and bones, including genetic fingerprinting, computer tomography or CT scans, and DNA testing. They have shed new light on the life and death of this young pharaoh, and enable us to see a more precise five-generation family tree that now includes the young man's parents.

The purpose of this novel is to include some of this latest research in explaining events in the life of the nineteen-year old king who lived during Egypt's Eighteenth Dynasty. The story is told through the eyes of one of the principal players in this drama named Horemheb. He served three pharaohs and became a member of their royal families.

The nickname "Tut" has been avoided, because historians believe such a nickname for the king would never have been used. Common folk, however, must have used shorter versions of these long complicated names. Those in this book are my own invention. To distinguish the special Egyptian spoken by the royals, I have chosen to have them speak formally, avoiding all contractions.

The name of the eternal river would not have been referred to as the "Nile," since the Greeks introduced the name in later Egyptian history. To the sons of *"The Black Land"* or *"Kemet"* it was simply *"the river"*—giver of life and sustenance.

This is a work of fiction, and while based on the latest scientific observations and interpretation of historical facts, it is the author's limited imagination that has brought these characters to life. Any inaccuracies are mine alone.

CHAPTER ONE

NEN-NESU

Horemheb couldn't sleep so he left his bed early. Leaving the house, he walked to the water's edge and sat on a flat boulder, gazing up at the stars. It always took his breath away to see how many lights there were in the night sky. Their reflection in the water only added to their unimaginable number.

Nearby a crocodile splashed into the marshy lake chasing an early breakfast. The young warrior had come home to Nen-nesu, the village of his birth with his friend, the son of an important court official. The sun, almost above the horizon, provided enough light for him to see his reflection in the murky water. As he leaned over, the ruggedly good-looking image of an eighteen-year old stared back at him. Its dark eyes sparkled from a pleasant face. The well-muscled chest and legs bore many small scars; evidence of skirmishes with other soldiers his own age. Grinning at the image, he destroyed it by running his hand over the surface of the water.

"There you are," someone shouted. Horemheb recognized Ramose' voice. "What awakened you so early?"

Looking at him over his shoulder Horemheb said, "Don't know. I just couldn't sleep." Picking up his spear and constant companion, he stood beside his childhood friend and sniffed the gentle breeze. "Can you smell that, Mose? The river will flood soon. I can sense it."

"And I need to go back," Ramose said. "My parents will think I've disappeared for good."

His friend laughed. "Maybe we *should* disappear. Let's run away and follow the river to the Great Sea. Let's find out what's out there."

"Harm, always the dreamer. You know I've got to get back to my studies. Besides, my father would kill me." Ramose felt privileged to be one of the few people the soldier allowed to use his old nickname. His birth name had been Haremheb but as he grew older he changed it to honor Horus.

Horemheb grumbled. "A man without dreams might as well be dead. He'd be as lifeless as stone." Suddenly walking to the water's edge, he used his spear to scare off a crocodile that had become too curious. Turning to face Ramose he waved his arm and pointed at him. "Look at you," he continued. "You don't *need* to dream, brother. You're a nobleman's son and will follow in your father's footsteps. Don't you ever want to be something different?"

Ramose frowned and didn't know how to respond. His clothes revealed the truth of it. His kilt was of the finest linen and he wore a gold collar around his neck. A wide gold band clamped to his right arm gave evidence of his social standing. Even so, the young man felt insecure. He stood almost a head shorter than his friend, and his body revealed he had never done any hard work in his life.

"Now look at me," Horemheb continued, pointing to himself. "I'm the orphan of ordinary folk. They weren't cheese makers as some of my enemies have said. My father had a good business as a stonemason, that is until he and mother died of the fever two years ago."

"I know," Ramose said. "Why didn't you take over his trade? How did you end up in Thebes?"

Horemheb scowled. "My stomach's growling so loudly I can't hear what you're saying. Let's get some food first." Using his spear as a walking stick, he led his friend back to the house. The most wonderful aroma from the kitchen greeted them and made their mouths water.

"Morning, young Lords," Menefer called to them, placing fresh bread and a pot of honey on the table. They greeted her happily and washed their hands in a basin sitting near the entrance to the kitchen.

"You two were up early," an older man said. He took his place at the table.

"I felt restless, good Father," Horemheb replied, using the honorific title for his father's partner with whom they had been staying. Buneb had taken over the house and business for a sum given Horemheb, enabling the young man to become an army recruit in Thebes. Joining their host at the table, Menefer brought them some cheese and broiled fish. A jar of homemade beer helped wash it all down.

Later, his wife cleared the table. Buneb said, "You must tell your father, my Lord, that we send him our sincerest greeting."

Ramose bowed his head courteously. "He'll be honored, friend Buneb." His father had sent several kidets of gold to pay for their food during the young men's visit, as well as for any inconvenience in housing them.

"We'll be leaving tomorrow," Horemheb said. "Ramose needs to get back, and my captain will be sure I've gone missing."

"Is military training all you had hoped it would be, my son?" Buneb asked.

"Even more than I had hoped. We've already had two engagements with desert marauders. The hand-to-hand combat with the bloodthirsty jackals proved we are ready."

"Yes, and he even brought back a souvenir," Ramose bragged. He made Horemheb turn his back so their friend could see the scar.

Embarrassed, Horemheb said, "It's nothing. The dagger didn't go in very far."

The stonemason laughed. "If I know anything about soldiers, Horemheb, that will not be the last scar added to your collection. In fact I know where there are more on that body of yours from when you were in the village militia." He saw Horemheb's face turn red and added, "It's somewhere on that backside of yours if I remember."

"Seth's foul breath. I get enough teasing about it from my comrades, Father," Horemheb said.

"Enough of that swearing, young man," Menefer chided.

"All right, I'm sorry. I'm just glad I can say it wasn't a coward's scar but a lucky shot by a pair of thieves." Buneb laughed as he left them and headed out to work.

The captain of *"Ra's Glory,"* seeing the obvious nobility of Ramose, pestered him for the latest news from Thebes. Horemheb chose to stand at the bow, taking in the pungent fragrance of the water as it flowed past. He laughed at a herd of hippos angrily flapping their ears at the ship for interrupting their nap. Naked children running along the shore waved to him.

The voyage south to the capital would take three days. They were sailing against the current and it would also mean two nights ashore. Navigation on the river at night could be dangerous if not impossible. The merchant ship, while smaller than pharaoh's galleys had a similar construction. Boards brought from lands in the north were assembled using strong new ropes, then sealed with pitch. The larger ships of the king now used wooden pegs, which swelled, tightening the boards. It made them stronger and watertight—a skill developed by the Phonecians.

Captain Metjen told his passengers, "We'll dock at Khmun tonight. The Inn of the White Lotus will have a room for you I'm sure."

"It's where we stayed on our journey here," Horemheb said. "You're right, they have good food and beer." The young soldier would have preferred sleeping on deck and sharing the sailor's food, but Ramose wanted a good bed with feather pillows. For some strange reason he preferred them to the wooden headrest used by most Egyptians.

By late afternoon the rudder men maneuvered the ship toward the dock of the ancient town. Khmun, situated on the border between Upper and Lower Egypt had become a wealthy opulent city. It drew thousands of scribes from all over the country, to the great temple of Thoth. The Ibis bird, symbol of the god, lived here by the thousands. The long down-turned billed creatures are honored and protected by law. The top of the temple of Toth came into view and the sailors threw their mooring ropes to men on shore.

Taking his ever-present spear with him, Horemheb led the way to the inn. The proprietor greeted them happily, knowing they paid well before. Ramose had entrusted their small purse to his friend, and in addition to the spear, Horemheb kept a dagger strapped to his thigh just in case.

"More beer," Ramose ordered half way through the meal. When they finished, he ordered more drinks, but couldn't make himself heard above the noise of the other customers.

"You've had enough," Horemheb grumbled. Making Ramose lean on his arm, they climbed the stone steps to their room. They had no sooner gotten inside than they were attacked. Throwing Ramose onto the bed, Horemheb stabbed the man who attacked first. Anticipating a second intruder, he crouched down and thrust his dagger into the man's side, slicing him open. Another man headed for the door, but Horemheb blocked his way and stabbed him in the chest, killing him instantly.

Ramose groaned and Horemheb realized one of the dead thieves had fallen on top of his friend. Pulling the body from the bed he dragged it to the door, his only source of light. The second man started moving again and Horemheb finished him off. Once he laid all three bodies outside their door, he rushed downstairs and yelled for the proprietor.

"You'll die for this," Horemheb yelled. "You're responsible for the safety of your guests." Turning to those still in the dining area he shouted, "Someone bring the Medjays. Hurry" Pharaoh's personal police force consisted of volunteers who made up the king's strong arm of the law. They had a reputation for being extremely ruthless with criminals.

"Please my Lord," the owner of the inn begged. "They'll shut us down."

"As they should," Horemheb yelled back. "My friend and I could have died tonight, and he is a member of pharaoh's court." At those words the man fell to his knees and begged for mercy.

"What's the trouble here?" a large burly guard asked, entering the inn. Three others came with him and all four were taller than Horemheb.

"Upstairs," Horemheb said. "And this man's responsible." The officer in charge went up the steps and quickly returned, not pleased with what he saw.

"Who's done this?" he asked. When Horemheb told him he alone had dispatched the thieves the man rubbed his small goatee and said, "It looks like you didn't need *us* after all!"

The Medjays carried the bodies down to the entrance but Horemheb sensed something not quite right. He counted four bodies. "Wait!" he exclaimed. Kneeling over Ramose's body he started to laugh. "This is one of the king's courtiers, my friends. He's just drunk and that's the blood of one of the attackers all over him." Horemheb shook his friend who groaned in protest. "I'll put him back to bed." Lifting him onto his shoulder, he carried his unconscious companion back to their room.

"By the gods," Ramose exclaimed when he awoke and found himself covered in blood. "Horemheb, by Seth's breath. What happened?" Suddenly his hangover hit him and he groaned, "Oh my head's going to explode!"

"Quiet," Horemheb growled. He was still trying to sleep on a makeshift bed on the floor. "Go have a bath." Pulling the covers back over his head he ignored the complaints.

Ramose went down to the bathing area behind the inn. There were no servants to help him as he entered the tiled pool at the rear of the garden. That surprised him, as did the Medjay stationed at the entrance. When he finished, he wrapped a towel around his waist and returned to his room.

Horemheb tried to tell him what happened in the night, but Ramose wasn't listening. He could only complain, "I'll have to buy another kilt."

"Mose, will you listen!" Horemheb insisted. "I killed three thieves who were waiting for us when we came upstairs last night. We could have been murdered."

A blank look remained on his friend's face. "You mean that blood wasn't *my* blood?" He suddenly caught on and said, "My father would have killed me." That made Horemheb burst out laughing, releasing some of the tension of their brush with death.

Horemheb mumbled. "I'll go and find you a kilt. You can't walk around like that. The Medjays have closed the inn, and we need to get to the ship."

As her last two passengers hurried on board, The "*Glory of Ra*" began to lower the mainsail. Captain Metjen took them aside and asked, "What happened to you last night? My crew has been talking."

"Some thieves tried to get the better of us, Captain. We surprised them," Horemheb explained. Ramose felt they didn't need to explain their actions and walked aft. He enjoyed watching the rudder men navigate the ship out into the middle of the current.

"That's not all my men heard, young man," Metjen objected. "You killed them by yourself."

Horemheb nodded. "That's what army training does for you, Captain. Trying not to grin he said, "They didn't stand a chance!"

Laughing and slapping the warrior on the shoulder Metjen said "Ramose is lucky to have you as a friend!"

"Well, I'm not so sure he thinks so," Horemheb chuckled. "We should thank Horus for saving our lives."

"Even so," the captain declared. "All honor to your god."

The day's journey to Qua proved uneventful except for a belligerent encounter with a floating herd of hippos. Captain Metjen made sure he gave them a wide berth. The hills around the valley gave the town its name. However, because of its small size, it could not provide accommodation for the passengers. They would have to sleep on deck that night.

Next morning, at sunrise, they sailed for Abydos half a day away. The ancient city claimed to be the final resting place of the sacred head of Osiris. A large necropolis just outside the town provided a door into the afterlife. Many pharaohs of the past, including Narmer, son of the Scorpion king were buried here.

Lord Anen, distant cousin of the reigning Pharaoh Amenhotep welcomed the two young men. As administrator of the city and a good friend of Ramose's father, the nobleman welcomed them to his villa. Lady Nithotep arranged for two young women to join them for the evening. Ladies Nofret and Mereryet were excellent companions and while they spent more time entranced by Horemheb, Ramose just liked being in their company. Lady Mereryet proved an accomplished harpist, calming them with her relaxing music.

Later, when they retired for the night, Ramose said, "Nofret would make a beautiful wife don't you think?"

"Not for you, brother. Your father will choose the woman for you and you know it."

Ramose grumbled. "Like you always say, brother—I can still dream can't I?"

"Yes, but when it comes to you and women, that's a dream that will never come true." Horemheb hadn't intended for his words to sound so unfeeling, and regretted them as soon as they left his mouth.

"And what about Lady Mereryet?" Ramose asked. "I saw you smiling at her."

"She pleased me, that's true, but I'm not yet of noble blood. She's out of my reach. I'm just being realistic."

"When you say 'not yet,' what do you mean, Harm?"

"Horus will bring me to a place of leadership which will change my humble origins, brother. One day I will be someone of nobility."

Ramose chuckled. "Ah, I see, another dream, is that it?"

"The *only* dream my friend," his companion sighed, "now go to sleep."

"We'll reach Thebes by midafternoon, young masters," the captain assured his passengers. About twenty other travelers had come on board at Abydos, including an officer of the Royal Guard Horemheb knew.

As they stood watching the capital grow larger on the horizon, Horemheb addressed the officer. "What took you from your unit, Captain Khui?"

"My father's burial at Abydos, may his name be remembered," Khui said. "At his advanced age, the gods were merciful in taking him in his sleep."

"I rejoice with you, my Lord that he has reached the golden afterlife," Horemheb said.

"I pray it is so. Perhaps one day when you've finished your training, you might consider serving in the king's Guards. Your captain has told me good things about you, even if you are only a fledgling."

Horemheb laughed at being reminded that he was not yet a falcon. "I can think of no higher honor, Captain. Please remember my name."

Grinning, Captain Khui answered. "Who else *could* have such a name? I'm glad you are Horus' man. I *will* remember."

"Thank you, my Lord. It would be my greatest honor to serve the king. When I've finished my training, I'll seek you out."

Ramose interrupted to say the ship had docked and he could see his father's servants waiting for him. "Be sure to come home when you have your leave, Harm. We'll have much to talk about. Thank you for taking me to your village, and for saving my life. I owe you a great deal."

"Yes you do, Mose, and don't forget it."

Suddenly a commotion on the dock caused Ramose to rush to the railing. One of the sailors hurried ashore and when he returned shouted something to the crew. Ramose approached the captain then walked over to tell to his comrades.

"It's pharaoh," he told them. "He's dying!"

CHAPTER TWO

THUTMOSE

Lord Aperel embraced his son as soon as he entered the garden. The beautiful villa stood on an elevation overlooking the river to avoid the annual inundation. The family enjoyed sitting on the veranda watching the mighty river race to the Great Sea.

After they greeted each other Ramose had to ask. "Is it true? Is Amenhotep dying?"

Lord Aperel sat down on one of the benches and shook his head. "Lord Ibebi thought at first his majesty had been poisoned, and a foolish servant spread the rumor. Everyone believed it, but the physician told the royal family he'll recover."

"Thank the gods," Ramose said. It sounded like prayer.

"Let it be so," his father intoned.

"Mose," his mother said. Her pleasant voice called to him from the house as she hurried out to join him in the garden. Her son stood and lovingly embraced

Lady Kasmut. She seated herself beside her husband in the cool shade of their private oasis. A small oval pool filled with small colorful fish completed their delightful paradise.

His father said, "You look good. The journey must have agreed with you."

"Very much, my Lord. Horemheb's village proved a pleasant change from the city." He went on to tell them everything, including how he helped Horemheb thwart an attack by thieves.

His father only smiled, knowing the opposite might be closer to the truth. Horemheb had always been the stronger of the two. He would wait to get the real story from his son's friend.

His mother didn't like to hear such things. "How shocking! I'll have to speak to Horemheb about putting you in that kind of danger."

"No harm done, Mother. The Medjays did what they always do."

His father changed the subject. "You will be pleased to learn, my Son, that his majesty has asked for you by name. We'll go to him when his health is better. I suspect he wants you to accompany the Crown Prince to Mitanni on a special mission."

"Mitanni?" his wife said. "Those barbarians. Why didn't you object, Husband?"

Lord Aperel laughed. "One doesn't object to a god, my Love. Anyway King Shuttarna is our ally and has wanted this diplomatic mission for a long time."

"Do you think I'm ready, Father?" Ramose asked. He sounded unsure of himself.

"I've taught you everything, Mose. The Prince likes you and pharaoh himself chose you." Ramose and his mother could hear the pride in the man's voice. Suddenly his father had an afterthought, "Now if we could only get Horemheb to accompany you, it would put me at ease."

Ramose jumped up. "I can arrange it, Father. We met Captain Khui of the Guards on the ship today. He wanted Horemheb to join them when his training is over. I'm sure he can arrange for him to come with us. It's a great idea."

"You see, Mother, this boy's mind is always working—just like his father."

Lady Kasmut scowled. "Yes, dear, whatever you say. Now come along, our boy must be starving." Ramose kissed her on the cheek as he lovingly put his arm around his mother's waist and walked with her into the house.

"Are you certain he's ready, Khamet?" Captain Khui asked.

"He's my finest trainee," Khamet said. "Regrettably I don't like the idea of his leaving the Fifth Regiment so soon. He'd make a good officer."

"Excellent. I've heard good reports about him from my guards. Send him to me officially at the end of the week. Prince Thutmose has asked for him specifically."

Such a request carried the weight of a royal command, and Khamet knew he had no choice. He slapped his fist across his chest in salute. "I hope this doesn't go to his head. He's a very ambitious young man and already has a high opinion of himself."

Khui laughed. "As we all did once, brother. But I'm sure the Guards will clip his wings if he gets too high and mighty."

When Khui had gone, Khamet sat for a moment regretting the loss of the young man he also considered a friend. Finally, he sent his aide to call him. When Horemheb arrived the young man saluted and stood at attention.

"Well, it looks as if your god is watching over you, spearman. On the last day of the week, you will report to Captain Khui of the Royal Guards. He'll give you a document officially transferring you to his service." He grinned, waiting to see how the young man would respond.

The young man shouted, "Horus be praised. I thank you too, Captain. I know you must have recommended it, and I'm grateful."

"Just make us proud, soldier. You're the best swordsman and archer this unit has seen in a long time. Your prowess as spearman is unsurpassed by anyone I've known. I'll be sorry to see you go, but I certainly won't miss your loud snoring on patrol." Horemheb burst out laughing as did the commander.

Khamet called for his aide and ordered a jar of beer for them both. The two men shared a drink, not only as friends, but as warriors in the king's service.

"Let me give you a bit of advice," Khamet said. The older warrior wiped his mouth with the back of his hand. "Prince Thutmose will be our next pharaoh, so try to impress him—he could take you far in achieving that dream of yours."

Horemheb stretched out his long legs because the chair was too small. "Tell me about him, Commander."

"Amenhotep has trained him well. The courtiers respect him, and he is just in all his decisions. He's ten years older than you and does not like anyone getting close to his sisters, and don't forget he has four of them. Be especially wary of Princess Sitamun. Some say she will become one of his wives."

"His sister?"

"Yes, pharaohs have done so in the past, although many believe it weakens the royal bloodline, and children of such marriages are not always healthy." The officer took another swig of beer and went on. "Oh, and don't be too friendly with his young brother Amenhotep. They are only five years apart, but there's a strong rivalry there. Even though pharaoh has named Thutmose his successor, many of us believe the crown prince fears his younger brother."

Horemheb tried to get comfortable on his chair but found it impossible. Leaning forward he helped himself to some more warm beer. "Thank you, Sir. I'll remember your advice. My greatest wish is to serve the royal family in some way."

"Horus will protect you, little falcon," Khamet said. He teased him, now mellowed by the beer. He knew that his young colleague felt guided by Horus, thus the reminder that Horemheb was only a fledgling and had a long way to go. "Be sure to turn in your weapons to the armory when you muster out."

"All but my spear, Captain." Horemheb stood slowly but couldn't salute very well, so he steadied himself for a moment, and then left the officer's quarters.

Ramose's nerves were getting to him as he made his way to the king's council chamber. Fragrant cedar wood covered the walls of the large room that contained an enormous table and chairs. Colorful paintings of pharaoh's exploits adorned the bright blue ceiling. When the Crown Prince came in, the young man did obeisance on the polished floor awaiting permission to stand.

"Arise my friend. When we are alone or in council you will not be required to prostrate yourself before me." Thutmose sat in the beautifully carved chair at the head of the table and looked closely at the young man. "Do you know why I have called you?"

"Only that it involves the Mitanni, Highness." Ramose took care not to look the prince in the eye.

"The Lord Chamberlain tells me you have studied their ways and know some of their language." The prince's inflection made it a question.

"Yes, Highness, and I know they were once our enemy."

"True enough, but for now my father wants closer ties with them. Our Vizier, your father, speaks highly of your knowledge and that pleases us. If and when we are pharaoh, we will need someone like him as *our* Vizier. I will be keeping a close eye on you." The prince then did the unthinkable—he motioned for Ramose, an ordinary commoner, to sit down. Ordinary persons were never allowed such a privilege in pharaoh's presence, or with any member of his family.

"Now, you have our permission to look at us directly when we are alone or in a meeting. In public, however, it will not be tolerated."

"You are most kind, Highness." This time Ramose looked directly at him.

Shifting from the royal we, the prince said, "I will call you Mose since all your friends do, and I too would like to be your friend." Thutmose's tone left no room for objections.

"Of course, Highness."

The prince now got to the real reason he had summoned Ramose. "Now tell me about your friend Horemheb. Can he also be trusted, with our lives I mean?"

Ramose relaxed, happy to talk about his childhood friend. "He's a good warrior, Highness. His parents owned a stonemasonry and died when he was a boy. He's an expert with spear, bow and sword. In fact, he recently killed three thieves single-handedly when they tried to kill us in our sleep"

"Single handedly?" Thutmose repeated. "But you were with him."

Ramose's face turned red. "Yes and no, Highness. I was so drunk I don't even remember. It was the Medjays who told me the next morning and showed me the bodies."

The prince burst out laughing. "Indeed. Remind me not to give you any strong drink if I am ever in danger." He meant it as a joke and laughed again good-naturedly. Ramose laughed too, but lacked the prince's enthusiasm.

"Well, I am pleased to tell you that Horemheb will join my personal guard and with you as my interpreter we'll leave Thebes in two days. Bring whatever documents you may need for translation, and personal items you deem necessary."

Ramose liked the prince. Tall like his father, his chest muscles were chiseled and he had a pleasant face. With his head shaved, the custom for men of the royal family, he wore the princely braid on the right side of his head. It designated him pharaoh's successor with the golden symbol of the Aten attached to the end of it. His large eyes were a mixture of brown and malachite green and they gave his face a pleasant friendliness. His eyes put everyone at ease.

Ramose forgot his place for a moment, then suddenly realized his audience with the prince had ended. He stood and bowed his head politely. "Highness," he said, and Thutmose nodded as he watched the young man leave.

The transition from the army to the guards did not prove easy. Horemheb's new comrades let him know they didn't think he deserved such a promotion, and were eager to make him prove himself.

"I'm pleased you're coming with us Harm," Ramose told him the morning they left Thebes. They stood at the railing of one of pharaoh's galleys given to the prince. The men of the regiment took their places in the hold prepared for the journey north. Some came on deck to assist the sailors in storing the prince's belongings.

As Horemheb and his friend watched the prince come on board, Horemheb spoke in a quiet voice. "I have a lot to prove on this journey, brother." The sailors brought Thutmose's chariot up the walkway and lowered his two white horses carefully into the hold where they could be kept calm. The ship's crew prostrated themselves as the prince walked on deck, while the guardsmen knelt on one knee, saluting him with their fists.

The prince addressed the ship's captain, motioning for him to stand. "Greetings Lord Neferu. We are in your hands."

Neferu bowed his head slightly. "Welcome, Highness, and may the gods give us a fair wind."

"May Shu be listening. Take us out when you're ready."

Neferu gave the signal, and the mooring ropes and gangway were pulled onto the deck. The great rectangular sail lowered from the top spar, as the crew pulled on ropes and pulleys, engaging more than thirty men. Its canvas filled with the morning breeze. With assistance from the strong current, the *Dazzling Disk of the Sun* left Thebes to the cheers of the crowd who came to see them off.

Horemheb looked up at the sail. Normally the royal galleys carried a falcon on their sails. Instead he saw the symbol of the Aten, the sun disk. "Why has pharaoh placed that symbol on the great sail instead honoring Horus, Captain?"

Neferu scowled and put his finger in front of his lips. "Amenhotep is loyal to Amun *and* Horus, but has recently adopted the sun disk for his special veneration. You mustn't question such things openly, guardsman. There are too many ears on this vessel." Horemheb nodded and said no more.

"I see pharaoh has sent your friend Mose as well," Neferu said. "Does he speak Hurrian?"

"Yes, his father made him learn it last year. Pharaoh's Vizier has had to use it himself in negotiations with the Mitanni over the years."

"Look at that," Neferu said turning his head toward the upper deck. Thutmose and Ramose sat under the shade of a sail rigged to protect them from the sun. "I envy your friend's chance to sit across from the prince and converse with him as a friend."

The prince sipped some wine while a servant brought freshly baked bread. Thutmose helped himself to a slice, lathering it with golden honey. "Let me tell you about this mission, Mose," he began. "Our father and King Tushratta have agreed to a marriage between our two countries. Our task is to bring Princess Tadukhepa to Thebes, it's as simple as that."

Ramose didn't respond. He knew he must wait for the prince to let him speak.

Thutmose added, "We will dock at Awen and continue through the delta and into the Great Sea. From there we will sail north to Ugarit where the princess's party will be waiting for us."

Ramose simply nodded and helped himself to some bread and honey.

Late in the afternoon their ship arrived at the ancient city of Awen. It was the oldest center for the worship of Ra—the god of the sun. As soon as the crowds saw the royal galley with the Aten emblazoned on its sail, they began cheering and clapping their hands.

"We will not go ashore," the prince told Captain Khui and his men. "We'll leave tomorrow at first light. Make sure any supplies we need are brought on board immediately."

The Captain of the Guard risked his life by interrupting. "Very good, Highness. I would only suggest your stallions be brought up and allowed to graze. My men will take care of them if you agree."

"Of course, Khui. Thank you for reminding us."

Horemheb supervised bringing up the horses from the hold with ropes and pulleys, and two guards walked them down the walkway to a field of grass nearby. At least two hours of sunlight remained. The newest guardsman stood at the railing watching the dockworkers carry cargo onto the deck. He grinned with pleasure when he saw that the prince had ordered plenty of clay jars filled with beer.

Suddenly, something caught his eye. On one of the dockworker's clothes a shiny object flashed in the sun. Horemheb turned toward it and watched in horror as the man dropped what he was carrying and leapt across the railing heading for the royal cabin.

Jumping over the barrier he ran after the man, bringing him down only a few feet from the prince. The man cried out and stabbed at the guardsman with his dagger trying to get to the royal person. Horemheb knocked him out with his fist unaware that blood began to flow from a wound on his own chest. Thutmose saw it and rushed to his side.

The prince pointed to the dockworker. "Take that jackal away and restrain him. "We'll decide what we will do with him. Send for the physician."

"That was quick thinking, my friend," the prince declared, helping Horemheb sit down. "Our archers didn't even have a chance to react." Throwing formal language to the wind he exclaimed, "You've saved my life, by the gods." Horemheb simply nodded but was beginning to feel woozy. Another guardsman pressed a cloth onto his stab wound and helped him down to the main deck where the royal healer waited.

An object had fallen out of the assassin's tunic and landed on the deck. Thutmose picked it up and examined the piece of papyrus. Some words had been scratched on it, and as he read them his face drained of color. Closing his eyes in disbelief he opened them slowly and read the words again:

"Death to the sons of Aten!"

CHAPTER THREE

UGARIT

    The physician cleaned Horemheb's wound and before stitching it up made him drink some wine. "You are fortunate the gods were with you, son," the old man said. "The wound is deep but the dagger didn't puncture your lung."
    Horemheb growled in pain, his words slurring. "Bless Horus."
    Pouring wine from a skin, the healer mixed white powder made from willow bark into his cup. "Drink more of this," he insisted. "It will help the pain."
    Captain Khui stood beside his guardsman. "The prince wants you to come to his cabin. Can you walk?"
    "Yes, Commander, but I'm a little drunk. I'm not sure what the healer put in my wine so I'm not responsible for anything I say."
    Khui chuckled as he helped him stand. Horemheb leaned on the captain's shoulder as they climbed the steps to the royal cabin.

Thutmose seemed genuinely concerned when he saw the size of Horemheb's bandage. "How is he really, Khui?"

"His head is a little fuzzy from the wine and sedative, Highness, but his lung has not been punctured. The healer told me to keep an eye on him when the fever starts."

Thutmose nodded. Infection claimed too many lives. "Bring his bed here, Captain, and I will watch with you."

"As you say, Highness." This surprised the officer. The royal family did not allow physical contact with the common people. One could not sit in their presence or touch them on pain of death. Khui signaled for two of his men to bring a cot to the prince's cabin, and as the sedative took full effect, they helped Horemheb lie down. Thutmose brought his chair closer to the small bed so he could sit beside the wounded man. The crew and guardsmen couldn't believe what they were seeing. That pharaoh's son would do such a thing became the main topic of conversation.

"This may not be the time, Highness," Khui said, "but a delegation is here led by the governor of the city. They've been disgraced by what's happened, and the fact that a worker from Awen has done this is beyond their understanding."

Thutmose frowned. "We are *not* pleased and will *not* receive them, Captain. We have had time to reflect on the matter and are convinced their security failed us. We want the Medjays to get to the bottom of this attack. Tell them the city will feel our father's wrath when he learns what happened here today."

"And rightfully so, Highness. Each dockworker is to be checked before coming on board the royal galley. The local guard have failed us. We will give those arrested to the Medjays for interrogation. What about the assassin?"

"He will be cut in pieces like our Father Osiris, beginning with the least important body parts," the prince said. "All pieces will be thrown to the crocodiles and may his Ka disappear into Seth's darkness forever." It took him a few minutes to control his temper before continuing. "Bring Ramose here—he's Horemheb's friend after all, and let him sit with us."

"Highness," Khui saluted as he left the cabin.

The galley sailed from Awen even before Ra appeared in the east. At the place where the giant river enters the marshy delta, it divides into seven branches.

Captain Neferu navigated his ship to the westernmost tributary. Once at the Great Sea, they would follow the coastline north.

Horemheb and his friend couldn't believe it when they saw the endless expanse of the sea. Most of the soldiers had never seen a horizon without land, and a much cooler wind from the northern mountains filled the sail. It also caused large waves to rock the ship in ways only experienced sailors could handle.

At midday an unusual thing happened. Drops of water began to fall gently from the sky—a phenomenon most had never seen in their lifetime. Rain rarely fell in the Black Land of home. Ramose noticed a change in the color of Horemheb's face, and reached out and touched him. "He's very hot, Highness."

Thutmose walked over and felt the young man's forehead and chest. "He's burning up."

Khui had seen this many times before on the battlefield and spoke up. "We must keep him cool, Highness. We'll have to bathe him with water here on the deck."

"Yes of course. Carry on," Thutmose said. He too had seen enough wounded men in battle to know what this could mean. Carrying the semiconscious Horemheb down to the deck, they removed his clothes, then, lowered buckets over the side to collect water. They poured it over him, keeping it up through the night until the physician announced the fever had broken and the danger passed.

Ramose helped him dry him off and handed him his kilt. The elderly healer wrapped the wound with clean bandages, and even though his chest was very tender, Horemheb walked slowly back to the cabin.

"Horus continues to help you, Harm, if you'll permit me to address you so," Thutmose said. Horemheb nodded, and the prince continued. "First that encounter with the three thieves, and now this. The gods must like you."

Horemheb smiled a little, touched by the prince's kindness. "It is more important for me, Highness, that I find your favor," he said. "Of course my mother had told me ever since my birth, that Horus had something special for me. It's just not my time to die."

"Well your mother, may her name be remembered, told you the truth because as of this day, you are Captain Khui's assistant. When we return to Thebes, we will see that pharaoh honors you more properly for what you've done!"

Horemheb simply nodded, but when he saw the big grin on Ramose's face, he grinned back.

They spent their first night in the safety of the sheltered port of Sidon. No one could go ashore. The mooring provided calmer water and the passengers and crew were relieved the rocking and tossing had ended.

Three days later, they reached their destination and the sudden arrival of such a magnificent galley at Ugarit drew large crowds. As soon as the ship had settled in its berth, the royal guards disembarked and formed a defensive line on the dock.

The prince's chariot and horses were brought ashore, and his driver led the animals to some grass nearby. The groom rubbed the animals' necks and muzzles to help calm them in their new environment. With the climate so much cooler, the Egyptians, now uncomfortable to be bare-chested, accepted the prince's suggestion that Khui purchase suitable clothing at the market.

"No delegation from the city has come to greet you, Highness," Ramose said. "Don't you find that unusual?"

The prince scowled. "Something must be wrong. Take some men and find out."

Khui saluted. Ramose went with him down the gangway. Choosing twenty well-armed archers, the Egyptians wanted to let onlookers know they would not tolerate interference.

Horemheb suddenly spoke up. "The princess cannot come Highness, of course." He spoke as if he had seen a vision. "She is being prevented from meeting you—I'm sure of it."

His words stunned the prince. "Perhaps she's just been delayed on her journey," Thutmose said. "It's a long way from Washshukanni to the coast."

Horemheb nodded, choosing not to argue with his friend. The prince invited him to join him for the morning meal and Horemheb accepted politely. A servant brought bread, cheese and fruit juice. The prince and commoner shared the morning meal.

Afterward, Thutmose confided the details of his father's forthcoming marriage. Then he added, "Pharaoh will be sending me south to Nubia when we get back. There has been some trouble beyond the first whitewater rapids, and you will accompany me."

Horemheb's heart suddenly beat faster. He saw another opportunity to prove his worth. "I am yours to command, Highness. I have heard the People of the Bow are fierce warriors and giants compared to us." Admiring Egyptians had given the name to their African enemy to the south.

"Good. You and I will see if it is true. Father says they are the best warriors he ever faced, and they take no prisoners."

"They'll not be able to withstand your power, Highness," Horemheb said. He spoke with such conviction the prince could do nothing but grin.

An hour passed before Khui and his men returned. He and Ramose walked up to the higher deck and waited. Thutmose could see by their expressions that the news would not be good.

"The princess has been ambushed just outside the city and her guards are dead. We saw where the abduction took place, Highness. Her escort still lay killed on the ground, that is, all but one survivor. He walked into town and delivered a note to the city administrator."

Ramose handed the message to the prince. "It is written in Hurrian, my Lord. It says,

"Two wagons of gold.
cave of the Hawk tomorrow
when the sun is high."

Captain Khui continued. "The men of the local garrison know where the cave can be found, Highness, and the surviving guard told us there are about thirty in the band of thieves."

"By Seth's backside," Thutmose shouted. "Two wagons of gold. Where can we find such a ransom? It's pure madness. She's probably dead already."

Ramose allowed his friend's anger to subside. "Can't the governor of the city provide some gold, Great Prince?".

Khui, however, had been giving the thieves' demand a great deal of thought. "Perhaps they won't have to, my Lord. All we need do is try to fool these fellows into *thinking* the wagons contain gold. At least long enough for us to organize a rescue."

"Yes, yes, a good suggestion," the prince said. "Let's think this through."

Horemheb's chest hurt and he winced as he shifted his weight on his chair. "Khui and I can go back to the city officials and get more information about the cave, Highness. We'll also ask about the gold, with your permission of course."

Thutmose agreed. "Go and see what else you can learn. Surely these jackals will expect us to take at least a day to respond to their demands." Turning to Horemheb he asked, "Are you sure you're well enough to do this?"

"Yes, Highness, my chest feels alright. Just give me another chance to serve."

"As a guardsman, you know your body's strength. Go with Khui if that is your choice." Horemheb smiled. He bowed his head, stood slowly and saluted.

Ugarit was like all the other ports along the coast of the Great Sea. Its docks were filled with the merchandise of many countries; sweet-smelling spices and silk cloth from the east. The sounds of Phoenician, Hurrian, and Greek tongues selling their goods made a babble of noise as they passed by. Ramose joined his friends in case translation proved necessary. The three headed into the center of town.

"We have to talk to that surviving guard again," Horemheb growled. "He must know where the cave is located."

"He's at the city barracks," Ramose said. "We can start there."

When they arrived, Ramose explained in Hurrian what they wanted and took them to the princess's guard.

"Ah, my Lord you're back," he said addressing Ramose. "Have you brought the ransom so soon?

"It is being prepared," Ramose replied in the man's tongue.

"I worry about her Highness," the man lamented," and Ramose translated.

"I don't trust him," Horemheb grumbled. "Ask him about the cave, Mose."

When the man heard the question, he shifted his feet and wouldn't look them in the eye. He told Ramose he didn't know. He explained that he had been tied up and blindfolded before being beaten and abandoned on the road, far from where the ambush occurred.

"Bah!" Horemheb exclaimed. "Let's ask some of the men in the local garrison."

"Very well," Khui said. He led them to the garrison commander who received them cautiously. Egypt had been their enemy for many years.

"One of my sergeants knows that region well, Captain" the officer said. "I'll send for him." While they were waiting, he served his visitors some red wine, which the Egyptians found bitter, but drank it down so as not to offend.

A short while after, a young soldier knocked on the door and entered his commander's office. He responded to the officer's question, and Ramose translated. "He said he has a friend in the village near the cave."

"Horus has heard us," Horemheb said. "I think I should go alone." Before Khui could protest he went on, "Ask him if I can borrow clothes to hide the fact that I'm a stranger. I'll also need someone who speaks both languages."

Ramose asked the sergeant, who nodded his head.

Horemheb added, "I'll come back to the ship when I've finished, brothers."

"You'll do nothing of the kind," Khui shouted. "In your condition? What are you thinking? You'll go with me." Horemheb knew he had better give in, and nodded. They followed the sergeant outside and Ramose could only watch in disbelief.

Stopping in front of one of the barracks, their guide motioned for the Egyptians to wait at the door and quickly came back with another soldier.

"My name is Juva," an even younger man introduced himself in Egyptian, and Horemheb breathed a sigh of relief. He handed the Egyptians some clothing, which they pulled on over their heads. Khui helped Horemheb pull it over his bandaged chest.

Horemheb smiled. "From a distance we might pass as local soldiers."

Juva said, "That's a great spear you carry, soldier. Can I hold it?"

Horemheb handed it to him. The young man moved it about trying to find the balance point. "It's a good spear," Juva said.

Horemheb took it back. "Can you take us to the village?"

"Follow me," he answered, and led them up the street leading from the sea and passing through the city gates. Juva explained to the guards on duty their destination. As they left town, Horemheb could see in the distance the foothills of some very tall mountains.

"There are many caves in those hills," Juva said. "There is one large enough to hide the bandits you're looking for."

As they walked along Horemheb noted the sun's position in the early afternoon. About what seemed a long time, they reached a small village encircled by a thick forest. Entering the clearing, children surrounded them, wanting to look at the strangers. Juva said something to the oldest boy who ran off.

When a young boy about ten years of age came toward them, Juva said, "This is Babu." He explained to the boy what Horemheb wanted. Babu listened carefully and answered Juva's questions. "He knows the cave very well and has even seen the bandits coming and going, he says. There is no way to attack them from the front, but he knows a secret entrance behind the cave. He and his friends often play there."

"By the gods," Horemheb swore. "Tell him we'll give him a big reward if he'll take us there. We can even present him to a real prince."

When Juva repeated the promise, the boy's face lit up.

"Follow me," he told them.

By the time Horemheb and his commander made it back to Ugarit, the prince had worked out a plan concerning the ransom and was on deck waiting for them. "We will fill the wagons with brass objects which from a distance look like gold. They will only get a glimpse of what is under the wagon-covers when they bring out the princess. Pray she is still alive."

Khui made his report, which pleased the prince. He then presented Juva and Babu to him and Thutmose ordered a reward of food for them. After some refreshments, the prince wanted to know if his men had made a plan for the rescue.

"This is our plan, Highness," Horemheb said. "Tonight when it's dark, we'll hide in the forest around Babu's village, close to the cave. At midday, you, Highness, and Ramose, along with perhaps as few as twenty guardsmen will arrive with the gold, distracting the kidnappers. The rest will remain hidden in the forest facing the cave, waiting for Khui and me to enter it from the rear. When we hear the cry of the falcon, we'll rescue the princess. The rest of our men will rush in with arrows flying." He watched the prince's face, hoping for his approval.

Thutmose frowned, unsure of the plan. "Can it work, Khui?"

"Yes, Highness. Slipping into the cave from behind might guarantee the Princess's safety. Otherwise, they might end her life once they think they have the gold."

"I agree," Thutmose said. "But just remember all of you—this is *my* plan."

They smiled because he grinned as he said it.

"Pharaoh is the only one who has ideas given him by the gods as you know. No one can ever tell him what to do. That's the law, so just remember it."

His men burst out laughing at such a ridiculous law.

That afternoon, thirty of the prince's archers made their way behind Babu as he led them through the hills to the forest. It proved to be difficult terrain for the Egyptians who had never walked through a forest. There were few hardwood trees at home, and those that existed were often sacred like the sycamore and willow. Now to find thousands of pine and fir trees covering the hillside became intimidating.

As darkness fell, the archers advanced to their hiding places for tomorrow's rendezvous. Horemheb and his handpicked archers followed the boy to the hiding place behind the cave. He carried his trusted spear in one hand, and his sword in the other. They would not enter the cave until they heard the signal.

Hapu, the prince's chariot driver, hitched the horses and positioned them close to the ship awaiting his master's departure the next day. Guardsmen lined up on shore, prepared to follow him. Captain Neferu would move the ship out into the harbor to prevent anyone from boarding her. The crewmen were armed and prepared for just such an eventuality.

Ramose rode with the prince in his chariot and they left Ugarit with the small contingency of guardsmen. Curious passersby came to the highway to see the Egyptians marching away from their city. In the middle of the guards were the two wagons of fake gold—fake in the sense that only a layer of real gold bars covered the brass items beneath. The local treasury loaned the real gold to the prince. Earlier, Thutmose had conducted tryouts among his men to see which of them could give the most authentic-sounding falcon's cry. Everything had been worked out.

When Thutmose approached the field that faced the cave, he had his driver stop. He and Ramose stepped down as the twenty guardsmen took their positions in front of the wagons.

"Here they come, Highness," a soldier shouted. They watched as perhaps twenty of the bandits emerged from the darkness, following a man who was undoubtedly their leader. Thutmose removed the canvas cover of the first wagon so only the real gold became visible.

"Do you have the gold?" the man shouted, and Ramose translated.

"Yes," Thutmose answered. "Where is the princess?"

The bandit clapped his hands, and two of his men emerged from the cave pushing a woman in front of them into the sunlight.

The prince said to Ramose, "How do we know if it really *is* the princess? I've never met her. It could all be a trick."

Ramose said in a soft voice. "It must be her, Highness. These jackals saw a good opportunity and took advantage of it."

"Very well." Walking over to the second wagon, he removed its cover giving the signal and the high-pitched staccato screech of the falcon echoed across the field. As swift as striking cobras, Horemheb and his men raced through the back of the cave and cut down the bandits still inside. Archers, hidden on each side of the field, stood and released their arrows. Horemheb and Khui rushed to the princess, killing the two men behind her. Thutmose moved quickly and cut down the bandit leader completing the rescue.

Ramose rushed to the trembling princess who collapsed in his arms. He assured her that she had nothing more to fear. When she could stand, he led her to the prince. "This is pharaoh's son, your Highness," he explained in Hurrian.

The prince came toward her, and she bowed low before him. Ramose began an introduction but to he could tell she somehow knew the tall one *had* to be the prince.

"You've saved my life," she said in almost perfect Egyptian, "and I am grateful to you. But I beg you, my Lord, please say nothing of this to my father. I will only bring shame upon him for allowing this to happen."

"As you will, Princess," Thutmose replied, delighted the woman spoke his language. "Come, you'll ride with us." He gave her his hand and helped her up into his chariot. When they were ready for the ride back to Ugarit, he turned to Khui and said, "My congratulations to all of your men. There will be extra beer for everyone." His men cheered and quickly helped turn the wagons around, and the guardsmen who had been in the forest formed up behind their comrades.

Horemheb grumbled. "And that's all the thanks we get?"

Khui overheard him, "Enough. He must show the princess that he is in charge. You would agree with him, wouldn't you, soldier?"

"Of course, Commander," Horemheb said. He showed his displeasure by being overly formal. "All plans and strategies come from Pharaoh—isn't that what he said?"

Horemheb stopped to plunge his sword into some sand to clean off the blood. "Well, Captain, be sure to tell him this—I'm convinced the surviving guard back in town had to be in league with the bandits. Old King 'what's his name' of Mitanni has a traitor in his midst."

CHAPTER FOUR

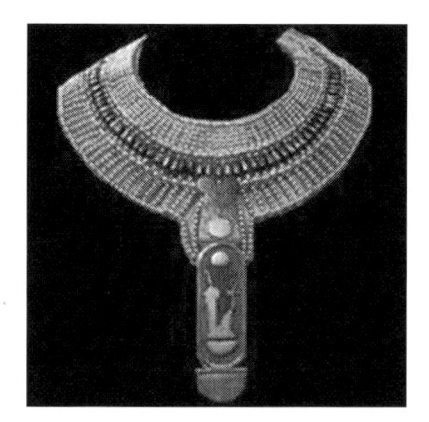

GOLD OF VALOR

The king's ship made good time on its return voyage. The crew cheered as they entered the sacred waters of the river. Princess Tadukhepa, or Tadu as she liked to be called, occupied the prince's cabin. Thutmose moved to the captain's smaller one. He didn't seem to mind, because he had grown quite fond of the Mitanni princess.

"It's a shame my father gets to marry her," he said to his friends. "I rather like her myself."

"She is beautiful," Ramose said. "But your first wife must be Egyptian, Great One."

The prince grimaced. "Stop calling me that. You know that title's reserved for Pharaoh. As flattering as it is, you better get out of the habit—it might just slip out in court by mistake."

Ramose laughed. "To hear is to obey, Glorious One."

"Why not tell your father you like her? Horemheb asked.

The prince frowned. "I will not interfere with the king's marriage. He is permitted to choose a foreign wife if the marriage has political value."

"Not me," Horemheb argued. "I will marry whomever I please."

"Ha." Ramose scoffed. "That's certainly true. There've been so many women."

"Don't start on me, Mose, or I'll tell the Prince about Lady Herit."

"Gentlemen. This discussion is pointless. Tadu is my father's bride. Now we must let Thebes know we are coming. There will be a grand welcome for his new wife."

The sailors took up their long oars for the return up river, using them to propel the ship against the strong current. The journey home would take an extra day. Messenger pigeons would carry the news of their approach to Awen, and other birds would relay the message along the river to the capital.

The princess came out of her cabin and sat watching the oarsmen. Thutmose could see the river fascinated her. "I love to watch the river flowing past," she told him. When the prince approached, she invited him to sit with her. A gust of warm air from the red lands filled the great sail and the ship picked up speed.

"What do you think of our sacred river, my Lady?"

"It's much bigger than our holy Euphrates, Highness," she said. "It is so powerful." She watched some flowers moving with the river and said, "Tell me about it."

Thutmose sat down and began. "The river is our god Hapi, Princess. He is depicted in paintings as a man with a large belly and breasts to show the fertility the river brings. It is he who provides life, water, food, and a yearly flooding of his banks to nourish our farmland. The children know him as The Lord of the Fishes and Birds and Marshes."

The Princess smiled. "It sounds similar to some of our stories."

"Without him, my Lady, Kemet, our black land, would have died, and so Hapi is revered even above Ra, the sun god." He stood and leaned against the railing. "We do not have the blessing of the gods you call 'rain,' and so if we go but a short distance from the river it can mean death. Away from it there is nothing, only desert which we call the red land."

She stood and joined him at the railing. "I have so much to learn, but I have heard a lot about Egypt from my cousin, Princess Gilukhepa, third wife of your king."

Thutmose, mortified that he had forgotten about the marriage made many years ago, didn't know what to say. He had seen Pharaoh's Mitanni wife on state occasions and religious festivals, but never made the connection until now. "Of course," he responded sheepishly. "I had forgotten."

Suddenly she laughed. "What are those?" She pointed to some large animals floating on the water. They were wagging their ears and snorting at the ship's intrusion into their world.

"More of our river-god's servants, Princess," Thutmose replied. "Some call them water-cows, but they are hippos, servants of Hapi. They may appear fat and amusing, but those teeth are deadly." Tadu laughed at their comic antics. Ramose approached and waited for his friend to recognize him.

When the prince beckoned, he bowed politely and took Thutmose aside. "I hope you're telling her about your mother, my Lord," Ramose suggested. "You and your father cannot throw Tadu into that den of vipers without warning." He referred to Queen Tiye, the Great Royal Wife, who ruled everyone at court, even her husband. He knew the prince respected his mother, but her network of spies reached everywhere in the palace. She had to know everything about everybody, and usually did.

The prince nodded. He spoke in a quiet voice. "I'd forgotten that one of my father's foreign wives came from Mitanni. Perhaps the two wives can commiserate with each other." Turning to see if anyone might be listening he continued. "I would also like some suggestions from you, as to how best to honor Horemheb."

"Gladly, Highness, you mean apart from throwing him to the crocodiles for being arrogant and stubborn and wanting to take all the credit for your plan to save the princess?"

Thutmose laughed. "Well said." Ramose left him and headed back to the main deck. The prince walked forward and found a long staff to which some sailor had attached a small net. Watching the water carefully, he plunged it into the water and scooped up an object. Taking it out, he walked back to the princess and handed it to her.

In a voice soft and lilting she said, "Oh, it's beautiful."

"It's a lotus flower, my Lady. For centuries men have given these to beautiful women." She blushed and sat down close to the railing. "Now I must warn you about something." Over the next hour she listened as he told her about his mother's love of intrigue.

When he finished she said, "You've not only given me something beautiful, but important knowledge that could save my life. My father, the king, taught me that to be forewarned is to be equipped for battle. Thank you, your Highness."

Thebes celebrated the arrival of Princess Tadukhepa with feasting and dancing. Pharaoh however, appeared to be the only member of the royal family happy to see her. If not for Lady Gilukhepa, third wife of pharaoh, the first week for her would have been a very unhappy one indeed. Thutmose saw to it that Tadu attended every celebration and encouraged his father to include her at official audiences at court. At least for the moment, she seemed to settle into her new life satisfactorily.

Horemheb, the hero of the great rescue, didn't like having to sit in the royal physician's surgery. He considered all sickness a sign of weakness, and to be forced to wait in such a place didn't agree with him.

The elderly healer entered and made him sit on the examining table. "Hmm," the man mumbled as he poked and prodded the guardsman's chest. "Yes, this looks good. Try not to lift or carry anything for several more weeks. The muscle tissue needs to rebuild here." He poked the tender scar, making his patient wince. "Do you understand?"

"Yes my Lord, but I feel fine."

The old man growled. "All right. Don't listen to me then. You warriors are all alike. I don't expect any of you men to take my advice seriously. Then your commanders complain that their men are unfit for duty."

Horemheb laughed. "I'm sorry, respected healer. I'm grateful and will do as you say. I count on Horus, may his name be honored, to help me, but this healing I must do myself. I need to know if I'll be ready when pharaoh goes to the Land of the Bow."

The physician mellowed a bit and smiled. "I don't see why not. You'll be hacking away at the enemy in good form I should think." He turned and was about to leave when he added, "You *were* protected by the god, my friend. The dagger didn't injure any organs, and that is why you're still alive. May your god go with you to the Land of the Falling Waters." Horemheb nodded, picked up his omnipresent spear, and left the small surgery.

In the palace, Prince Thutmose felt nervous. His father summoned him, something the king had not done in a long time. For moral support he decided to take Khui with him. As the two friends made their way through the long polished hallways, a young man stepped out in front of them.

"Welcome home, Brother," Prince Smenkhare greeted his older sibling.

Captain Khui knelt and saluted the prince, who waved his hand for the soldier to stand.

"You brought back a fine catch this time," his younger brother added, referring to Princess Tadukhepa.

"You think she's some kind of fish, Khare?" Thutmose snapped. His brother, eight years younger than he, already acted like their father's successor rather than the youngest son.

"Well," Smenkhare said. "We do catch these women the same way don't we? We baited the line, in this case a treaty of peace with the Mitanni, and you went to haul her in. But I'm sure when you're pharaoh you won't do anything so political."

Thutmose stepped closer to his brother and looked him in the eye. "Until one actually becomes Pharaoh Khare, one cannot know what he will or will not do. But you'll never have to worry about that, will you?" It was a cruel thing for Thutmose to say, but true. Another brother stood in line before Smenkhare.

"Bah," the young man grumbled as he turned and walked away.

When they reached the king's private quarters, two guards saluted the prince. One of them opened the door allowing him and Khui to enter the foyer. A household steward went to announce their arrival. When he returned, he told them his majesty would receive them in the garden.

As a boy, the prince loved the palace garden. A large pool in the center provided water for flowerbeds and rows of sycamores, palms and willow trees. His parents were sitting in the shade near the pool. Queen Tiye smiled at him as he approached.

"My boy," she said. Then she motioned for him to come closer. "You've made us very proud."

"And you, Captain," Amenhotep said raising his hand so the soldier could stand after his salute. "You and your men are to be commended."

"They are excellent archers, Majesty, and proud to serve."

Lady Tiye said, "Only as good as the commanding officer who trained them, Khui. You must give yourself credit, and we are grateful for what you did."

Khui bowed his head in response.

The queen had lost her beauty years ago, but used every cosmetic her ladies-in-waiting could provide to hide the truth of it. A tall woman, she continued to intimidate everyone she met.

"You have our permission to withdraw, Captain," Pharaoh said. Raising his hand again, the officer saluted and left. Thutmose moved closer and sat on the edge of the pond beside his parents.

"Now," Pharaoh said, "tell us about Horemheb."

"He proved an invaluable aide to me, Father. He's highly intelligent and very clever. The plan to rescue the princess came from him, although I would never tell him so. When the assassin leapt across the railing to attack me, Horemheb instinctively sprang like a young lion and blocked him—giving no thought to his own life."

"Then he must be honored for it." the king exclaimed. "The people love a hero—let's give them a new one." The king, now in his fifties, had lost his virulent charisma. His body had become thick and he sported a double chin, yet his strong face still made people believe that he looked like a Pharaoh.

Queen Tiye seemed thoughtful and reticent to share her husband's enthusiasm. "He is not of noble blood. The courtiers say he is the son of a cheese maker."

"Not so, Mother. He's the only son of a stonemason; a well-respected tradesman in the province of the Fayouim."

"You will organize the ceremony to reward him, my son," Amenhotep commanded. "Ramose will assist you. Honor your guards too in such a way that your place as heir will be strengthened. You have chosen these two young men to be at your side, now let there be no doubt that you are confident in your choices."

Thutmose bowed his head. "As you say, Father." Realizing his parents had nothing more to add, he withdrew.

The royal couple remained by the pool a little longer lost in thought. Then, the queen stood as if to leave, but turned and looked into her husband's eyes. "There is something you should do, beloved," she said, "and only you can do it. Remove Horemheb from the Guards and put him back in the army." She saw the questioned look on her husband's face and continued. "If he is as sharp and as clever as your son finds him to be, we need more generals like him. Just a thought," and with that she headed back toward their apartment.

Amenhotep smiled. He loved Tiye and trusted her judgment more than that of many of his advisors. "The army? Hmm," he mumbled aloud. "Yes, of course. I'm so glad I thought of it." Then he laughed as he ran his fingers over the water, startling a small turtle below the surface.

A week later, the feast to honor Pharaoh's Guards convened in the inner courtyard of the palace. Leaders of the Army and the king's councilors were in attendance, as well as most of the royal court. The shade from the palace walls made the midmorning outdoor ceremony comfortable. A large red canopy had been placed for their majesties and as time to begin approached, the Royal Guards marched in and stood at attention facing the royal platform. Their arrival signaled for all other participants to enter, and the courtyard filled quickly.

Even though the Crown Prince had planned the event, Pharaoh would preside. A loud flourish of trumpets announced the arrival of the king's chamberlain. His counselors moved to either side of the royal dais. More trumpet blasts announced the arrival of Prince Thutmose. Everyone made obeisance to him, prostrating themselves, turning their palms toward him as he took his place. Queen Tiye followed, dressed in a gold and ruby covered gown. When the crowd stood once again, the room was abuzz with compliments about her gown.

A drum roll followed, and a much longer flourish of trumpets signaled Pharaoh's entrance. Guardsmen knelt on one knee, with bowed heads. The courtiers made obeisance again, their palms turned toward the living god. The chamberlain then tapped his staff, the signal for everyone to stand.

Before speaking, the Ruler of Egypt walked forward to be close to his courtiers. He paused, looking over his subjects, then spoke in a loud, clear voice. "We honor our warriors today by our presence. We give praise to the valiant service of the Royal Guards." Enthusiastic applause greeted his words. He continued, "Recently in the land of Mitanni, they rescued the daughter of my brother, King Tushratta. Through the courage of our beloved Son and Heir, and his men, the rescue succeeded." Thunderous applause erupted, louder than before, and the cheers from the court made Pharaoh smile.

"Know then, that I Amenhotep, third pharaoh honored with that name, Ruler of Thebes and The Two Lands, Son of Amun and blessed by the Aten, give five kidets of gold to every guardsman."

The men shouted and stomped their feet at the king's generosity. It was an enormous sum, almost half a year's wages, and they continued cheering until he raised his hand.

Pharaoh motioned to his chamberlain who brought a box of thin cedar wood and handed it to Prince Thutmose. The young man took it and walked over to stand beside his father.

"We have chosen to honor another," Amenhotep announced.

Thutmose nodded to his father then said clearly, "Horemheb of the Royal Guards. Stand forward."

The eyes of all the guards turned toward their comrade, stomping their feet in rhythm as he walked forward. Climbing up the steps to face the king, Horemheb knelt down on one knee, bowed his head and slapped his fist across his chest.

Pharaoh declared loudly, "For courage beyond duty, and for taking no thought for his own life, Horemheb, son of Kheruef, member of the Royal Guard, is awarded the Gold of Valor. It bears our name so that all may know that where he stands, we stand." The warriors couldn't contain themselves, and began to applaud and cheer for such an honor given to one of their own.

Removing the gold chain from its box, pharaoh carried it toward the guardsman and carefully placed it around Horemheb's neck. Thutmose closed the clasp and stepped back. A gold cartouche, weighing a full deben of the precious metal, bore the king's name suspended on the chain. Whenever anyone saw the king's name, the law compelled all present to treat the bearer as if Pharaoh had appeared in person.

The courtiers suddenly stopped applauding, causing a hush to fall on the courtyard. Pharaoh had done something unheard of—he touched Horemheb. He placed his royal hand on the man's shoulder. Then the king turned the guardsman around so everyone could see the Gold of Valor. They cheered even louder.

Ramose, so proud of his friend cheered the loudest. All of Egypt wanted to honor the stonemason's son. Pharaoh raised his hand again and there was complete silence.

"It is our desire to place this valuable warrior where we can best use his talents and abilities. As Ruler of the Two Lands, and Commander of all the Armies, we promote Horemheb Captain in our Army."

The Chamberlain struck the ground three times and shouted, "As it has been spoken, so let it be done." The crowd applauded and watched as the astonished Horemheb knelt once more in front of Pharaoh.

Later, at the banquet given in honor of the Guards, Captain Khui said to the prince, "Well I didn't know *that* would happen."

"Nor did I," Thutmose said. "I hope it's not a mistake. He's a good guard, and if the common people no longer have any fear of attacking their pharaoh, we will need more like him."

Contrary to what his friends thought, Horemheb felt embarrassed by all the adulation. Returning to the army pleased him, but with Prince Thutmose now his friend, he still longed for combat.

A woman standing next to Horemheb said, "Your mind seems a long way off, my Lord."

He turned and found an attractive courtesan standing at his side. He quickly assumed the stranger to be the wife of one of the king's advisors or court officials. As he got his first good look at her, he regretted at once not having noticed her.

"I'm sorry, my Lady. My mind took me back to my village. I wished that my parents, may their names be remembered, could have been here today." He looked intently into her greenish-brown eyes. "I'm sure you and I have not met because I would definitely have remembered you."

The young woman blushed slightly and laughed. "I am Amenia, Captain, and I didn't mean to appear forward. My father is Lord Amenken, Treasurer to His Majesty."

"I am pleased to meet you on this, the happiest day of my life," Horemheb said. Then he bowed his head politely.

A young man ran up to them and interrupted. "Come on, Menia," he said rather loudly, pulling on the lady's sleeve, "Father's looking for us."

"You'll have to forgive my brother, Captain," the young woman explained. "Go on, Maya. I'll catch up." Turning back to Horemheb, she said, "I must bid you farewell, my Lord. I pray for you all the blessings of the gods."

Her brother suddenly realized to whom she had been speaking. "You're the one." he said. "Look at that, Menia! All that gold." He leaned closer to get a better look at the golden necklace, but his sister grabbed his arm and moved him along. She smiled back at Horemheb as she hurried off.

Captain Khui came up behind him. "Who was that?"

"Lord Amenken's daughter," Horemheb answered. "I wish I had time to get better acquainted, but there won't be time for that I'm afraid. I have to report for duty in the morning."

Khui cleared his throat. "Horemheb," he said. He found it difficult to share what their bond of friendship meant to him. "I must tell you how much I regret the king's decision to transfer you, but I wish you all the best."

"I wouldn't be worried, my friend. Who knows? You too could get transferred to the army." That made them both laugh as they headed for the tables of their comrades. Soon they were lamenting the sad uncertain life of a soldier. Several of Horemheb's friends offered to be his bodyguard whenever he chose to wear the king's necklace, and the fact he might need a bodyguard made them laugh all the more.

A short toad of a man named Mena watched everything from the shadows. Queen Tiye's servant could have been a mole since he loved the dark and dirty places around the palace. He had hidden himself in the bushes near enough to hear everyone's conversation. Mena had served the queen for twenty-years, managing to survive an endless number of her palace intrigues. He would remember everything that was said and repeat the words to his mistress. When the guardsmen returned to their barracks, the queen's servant moved as stealthily as a cobra back to his lair below the palace.

CHAPTER FIVE

WHITE-WATER RAPIDS

Six months later, Pharaoh Amenhotep's southern campaign against Nubia began. Instead of the crown prince leading the troops as his son had hoped, Pharaoh chose General Minnakf, a seasoned commander.

"I can't believe he chose that old war horse," Horemheb snarled. He didn't like the fact Prince Thutmose would not be with them. "The Ptah and Horus Regiments will lead the assault at Swentet. I've been told it's the location of the first whitewater rapids."

Captain Khamet, who had stretched out on the only chair in Horemheb's room, spoke up. "There are two forts already in the area. "The first is on Abu, an island in the middle of the river. It's named for the large animals living there. The other fortification is at Swentet."

Horemheb liked the fact that as captain of the Horus Regiment, he would be fighting alongside his former instructor.

Before the departure, the Vizier of the South invited the general and his two officers to his home for an evening meal. The two younger warriors were surprised the man resided in Thebes, and not in the south where he belonged.

As they met outside the Vizier's residence, the general gave them a warning. "There will be no comments from either of you men about the campaign."

His officers saluted, knowing better than to open their mouths.

Lord Merimose met them in the foyer and led them into the large dining room. "Gentlemen, may I present the light of my life, Lady Nebt."

His guests nodded politely and the general moved forward to greet her. "Dear Lady, it has been much too long. My beloved Kawit sends her greeting."

"You are most kind, General. It's good to see you again, and your commanders." Normally she would join them for the meal, but because of the nature of their visit she invited them to be seated and left the room.

Servants brought in the food and Lord Merimose's table presented a wide variety of choices. Several kinds of meat filled the table including duck and goose, along with various vegetables, steamed to perfection. Fresh bread had been placed on the table and the aroma of cumin, dill and rosemary seasonings filled the air.

Not accustomed to such abundance, the two younger officers couldn't decide what to select first. Even though offered wine, all the men chose beer.

When they finished, they retired to the coolness of the formal garden—an in vogue feature in noble villas of the capital. A full moon provided enough light for them to see each other's faces clearly.

"Let us speak of the Nubians," Merimose began. "We must put an end to King Ikhey's incursions below the first whitewater." The Egyptians referred to the rocky outcroppings forming six barriers of rock along the upper river as "whitewater falls or rapids."

"What kind of attacks, my Lord?" General Minnakf asked.

"There have been raids on the towns of Edfu and Swentet, and even the small island settlement and fort on sacred Abu," Merimose replied. "We must push them back beyond the falls."

"Hmm," General Minnakf murmured. "We can send our two regiments immediately, Lord Vizier, but we'll need to requisition all merchant ships for their transport. I recommend we assemble at Swentet in two weeks' time."

"Make it so, General," the politician said. "Pharaoh has given us one of his galleys and you and your staff will sail with me. We'll be there ahead of most of the troops, giving us time for reconnaissance."

Horemheb looked at Khamet and smiled. Glad the army would be going by ship. No one in Egypt liked to walk with the river close by. "Who is this Ikhey, my Lord? Is he their king?" He had no sooner asked than he remembered the general's warning. "Apologies, General," he added, but Minnakf only frowned, ignoring him.

Merimose answered. "Our sources from Edfu tell us he is the king of the Nubians who lives in the hills, some distance from the river. They actually plant crops and live like the people of the red lands. Rumor has it he's more than four cubits tall and has proven to be a fierce and merciless warrior."

Minnakf shook his head angrily. "Not for long, Excellency. My men will cut him down to size and put an end to his troublemaking."

"That's the spirit, brothers. May the gods help us," Merimose said.

"*Bak-her*," his guests replied. "May it be so."

Merimose stood, then, remembered something else. "We have been told the Nubians are the finest archers anyone has encountered. We must show them what Egyptian bowmen are made of, General."

"And we will, my Lord Vizier. We'll prove ourselves to you and his Majesty." The veteran soldier said it was absolute confidence.

His two subordinates did not share their commander's enthusiasm.

Moving thousands of soldiers south would prove difficult. Three thousand men in each regiment needed passage, and the most a commercial ship could carry might be two hundred at a time. A military quartermaster assigned to each unit paid the captain of the conscripted ships. The sailors and crew greeted the soldiers cordially, grateful for the added income.

The morning the royal galley *Breath of Horus*' departed, Ramose, the new assistant to the Vizier of Thebes, came to see Horemheb off. "Horus go with you, brother. May the enemy's arrows avoid you, and may the women of Abu keep you happy."

Horemheb laughed. "And may all evil courtiers who are even now plotting your downfall, meet a horrible end." They continued laughing all the way to the ship.

"Now listen to me, Horemheb. That spear of yours may be your lucky charm, but don't volunteer for any unnecessary dangers. No princesses from caves. Don't tempt the gods."

"Yes, mother-hen," his friend growled. "Now get off the ship so we can sail."

Ramose wished both officers well. Horemheb watched his friend's chariot head back toward the palace.

"What about the General?" Khamet asked.

"He's not onboard yet, Captain," Horemheb said.

"You can address me by my name, Captain."

"As my instructor, Sir, it would be impolite for me to address you in such an informal manner."

"I understand, but you could at least try?"

Horemheb grinned. "Yes . . .Khamet, as you command."

"Better. Now, are all our men onboard?" He referred to their own companies of two hundred archers and swordsmen.

"All in place, including my trusty companion." Horemheb grinned as he held up his spear. Thrusting it high into the air, he yelled, "For Horus and the king."

"You had me worried for a moment, Harm, but now I'll rest easy."

Making their way up to the royal deck, they avoided the crew readying the galley for departure. The large rectangular-rigged sail took fifty sailors to lower it from the top spar. The crew had to be also good oarsmen because the ship would be sailing up river.

It took three days to reach Edfu. The warriors divided into groups, taking turns sleeping on deck. When they docked, the general and his commanders went to the fortress to gather first-hand information. Offered a simple meal of grilled fish, leeks, bread and beer, General Minnakf and his officers listened to the report of the Nubian attacks below the waterfall.

"They attack at night, General, when the villagers are asleep," the fort's commander said. "They come like jackals. May Seth destroy them. We've killed a few, but they don't look like any Africans we've seen before. They dress like nomads and their bows are well made. Their arrows can reach long distances."

"Any captured alive, Captain?" Minnakf asked.

"No, General. They choose to die rather than surrender."

Horemheb asked to speak. The general nodded. "Why are they attacking, Captain? Your villagers are not harvesting any crops, and don't raise many cattle from what I see. Why would so few men attack so many?"

"No one can say," the commander said. "I think it's just because we're here."

Later, as the general's team walked back with him, he shared his frustration. "The reason this fortress is here in the first place is to prevent these kinds of attacks. There's always been an uneasy truce at this border crossing.

"But there's nothing here for the Nubians, my Lord," Khamet said. "Look at the soil." He pointed to the infertile land close to the river, covered with gravel and rocks. "It's so unlike the rich black earth of home."

"Maybe it's a test, General," Horemheb suggested. "Perhaps their king is trying to find out what we will do. He's like a child trying to see how far his parents will let him go before they punish him."

"Well, they are about to find out when we come face to face, Captain. They'll get more than they bargained for," the general roared.

That night Horemheb stretched out on deck outside Lord Merimose's cabin. "There's something not right about this whole campaign, Khamet. I'm afraid we're underestimating the Nubian's will to fight. We should proceed carefully."

Khamet whispered, "You know how generals are, Harm. Attack and destroy. That's their only strategy."

"You're right, but if this giant draws us out into the red land, it may be we who are destroyed."

The next day they sailed from Edfu farther up river to Swentet at the first white rapids. Many Egyptians considered the waterfall to be the sacred source of their river god. As the *Breath of Horus* approached the dock, thousands of soldiers crowded the river's edge and cheered the arrival of their general.

Vizier Merimose stood beside him, encouraged by the enthusiastic welcome. "I didn't realize so many of our men would already be here, General. Who is the fort commander?"

"Captain Raia, my Lord. You know him. He's the son of Lord Merine, one of Pharaoh's counselors. He's a good soldier and officer."

"We shall see," Minnakf growled.

When the ship docked and the gangway put in place, the crew off-loaded both chariots and horses for their important passengers. The animals were glad to be on solid ground once more and pranced about.

"And so it begins," Horemheb said, more to himself than anyone.

"Yes it does," Khamet whispered. "But where will it end?"

When Horemheb first set eyes on the white-water rapids stretching across the river, he couldn't believe it. As they approached, the sound of the rushing water became so deafening he understood how the ancients might believe gods lived there. It was believed that the goddess Anukis, who created the waters of the river of life, lived in a shrine near the river.

"There are five more rapids up river, each a barrier to navigation. If you look closely, the bedrock has been eroded perhaps fifty cubits by the rushing water. You can see where the river has carved out these vast canyons."

"It's possible to sail beyond here when the river is in flood," Captain Raia told them as they walked closer to the turbulent water.

"You mean the river actually rises high enough to cover all this?" Horemheb asked, skeptically.

"Yes, my friend. All of these boulders will be covered leaving only the whirlpools on the surface. It still makes me nervous to sail over them."

Khamet joined them. "I can see why. Such a sound. It's as if there are angry demons in the water fighting each other."

As they started back, Horemheb spoke with Raia. "Why do you think the Nubians have been attacking, brother?"

The officer stopped walking and looked at him. "I think Ikhey wants to keep us from taking his gold and ivory. Our miners have not been able to pass beyond this point. All caravans that have tried have been turned back or destroyed."

Looking up at the high cliffs, Horemheb said, "They'd have the high ground and the advantage, my friend. Do we know where their camp might be located?"

Raia said, "At first we thought the raiding parties were coming from Meroe their capital, but Ikhey isn't there. Our spies haven't found his camp."

"You have Nubian spies?" Horemheb asked incredulously.

"Yes, gentlemen. Gold speaks even louder than the sword." They walked on a little farther, then he told them, "They speak Kenuzi, the local Kushite language, and are good scouts."

"When did the king last attack?" Khamet asked.

"Two weeks ago, and it cost us twenty men, our first losses. Their archers are incredibly accurate. Our men were shot through the neck at more than five hundred paces." Horemheb and his friend found it hard to believe.

"Were they up on the cliffs or near your fortress?" Khamet asked.

"Down here on our level, not far from the fort. They were so well hidden; we couldn't see them until they fired."

The discussion made Horemheb feel uneasy. They were too exposed out in the open. His spear would be no match for enemy arrows. He breathed easier when they got back to camp. Their men had already prepared a midday meal. The officers helped themselves to fresh fish grilled over charcoal fires, with bread baked the night before. They washed it down with water, choosing to save their beer for the evening meal.

Horemheb finished his last piece of fish. "Horses and chariots are no good here. The sand around the rapids is too wet and soft. We'll need camels whose padded feet are bigger around. I wonder if we could trade for some."

"I've never ridden one," Khamet said. "I think I'd rather march with my men."

"I've ridden one into the red land outside Thebes," Horemheb told him. "They have strong ankles and are surefooted. You ride high on top of them—a great vantage point when you're scouting around."

"But you're also a sitting duck," Khamet fired back.

"Maybe so, but we'll need them if we're going beyond the barrier." Horemheb gulped down the last of his water. As he looked out across the river, an idea came to him. "What about the men over there—in the fortress of Abu? Will they be joining in the fight?"

"I don't know," Khamet answered. "Perhaps the general will let us go over to the island and find out. I've never seen one of the great abus, have you?" Horemheb's eyes lit up, but he shook his head.

When Khamet asked, the senior officer told him to go and bring back the commander of the fort. "We'll need his men." Climbing onboard a small felucca, its tall triangular sail quickly caught the wind, carrying the two officers across the river. Once ashore they found the Island of Abu to be bigger than they had imagined. Named for the old Egyptian word for elephant, the well-fortified command post faced Fort Swentet.

An officer came out to greet them. "I am Captain Paser, welcome to Abu." When Horemheb told him why they had come the soldier shook his head. "I have only three hundred men in the fort, friends. We did not think we would have to join you." He saw Horemheb's frown and added, "But, we'll follow orders of course."

After some refreshing beer, Paser led his guests to three horses, and they rode to the center of the island. He tied his horse to a tall sycamore, as did his guests. "There," he said quietly, pointing to what appeared at first to be a thicket of trees. Horemheb looked more closely and realized some of the trees were moving.

"By the gods," Khamet shouted. "Look at them. They're gigantic."

"Quiet," Paser said softly, but the warning came too late. A large bull elephant turned toward the noise and flapped his enormous ears angrily. His trumpeting at the intruders caused the herd to bellow as well.

"I didn't believe the stories were true," Horemheb declared. "Look at him. He's as big as a house."

"Mount up," their host shouted. "The herd's following the bull toward us." Jumping back onto their horses, they kicked their heels in their mounts' flanks and galloped back to the fort.

"They are enormous," Horemheb shouted, laughing with exhilaration. "Do they ever come near the fort?"

"No, they like to eat the bark of trees and stay pretty much in the interior. But they have been known to swim across the river to the other side when the water is low."

Khamet shouted to his friend. "That's one animal your spear couldn't kill,"

Captain Paser sailed back with them and went onboard the galley to meet the general. In their absence, several more ships had arrived with troops. Their numbers were now more than five thousand. The regiments were finally complete.

When Paser came back he said, "The general orders you two onboard. It's been good meeting you and I have my orders to join you in the battle." He gave a brief salute and headed down to the felucca waiting to take him back.

"We'll look forward to it, Captain," Khamet shouted after him.

Horemheb cried, "Horus protect you from the elephants, brother," and he waved at their new friend.

"We never did get to ask him how to bring down one of those monsters," Khamet said. "Did you see the tusks on that bull elephant?"

"I don't think we'll meet any where we're headed, but who knows this far south?" Horemheb said. "Anything is possible."

As soon as they reported on board the king's ship, the general said, "Ah, there you are Commanders." They approached and saluted. "Men, there are fifty camels being sent this way. As soon as they arrive, I want you and your team to head up beyond the white water and scout out the land. See if you can spot these Nubians and their camp, but don't engage them in any way."

"As you command, General," Horemheb responded. "It will take us a day or two to feel comfortable riding them, but we'll go as soon as we can."

"You'll need supplies, of course, and remember camels can carry a lot. Take extra waterskins. You don't know how far away from the river you might have to go." When Lord Merimose came out of his cabin, Minnakf explained to him what the two officers were about to do.

"Avoid any contact with these people," the Vizier ordered. "Wait until you've sufficient support from us."

Khamet saluted. "Yes, my Lord."

"This must be how Seth's breath smells." Khamet growled to his friend. "These are the foulest-smelling animals on earth." He rode one of the beasts up ahead of the others. They took fifty of their best warriors—twenty-five from each battalion, and followed a narrow path around the rapids. The rocks and high cliffs leveled off until they were once again on flat, smooth ground beside the river.

Horemheb slapped his leg at several fleas crawling on it. "There are stowaways on these beasts."

"Up here, Captain!" one of the scouts shouted from up ahead. When the officers reached him, he pointed to the ground at what appeared to be a trail of some sort. "There are a lot of footprints, Sir," the man said.

"Excellent work, Sergeant," Horemheb replied. "Select ten of our best men and come along with us. We'll see where it goes." Turning to the others, he said, "The rest of you remain here for now. Be on the alert. These men are excellent marksmen, so don't make yourself a target."

Leaving the camels behind, the small patrol followed the scout up the path leading from the river. The soil began to change under their feet. The ground had become dry. Before long there were no plants or any evidence of life. "We're on the edge of the red land," Horemheb said.

After walking a good distance, they stopped to drink. The sun still hovered midway in the sky, so they drank sparingly. "I regret everything I said about those camels," Khamet grumbled.

Suddenly, dozens of arrows thudded into the ground making them jump. Horemheb realized the Nubians had fenced them in. They were prisoners within a circle of warriors blocking their escape. Reluctantly he let his spear fall to the ground. "Throw down your weapons, men. We're surrounded."

CHAPTER SIX

IKHEY

The Nubians rushed forward and bound the enemy's hands. Picking up the Egyptian's weapons, they forced the captives to follow a tall warrior.

"Are all of these men so tall?" Horemheb grumbled as he looked around.

"There's your answer," Khamet murmured looking at the dark-skinned warriors walking on each side of them. They were in fact, more than a head taller than the Egyptians.

Naked, except for a leather apron protecting their modesty, the Nubians carried magnificent bows over their shoulders. Daggers were tied to the upper arm. At just the right angle, the sunlight made the color of their ebony skin appear dark purple. Their feet looked to be as tough as leather.

As they moved along a well-worn path away from the river, one of Horemheb's men spoke to the Africans in their language. His attempts to communicate were ignored.

A Nubian beside them said in perfect Egyptian, "You are approaching our camp. You will not speak or look our king in the face. Prostrate yourselves before him and do not move." His use of their tongue convinced Horemheb the man must have been an escaped slave.

"Look at the ground," Khamet whispered. "The soil's moist again and richer."

"The trail must have turned back toward the river," Horemheb said. A few moments later they were astonished to find themselves walking through a field of corn.

Round huts with pointed straw roofs could be seen ahead. Children played between the simple structures as elderly women kept an eye on them. Suddenly, more warriors ran toward them crying out in an ululating chant, startling the strangers. A loud staccato beat of a large drum caused the Nubians to turn toward a giant of a man standing in front of the biggest house. A leopard skin covered his shoulder, convincing Horemheb that he had to be the king. Egyptian Pharaohs also revered the leopard.

A magnificent woman stood on his right, holding a spear. Even though the female form in Egypt is celebrated in art and sculpture, none of the Egyptians had seen such perfection. Well-muscled, she held her head proudly. Her firm breasts moved slightly as she turned her head to stare contemptuously at the Egyptians.

"Down," someone shouted, ordering the Egyptians to fall on their faces. The man who had spoken in their tongue moved forward and stood near the giant. The king spoke in a loud, angry deep voice, shaking his fist at the intruders. His people shouted in agreement when he finished. He raised his hand and waited for the translation.

"King Ikhey says you are his prisoners, and he will show no mercy," the interpreter said. "You have passed the whitewater and entered his land. Why have you invaded his country?"

When no one responded, Ikhey said, "Is there not a man of courage among you who will speak?"

When Horemheb heard the interpretation he replied in a loud voice, "I will speak, Tall One. But a warrior cannot speak while on his stomach."

Ikhey burst out laughing when he heard Horemheb's words. "Let him stand," the king commanded, and two men pulled the Egyptian to his feet.

"I am Horemheb, Great King. We have passed the whitewater to find you. We come to ask you the same question. Why have your men invaded our land beyond the water barrier? You have broken our treaty of peace."

"I can't tell him that," the interpreter whispered shaking his head. "I must put your words more politely." When he finally translated, the king let out a great guffaw, causing his warriors to imitate him.

"You are not afraid, Horem," Ikhey said. "You speak like a soldier. Because of this you will fight my champion. If you win, you and your men will live and be my slaves. If you lose, all will die."

When the interpreter finished, Horemheb felt as if he had received a swift punch to the stomach. He looked at his men lying face down. Would he be able to save them? His father always told him to stand up to bullies. He defiantly stuck out his chin and laughed. "Send your champion, Majesty," he shouted. "He won't last long."

This too amused the Nubian king who ordered the remaining prisoners be taken to a large cage beside his hut. The translator said, "The only weapon for this fight will be the spear." Horemheb's heart beat faster when he heard the choice of weapons, but his spear had been taken away.

"I will need my spear," Horemheb said. The interpreter repeated his request to the king, who now sat on a cleverly built chair made of just two pieces of wood. The pieces fitted one inside the other and the weight of the person maintained a perfect balance. He nodded and a warrior returned Horemheb's weapon. Two other women-warriors came forward and stood behind the king. "The first woman must be his queen," he mumbled. "These must be more wives." Like the men, the women were unclothed except for the small apron. Their long legs and firm bodies took the Egyptians' breath away. The manner in which they held their spears, however, left no doubt that all three were warriors.

An unarmed soldier approached Horemheb and untied him. Out of the corner of his eye, the woman who had been standing beside the king walked slowly toward him. He tried unsuccessfully to keep his eyes straight ahead. *She's beyond belief. Her body looks like our Mother Isis in the flesh.* He tried not to flinch as she reached out and ran her fingers through his hair. He could see by her expression that the feel of it surprised her. Her full lips curved up in a smile and she suddenly burst out laughing. Abruptly, she spat on the ground, turned around and walked back to her place beside the king.

The crowd began shouting excitedly again causing Horemheb to turn in their direction. Coming toward him loomed the largest man he had ever seen. *By the gods. This creature from Seth's bowels will be my doom. What a monster.* He could see the fear on his men's faces as one of the women warriors used a stick to trace a large circle in the dirt around their captain.

"For Horus and Pharaoh" Horemheb shouted raising his spear, shaking it at the king's champion.

Hearing his cry, the Nubians grew silent.

"May the gods give me strength," he added. The interpreter didn't translate his words, but everyone quickly moved away from the circle. Inwardly, Horemheb felt little fear. He prayed silently, *Horus give me strength. Help me save my men, Mighty god*. He looked again at the king. He felt deep down that the king has no intention of letting the Egyptians live. This has to be some kind of test of the king's honor.

Ikhey's champion entered the circle and removed his headband, arm bracelets and dagger. Turning to the king, he bowed his head slowly before facing his small foe. Letting out a blood-curdling scream, he lunged at the Egyptian but Horemheb easily stepped aside. Neither man wanted to throw his spear, lest he miss and become defenseless.

Horemheb had a plan. Faster than his opponent, he circled the man and thrust with his spear as he did fighting crocodiles back home. The tall warrior cried out as Horemheb sliced the back of the man's right leg, drawing first blood.

"Missed," Horemheb hissed to himself. He hoped the giant's anger would unnerve the man and make him take chances. That's what he did as he rushed at the Egyptian. Horemheb stuck his spear between the giant's legs tripping him. As the Nubian fell, his opponent moved to the other side of the circle, out of the man's reach.

Ikhey's champion got up quickly and took aim at Horemheb's head and threw his spear at lightning speed.

Horemheb jumped aside again but not quickly enough. The Nubian's spear grazed his head just above his ear. Blood flowed down from the cut, dripping onto his shoulder. The giant's spear now lay outside the circle and he rushed toward his opponent once more. The Egyptian knew he couldn't let his adversary get close enough to grab him. He would be easily crushed by the man's strength. With a quick jab with his spear he cut open a gash in the giant's side. The Nubian yelled in pain and lunged at his opponent's legs, trying to bring him down.

Using his spear for leverage, Horemheb jumped straight up into the air and over the man. He stepped onto the man's back and leapt to the other side of the circle, mocking the man with his laugh. "What's wrong great turtle? You're too slow for this jackal."

The giant roared even louder and ignoring Horemheb's spear charged at the smaller man.

Horemheb saw his chance and stabbed the Nubian in the abdomen, a blow that would have brought any other man down. The man swung and with his strong arm knocked Horemheb's spear out of his hand. It fell across the ground but stayed within the circle.

"By the gods," Horemheb exclaimed. "I must do this." He ran to the other side and picked up the weapon and turned to face his opponent again. Blood spilled from the giant's gut and from the deep gash on his thigh. "How can you still be moving?" Horemheb shouted at the man. *If I can only bring him down.* Looking for an opening he saw how the Nubian had trouble with his stomach. As the giant neared him, Horemheb used the full length of the spear, striking the Nubian once more deep into his stomach making him fall onto his side.

Shouting what must have been curses, the Nubian angrily shook his fist at him. The Egyptian quickly pulled back on his spear, tearing the man's gut, spilling his intestines onto the ground. Kicking the giant over, Horemheb struck him again, this time deep into his heart. The giant gasped and died. He deliberately stuck the blunt end of his spear into the dirt like a king's staff. Blood dripped from its pointed tip onto the ground. A great roar of anger grew from the crowd of Nubian warriors.

The noise of the crowd suddenly stopped and Horemheb turned to see the king walking toward him. Ikhey's face remained expressionless. He stood and approached the dead warrior. Stretching out his hand, one of the Nubian warriors handed the king the man's headdress, dagger and armbands. Turning to Horemheb, the king handed them to him. He spoke and waited for the translation.

The interpreter began, "The king says, 'These are yours. You will live, as will your men, but only to serve me. You are my slaves now and will be treated as such.'"

Two warriors pushed Horemheb roughly toward his comrades. They were taken out of the cage and forced into a fenced-in pen on the edge of the village. They joined several families of goats inside the enclosure. Ten guards were posted—one for each Egyptian.

"At least we're alive, thanks to you, brother," Khamet said." His men crowded around pounding him on the back.

"You will stay here," the interpreter told them. "Any attempt to escape will mean death." He spit on the ground, then, walked away.

"They weren't expecting this," Khamet said nervously. "They might still try to kill us when the king leaves the village."

One of his men said, "Well I certainly wish one of those female warriors would try to kill me. Have you ever seen such women?" He made a crude gesture, but Horemheb stopped him.

"Hold your tongue, Badru," he ordered. "Concentrate on finding a way to get out of here." The man nodded, moving away. "I disagree, Khamet," Horemheb responded to his friend's statement. "I don't think they'll try to kill us. I believe these people will keep their word. If not, we would already be dead. What we need now is to plan a way of escape." Sitting down on the ground, they put their heads together, hoping to come up with something.

On board the *Breath of Horus*, Merimose said, "It's been almost a week, my Lord. I'm concerned for our scouts."

Minnakf nodded. "I understand, Meri, but I still advise caution. They may have had to go farther inland than we anticipated." As they were speaking, Minnakf's aide brought a courier on deck.

"He says he came by canoe from Edfu, General," the aide said. "He's carrying an important message that arrived by pigeon this morning."

"Approach," Merimose ordered, motioning for the man to come closer. The messenger handed him a small rolled-up parchment with Pharaoh's seal.

"This can only mean trouble," Minnakf said. As Merimose read the message, his face turned into a scowl. He handed it over to the general.

When Minnakf finished reading he swore, "By Seth's foul breath." Shaking his head he added, "I pray it isn't true." The two men walked along the railing for a while, watching the river race past.

Speaking quietly, Merimose shook his head. "Young Thutmose has been stricken with a high fever. This means his majesty's plan to join us in our victory has changed. He must stay at his son's side."

The general nodded. "Rightfully so. These fevers blowing down from the delta can be dangerous. I don't trust Pharaoh's healers to find the cause. You never know with them." He paused, then, prayed, "May Horus and Amun help the prince."

"Let it be so," his friend replied.

After writing a response, they called for the courier and gave him a silver coin to ensure his fast return to Edfu. "It's better he return at once than stay around," Merimose observed. "Word could leak out and demoralize the men."

"Yes, good thinking," Minnakf said. Becoming thoughtful, he asked quietly. "If Thutmose dies, who succeeds him?"

"The next son in line is named after his great grandfather. He will be the fourth Pharaoh named Amenhotep."

The Egyptian prisoners in the goat pen were worried. "What about the men we left behind with the camels?" Badru asked.

"They were ordered to go back to the fort if we didn't return that first night," Horemheb said. "If they had been attacked or captured, they would have been brought here. I think we can safely say they made it back." Trying to refocus his men's attention he said, "What we need to do now is observe our guard's routine. Watch what they do all day. Where do they go when they are relieved of duty? Remember their pattern."

"We already know, Brother," Khamet replied. "When the sun comes up we are fed cornbread and given water before being marched to the fields. While we hoe and weed they stand nearby. At midday it's more bread and water."

"We work until dusk and are forced back here," another said. "It never changes."

"Of course," Horemheb said, "and maybe that can be to our advantage."

The next night, he surprised them with a plan. "It's dangerous, but it might work. We have no weapons so we're forced to be cunning. I've seen a small plant growing in the fields that grows in my village back home. When its clear sap is mixed with water, it makes you fall asleep very fast. I've already collected and hidden enough of them." Pulling one out from under the waistband of his kilt, he passed it around. "There are more under that flat rock in the corner of the pen. I propose that in the morning when the three of us are forced to go for water, we squeeze the sap into the skins when the guards aren't looking".

"It's risky," Khamet said, "but what other choice do we have?"

"None," Horemheb replied. "Tomorrow we cannot drink any water. The guards drink when we do, so only pretend to drink. Don't let them see you closing your lips when you do. After they've fallen asleep, take their weapons and keep low to the ground. Head for the river. If the gods are with us, we might get away."

"I'd rather bash them with my hoe," one his men grumbled.

"Speed is the key," Horemheb insisted. "Pray Horus will give us the strength of his mighty wings."

"I'm so sick of this goat smell," someone said. "I'm ready to eat one of these beasts." That made them laugh.

"Look at them," Badu said, pointing to the guards. "They don't even know what we're laughing about."

The next morning, everything went according to plan. The same three men were selected to go for water. Using the plants hidden on their persons they were able to squeeze the sap into the newly filled water skins.

As they waited at the river, one of the guards abruptly jumped in for a swim. Fortunately there were no crocodiles in the swift current. The distraction worried Horemheb. It meant there would be a delay returning with the water. The guard cavorted in the river for what seemed a long time before rejoining his comrades.

Lifting the heavy water skins onto their shoulders, the prisoners were glad to be finally heading back. Halfway there they encountered women coming for water and the guards stopped to flirt with them. Because the Nubians wore so little clothing, the advances by the guards left little to the imagination. One of the more nubile women welcomed their advances and teased them until her companions made her rejoin them.

Reaching the fields at last, the Egyptians were given their midday bread. The guards drank their fill of water first, leaving the rest to be passed around by the prisoners who only mimicked drinking.

It took a long time before the first guard slumped to the ground. His prisoner took the unconscious guard's weapons and hid him between rows of the corn. Then, keeping low to the ground, he made his way along the path. A second guard fell without incident, allowing another prisoner to disappear.

As Horemheb watched his men escape, he realized his own guard hadn't taken any water. His heart raced because if he were captured, his men would be executed. He had to get away. Offering the guard the water skin again, the man only shook his head. With no other option, Horemheb whacked his guard over the head with his hoe.

Horemheb's leg muscles protested the crouching and running as he hurried along the path. Someone up ahead moved toward him. "Is that you, Khamet?" he whispered. "What did you do? Wait until all of your men got away?"

"I thought that's what you would do, Harm," his friend replied with a grin. The first escapee had waited for them to catch up. Together again as a unit, they moved quickly toward the safety of the river.

"Quiet," Badru warned to those behind him. "Stop." To their dismay, they had come face to face with three women returning with jars of water. Horemheb's men rushed forward to stop them from crying out. The women, however, were fighters and pulled out their daggers engaging the escapees in hand-to-hand. The Nubians fought well, but were no match for ten opponents.

"Take one of them prisoner," Horemheb called to Khamet. Ruthlessly, two of the women's throats were cut, their bodies hidden off the path in some tall grass. Cutting cloth strips from their kilts they gagged the remaining woman's mouth before tying her hands. She tried to bite her attackers, knocking one, then, another to the ground. She fought savagely, equal to any of Horemheb's men. It took three men finally to keep her still.

"Hurry men," Horemheb said as he ran toward the river. "We're at risk of being spotted from the cliffs up ahead. Keep a sharp eye all around you." The woman continued to struggle, so Horemheb knocked her unconscious and threw her over his shoulder.

"Ah, rank has its privileges," Badru quipped.

"That puts you on guard duty, soldier," Horemheb growled back. He had to admit, however, the feel of such a beautiful woman so close to him, proved exciting.

Upon reaching the road around the whitewater barrier, they could see the fort in the distance. A trumpet blew in the fort's tower as soon as the missing men were seen coming down the road. Word spread throughout the camp causing a great roar of jubilation that became so intense it sounded like an approaching sandstorm.

Hundreds of soldiers ran to the roadside and gawked at the unconscious prisoner on Horemheb's shoulder. Everyone cheered and pounded their shields. Soon the crowd grew into hundreds, then thousands by the time they reached the fort.

General Minnakf heard the cheers and Merimose joined him as they walked out of the fortress gates to meet the lost patrol. Minnakf smiled when he saw that his men were uninjured. But when he saw the nearly naked woman lying at Horemheb's feet, his jaw dropped in surprise.

"Reporting for duty, Sir," Horemheb declared with a salute. "But before we resume our posts, General, could we have some beer?"

CHAPTER SEVEN

ABAR

The Nubian prisoner had been tied up near Horemheb's tent. He and his friend had decided to set up camp ashore so they could be near their troops.

"She's awake," Khamet said.

"Bring Shabaka," Horemheb ordered. Khamet sent one of his men and they returned a short time later.

The captive had been bound to a large post with her hands above her head to keep her from chewing through the ropes.

"She's *still* trying to bite us, Captain," Shabaka said. "I say throw her to the crocs."

"And what would *they* tell us?" Horemheb said. "We need to know more about what is going on in their camp. Will the crocs tell us that? Moreover, how could you throw such a beautiful creature to those slimy servants of Seth?" The translator shook his head, knowing better than to respond.

"Tell her we'll remove the gag if she'll speak to us," Horemheb commanded. "Try to find out who she is."

Shabaka walked over to her, keeping his distance. He spoke for a short time, then, removed the cloth gag. She spat on the ground immediately, then, began to speak. "That's a good sign," Horemheb observed. "Perhaps now we'll learn something."

The translator said, "She's asking for water, plus a dagger to kill herself. She's been dishonored."

"Of course she feels so, but who is she?" Horemheb insisted.

"By her answers, Sir, especially her choice of words, I know she's not like most of the women of my country. She's proud and arrogant. Qualities of a warrior, yes, but there is something more. I can't explain it."

"What do you mean?"

"Well, Shabaka continued, "Look at her hands. They're not calloused like other women's. It means she doesn't grind corn or work in the fields."

Khamet spoke up. "Maybe she's one of Ikhey's wives. They wouldn't do those things, would they?"

"Yes they would, Captain. Our women always prepare food for their own family, even the king's wives." Shabaka thought a moment and added, "There's also some kind of mark on the back of her neck. I've not seen one like it."

"Could the mark indicate she's one of his wives?" Horemheb demanded.

"It could my Lord, but I don't think so. I saw his wives at a celebration several years ago. Our women don't have such marks on their skin."

"I will speak to her," Horemheb said. "Will she answer me?"

Shabaka shrugged. "You can try, Captain."

The young woman frowned as Horemheb approached. She spat on the ground, causing him to turn and shout in exasperation, "Why do they do so much spitting?"

The translator laughed. "She curses the ground you walk on, my Lord. We believe our spit mixes with our Mother earth, invoking the curse of Ndombi, the god of darkness."

Horemheb smiled. "Ah yes, you mean Seth. That's what we call him. I want you now to interpret my words exactly."

"Yes, Captain."

Horemheb said, "We do not mean to harm you. We'll bring water and food if you agree to cooperate."

The woman looked at Shabaka and shouted angrily. Horemheb could almost guess what she said.

"She's cursing me, Captain. She says I have betrayed her and my people."

"You have, Shabaka," Horemheb replied. "Tell her to stand." The woman did so with great difficulty. With her hands to help her, she managed to lift herself up. Horemheb walked slowly around her as if inspecting a prize horse. When he saw the mark on her neck he stopped. "I've seen this before," he mumbled, "but where? Perhaps on the neck of the fallen champion? No. Why can't I remember?"

The woman spoke to Shabaka. "'My people will kill all of you,' she boasts, my Lord."

"Tell her this. She and all of her people will die unless she helps us." Horemheb turned and stomped away. Speaking to Khamet, he said, "When she's thirsty enough she'll talk."

Marveling at the beautiful display of colors in the sky as the sun rose in the east, Horemheb spotted a large galley on the river. Instantly he recognized it as Pharaoh's ship. "Pharaoh is here." he shouted.

General Minnakf rushed outside and leaned over the railing, not believing his eyes. "By the gods. His Majesty's here." Trumpeters sounded the army's call to assemble. Lord Merimose quickly changed his clothes, putting on his robe of office. He ordered his chariot brought to the gangplank, as did the General of the Army. The two men rode off to greet their sovereign.

When the royal galley arrived, Horemheb watched as lines were thrown ashore to moor the great vessel. The king emerged from his cabin and walked toward the railing. Horemheb laughed. "Look at him. Amenhotep couldn't be more pleased. He's taken everyone by surprise." Pharaoh waited with his hands on his hips at the top of the gangplank like an irate schoolteacher. His guards rushed to take up positions in front of the ship.

Horemheb and his friend waited on the dock as the ship's crew prepared for his majesty to come ashore. Unnoticed by the king, the two friends heard Pharaoh say, "Here come those pompous old fools." He said it quietly nodding toward his general and vizier. "Don't tell them I said that."

Horemheb smiled because he knew the king actually liked the two men heading his way.

"Your carrying chair is ready Majesty," the guardsman announced. The golden palanquin had been brought up from the hold awaiting the Divine Son of Ra's pleasure.

Lord Merimose arrived first and stepped down from his chariot, making obeisance before the king. General Minnakf saluted on one knee, his fist across his chest.

"Welcome, Divine One," Merimose began when the king allowed him to stand. "This is a glorious and unexpected pleasure."

"The Army is ready for your command, Great Pharaoh," Minnakf declared loud enough for everyone to hear. He gave a signal and trumpets sounded as the Ruler of the Two Lands walked slowly down the gangplank, stopping in front of his old friends.

Nodding, he said, "Word has reached us that the reconnaissance team has returned. Our battle with Nubia is about to begin. I want my pavilion set up here, and we will discuss our plans."

The king's words surprised Horemheb. "How could Pharaoh have already learned of our return?" he murmured to Khamet. "We've only been back two days." His colleague shrugged and with a look, warned his friend about talking.

"We'll assemble the pavilion at once, Mighty Lord." Minnakf said. He signaled for Horemheb and the rest of his staff to bring the great tent from the hold.

Everyone waited until Amenhotep stepped up into his carrying chair and sat down. "We are going to the temple of the goddess Anukis to give thanks for our safe arrival," he announced. The bearers lifted the chair and began a slow walk to the shrine. Warriors along the way knelt before him and cheered as he passed, careful not to look upon his face. His personal guards walked on each side of him forming a protective shield. Horemheb walked up on deck, and when he turned, he could see in the distance the priests preparing to welcome Pharaoh to the sacred shrine. They held bowls of incense for him to carry before the goddess.

General Minnakf supervised the raising of the king's pavilion even though Horemheb and Khamet's men did all the work. Once in place, the general growled, "This is a disaster. Pharaoh's presence complicates everything. We can't let him interfere with our war plans."

"We agree, General," Horemheb said. He was certain the general had not expected a response. "Only we have been beyond the white water, and the reconnaissance team knows where to go. We'll convince him of it if you agree, my Lord."

"No. You will not speak to his majesty unless spoken to. You will defer any questions to me. Is that understood?" He saw the two men glance at each other.

"And there's to be no mention of your Nubian prisoner either." Horemheb saluted and Khamet felt relieved. His friend would not be tempted to say anything stupid.

Lord Merimose sat down on one of the canvas chairs in the king's tent. "Well, we know Prince Thutmose has improved, or the king wouldn't be here." Turning toward the general, he said, "Pharaoh wants the glory of your certain victory, my friend. Pharaohs have done so for centuries." He frowned as he continued. "But how could he know our men had escaped? How did he find out?"

"A messenger pigeon must have been sent up to Edfu, my Lord," Khamet said. "From there another bird could have taken the message to Thebes. We can check to see who sent them."

The Vizier shook his head, "It doesn't matter now that he's here."

Minnakft looked at the younger officers. "Are we decided then on how the battle will begin?"

Captain Khamet nodded. "One half of each battalion will advance around the rapids, placing their archers at the front, General. Then the sword and spearmen will follow to finish them off."

"Khamet and I will hunt down the Nubian king, my Lord, and bring him to you for your pleasure—oh, and his majesty's, of course," Horemheb said. "I'm trying now to get information from the prisoner that might help us, but she's being uncooperative."

"Make her talk, Captain," Minnakf growled. "Or we'll do it for you. That's an order."

"As you command General," Horemheb said. "Our only reason for letting her live is to find out the location of Nubia's capital." He paused a moment not sure how to continue. "But there's another matter, my Lord. It concerns Pharaoh. You cannot guarantee his safety during the battle. He must be convinced to remain here."

"Gods," the general growled, clearing his throat. "You forget yourselves. No one can tell his majesty what to do, especially on the battlefield. I'm going to rely on you two to keep him safe. Put your best team around him."

"As you say, my Lord," Horemheb answered. "But only the gods can say what will happen. Ikhey's archers are skilled, so we'll need more shields around the king."

From the other side of camp cheers could be heard again as Pharaoh began his return to the ship. When his bearers lowered the carrying chair and his feet touched the ground, every soldier knelt down instantly. Like the ripples on a pond, row upon row knelt facing him. Lord Merimose fell prostrate before him once again. Giving his Vizier permission to rise, Amenhotep waved to the army, then, entered his tent, indicating for the four men to follow.

"Ah, Horemheb, Khamet. It is good to see you again," Pharaoh said. "Tell us about your escape from this Nubian giant."

"Majesty," Horemheb began, "he's taller than any man I have ever seen. He is as black as ebony and strong as an ox." Amenhotep's eyes showed surprise as the captain continued. "But I also believe he's a man of his word. He promised if I defeated his champion, he would let us live—and he kept his word."

"You fought knowing it would mean the death of your men?" the king said.

"Yes, Majesty, but Horus stood with me and my spear. Unfortunately, they took it from me after the fight. I've had it forever."

"It's like his right arm, Great One," Khamet said.

Amenhotep frowned and pulled on his small goatee. "What does the man who trained him say about all this?"

Khamet bowed his head slightly to the king. "We were outnumbered a hundred to one, Majesty. Horemheb is not only brave, but a clever fighter, as well. None of us would have thought of putting the guards to sleep."

"Indeed," Pharaoh nodded. "It would seem we must keep an eye on this spearman, General." Minnakf tried to smile. The king waved his hand dismissing the young officers, but indicated he wanted the other two to remain.

Standing just outside the tent, the two men could easily hear Pharaoh's words through the canvas. "We want that warrior at our side when we attack, Minnakf." A pause ensued, then they heard the king say "You look troubled. What is it? Tell me." Because the two men were friends, pharaoh had dispensed with the royal "we," relaxing protocol.

"Merimose and I are concerned for your safety, Mighty Pharaoh. Not your courage, but your person. If you permit us to say, you mustn't put yourself at such risk."

"No," the king shouted. "I am the Son of Ra. The gods protect me."

"Maybe so, Majesty," Merimose said. "But they have not always done so. Many Pharaohs have died in battle. Your son has just recovered from a serious illness, may the gods be praised. You cannot put the throne in jeopardy. Forgive me for my impertinence, Great One."

Horemheb moved a little closer to the tent and heard Amenhotep let out a great sigh. "My friends. I know you both only want to protect me, and I am grateful for it. But I want a personal victory to put on my monuments. One my family will always remember."

The general spoke in a kinder voice. "Rightfully so, Great Father. You will be with us at the moment of victory—and it will be yours. Trust us Majesty."

Outside, Horemheb whispered, "Pharaoh's not pleased. He's going to insist on coming with us." Khamet nodded. They heard the king say, "I will consider what you say. Now, when do we attack?"

"The day after tomorrow," Minnakf said. "Just before dawn."

"She won't talk to me, Captain," Kashta said. He walked away from the Nubian prisoner. "She wants you and you alone to question her."

"Me?" Horemheb said. "How am I to question her? Don't be ridiculous."

"It's all she will say to me, Captain. You must try."

Horemheb frowned and headed for where the woman had been moved. He found her sitting on a wooden bench, hands tied together in front of her. He could tell by bits of bread and an empty cup she had been allowed to eat and drink. Someone had given her a simple linen robe. *Probably one of the soldier's wives in Swentet.* She stood as he approached. The garment could not hide her beauty. He remembered her as she stood before him, touching his hair. It had been a sensuous gesture almost unnerving him.

He motioned for her to sit back down. "You've been given water and food because you agreed to talk to me," he said. She didn't respond but looked up at him with deep penetrating eyes.

"I know you can't understand a word I'm saying you poor, uneducated creature. But you must tell me the location of your capital city." When she still didn't respond, he turned to leave.

"Why should I betray my people?" she asked in Egyptian. Seeing his surprised look she added, "Oh yes, I speak your cursed tongue, may my gods forgive me."

Horemheb smiled. "I see the face of a woman," he said, "but hear the mind of a warrior." Standing a safe distance from her, he added, "First of all, who are you?"

"I am Abar," she answered. "Star of the Morning." Looking at him intently, she asked, "Why did you kill my companions?"

"I regret that," he told her honestly. "We could not stop to fight if we were to escape."

"They should have been allowed to die like warriors," she said angrily.

Horemheb shook his head. "Unfortunate casualties of war," he said. "All soldiers know this." Her eyes narrowed as she looked at him more closely. He could tell she wasn't aware he was watching her until their eyes met, making her look quickly away.

"Your king is here," she said. "I heard all the cheering." Horemheb didn't respond. "He too will die, your king," she taunted. The Egyptian didn't react. "I must walk by my sacred river. Will you let me?"

"Your river?" he protested. "This river is the Father and Mother of Egypt, our land."

Shaking her head, Abar said, "Not so. Everyone knows the river comes from the gods beyond the waterfalls in the south. Because he travels through our Land before yours, he is our River God."

Horemheb smiled at her for the first time. "I will not argue about gods with you," he said. He liked the sound of her voice. Her skin looked as smooth as polished ebony and her rounded breasts moved slightly when she turned her neck. "Guards," he called. "I will walk with the prisoner along the river. Perhaps I can draw more words from her with honey than with Shabaka's vinegar." She tried not to smile so the guards wouldn't see she understood what had been said. She wondered why Horemheb didn't tell his men she knew their tongue.

"She bites, Captain," one of the guards reminded him. "I have the marks to prove it."

"As do I, soldier," Horemheb shot back. "Let's take four men with us. That way I'll have nothing to fear."

Abar stood silently as the guards removed the ropes from her hands and feet. Gently pushing her ahead of him, Horemheb ordered his men to walk behind him. "I'm trying to understand her tongue," he told them. To the woman he said, "Speak softly. It may benefit us if everyone still believes you can't speak our language." She nodded and walked slowly, stretching her leg muscles. At the river's edge, she sat down on the soft grass, putting her hands into the water. She winced in pain when it flowed over the abrasions the ropes had made in her skin, but didn't cry out.

"How many are in your family?" Horemheb asked, sitting down on the grass a body-length away from her. "Not too loudly, remember."

"We were six," she replied softly. "Now we are four, since you killed two of my cousins."

He frowned. "I thought you said they were your sisters."

"Sister, cousin" she answered. "In our tongue they are the same word."

Horemheb, wary of getting too close to the woman, still felt a kind of magnetism radiating from her. It made him uncomfortable. "Where is your king's city? We know it can't be the village where we were held prisoner."

Abar laughed softly and turned her head to gaze across the water. "It is in the mountains," she told him. "But you'll never find it. This camp near the whitewater is only for raising corn as you saw. Our king will move on."

"You could take me to that place," Horemheb insisted.

"True, but why would I betray my king and people?" she said, lowering her voice in anger. Abruptly, before Horemheb could move, the prisoner stood and jumped into the river. She sank immediately and he dove in shouting for the guards to follow him. Swimming underwater, he felt her leg and grabbed an ankle. Pulling her up against the strong current, they reached the surface. "Swim," he shouted at her.

""I can't," she sputtered, coughing up a lot of water.

"Guards," Horemheb cried, "Grab her." He pushed her forcefully toward shore. "Such a stupid woman," he growled. She managed to slap him hard on the face as he helped his men pull her up onto the bank. In his struggle underwater, his kilt had been lost, making him self-conscious climbing out of the water. "Bring me a kilt," he ordered angrily, ignoring the amusement on the faces of his men.

When the prisoner had coughed up the rest of the water, she saw his nakedness and laughed. Horemheb ignored her, trying to understand why the woman had jumped. When he saw that his men were not close enough to hear, he said, "Why would a warrior jump into the river to kill herself? What kind of soldier's death is that?"

"At least it would have been by my own hand, son of a jackal," she spat at him. At that moment, the guard arrived with his kilt, and Horemheb dressed quickly.

"Tie up her hands and feet, and find something to gag her with," he ordered. "I don't want the whole camp listening to her curses. Tie her to the large post by my tent. Do it as if you were going to roast her over the fire. Do you understand?"

"Yes, Captain," his men replied. With her mouth covered, the guards lifted her onto their shoulders, heading back to camp. Horemheb watched as they tied her to the pole with her hands behind her. More ropes were added until she looked like an antelope ready for roasting. Saluting their commander, the guards left her alone with him.

Moving up close enough to whisper in her ear, he said, "Tomorrow your people will die. I will cook you here when I return. You had your chance to help me find a peaceful solution, but now Nubia will pay." Mocking her custom, he spat on the ground at her feet and walked away.

CHAPTER EIGHT

INTO THE BATTLE

Only two hours remained before sunrise. Khamet led the Ptah Battalion around the rapids and placed his archers out in front of them. The other warriors stood at the ready behind them.

Back at camp, Pharaoh's horse had been saddled. He would be accompanied by not only his general, but Horemheb who chose to ride his camel.

"Men of Horus Battalion!" Horemheb shouted, "Lead our Divine Pharaoh to the whitewater, and may the gods be with us!"

His men cheered in response and struck their copper shields with their swords. The thunderous sound echoed up through the canyon, reverberating over the water toward Abu. A company of fifty archers marched on each side of the king, as Horemheb led the way. The narrow trail proved to be slippery, dampened by the mist from the falls.

The horses and camels became skittish and Horemheb decided his majesty should dismount. The men led the animals individually, reassuring them with pats on the neck.

"I can see why people believe the gods stir up the water," Amenhotep yelled above the roar of the rapids. "It is a frightening sound." When the horses were calm again, the king and his aides remounted, moving forward toward the Ptah Battalion.

The sun had been up for a short time when a messenger from Khamet ran toward Horemheb, but fell onto one knee when he saw Pharaoh. "Captain Khamet has found the enemy, Majesty. Our scouts spotted them this side of the village. They're harvesting corn and are unaware of our presence!"

"Excellent," the general replied. "We'll take them by surprise. Tell your captain to begin the attack."

"Wait!" Pharaoh shouted. "We will go to the front, General! It is our rightful place."

"He's right, General," Horemheb declared. "When the men see Pharaoh riding in front of them it will stir up their utmost bravery."

Nodding to the king, Minnakf replied, "As you command, Great One. Clear a path for Pharaoh."

The warriors made way as the riders urged their horses into a full gallop. When they reached Khamet's position, the captain met them, and knelt to salute.

"Forgive me, Majesty, you must dismount. You're an easy target. Advance with us on foot, if you'll forgive my impertinence."

"Well spoken, Captain," Amenhotep replied with a smile as he got down. The horses and camels were quickly led back toward the river.

"Do they know we're here?" Horemheb asked.

"No, the sound of the waterfall has covered our movements, but we must go now or lose the element of surprise," Khamet told them.

"Then attack," Pharaoh ordered.

"Silence is the key," Horemheb interrupted, hoping to explain. "We use banners to communicate our commands, Majesty." He gave an order and a yellow banner waved back and forth. As if by magic, a cloud of arrows flew into the air raining down on the Nubians harvesting corn. Cries of pain and surprise rose from the field as hundreds of the enemy fell dead. While the archers reloaded, the swordsmen rushed in to put an end to those who might have been wounded.

Horemheb raised his hand again, and a red banner flew this time. Khamet, who had rejoined his men, led the Horus Battalion. It charged ahead toward the

INTO THE BATTLE

settlement where the Egyptians had been held prisoner. Catching the Nubians by surprise, they took them captive. As the gods would have it, they became Pharaoh's prisoners.

"Where is he?" Amenhotep shouted. Horemheb knew Pharaoh meant King Ikhey.

A messenger rushed toward them. "Horus' men have cut him off and blocked Ikhey's escape, Majesty. He's gone to a cave in the cliffs at the far end of the plain!"

"Take as many prisoners as you can, General," the king commanded. "These Nubians must be taught a lesson."

"We'll advance toward Khamet's position," Horemheb shouted to the messenger. "Tell him to wait for Pharaoh." The runner saluted and ran back to his company.

"Get down," Horemheb shouted, oblivious to the fact that he had just ordered his king and his general. "There are hundreds of archers in there with him. I do believe he is trapped, general."

"Good," Minnakf responded. "Let's send him a message! Bring the interpreter." When the man arrived, they asked him if he could also write in the Nubian language.

"I can, General, but have no materials," the man replied.

"Tear off a piece of your kilt," Horemheb ordered, and the man did so. Using the broken shaft of the arrow as a pen, the archer cut his finger with his dagger, and wrote the message in blood:

"Surrender the king. All will live."

Their best warrior chose an acacia tree near the cave entrance as his target. Wrapping the message around the shaft of his arrow, he used an unraveled piece of rope to tie it in place. Aiming carefully, he shot the arrow into the trunk of the tree.

"Raise the white banner," Horemheb commanded, and the rain of arrows ceased.

"We want their king alive, General," Amenhotep declared. "He must be taken to Thebes so all may see the fate of those who rebel against us."

"Let me bring him to you, Majesty," Horemheb suggested quietly. "I know what he looks like and he knows me. As one warrior to another, maybe he'll yield to me."

"Don't be foolish, Captain," the general growled. "We'll wait for a reply."

Amenhotep looked at the young officer with new admiration and respect. "We agree with Minnakf, Captain. We'll wait him out."

Horemheb nodded and leaned on a spear given to him by one of his men. The Nubians had kept his old one.

After what seemed a long period of time, the Egyptians became restless. The adrenaline rush from the battle subsided, and most now sat on the ground using their shields as protection from the sun.

"Someone's coming," a soldier shouted.

The interpreter rushed toward his commanders. He handed over the message the enemy gave him. He pointed to the writing on the back. Speaking loudly so all could hear he said, "This is the answer, Majesty. ' Send in the killer of champions. The king will surrender to him alone.' That's all it says, Great One."

"He means Horemheb," Khamet told Pharaoh.

"Yes, so we understand," Amenhotep replied. "But perhaps he wants to kill our best warrior as a last act of revenge!"

"No, Majesty. He is a man of his word. He *will* surrender—I believe him."

The king looked at the general and Minnakf nodded. "Very well, Captain, we agree. Horus go with you."

Horemheb saluted and took Khamet and five of his best men along with the interpreter.

A lone figure emerged slowly from the cave's shadows. His imposing stature indicated to everyone that he could only be the king. He stood straight and carried his spear defiantly. He walked toward Horemheb's party, which moved forward with the interpreter. The king's shoulder dripped blood. Horemheb could see the broken shaft of an arrow embedded in the flesh. When they were within ten paces of each other, the Nubian king spoke through the interpreter.

"Will my men be spared? Are you a man of your word?"

Horemheb nodded. "Great Pharaoh has so declared, my Lord Ikhey. But as for you, I can make no such promise." The interpreter translated and they waited for the Nubian's response.

"You've killed my wife and family, Egyptian. There *is* no future for me now. I yield to the will of Sebiumeker, my god." He threw down his spear. Horemheb picked it up, nodding to the defeated king. He then ordered his men to tie the king's hands in front of him. Ikhey winced with pain as they tied a rope around his neck, the end of which they handed to Horemheb.

"You have fought well," Horemheb said in a quiet voice. Your surrender will save the lives of your people. My king will honor his word." Ikhey listened to the translation but simply stared straight ahead. Horemheb led the way back to Amenhotep, pulling the defeated king behind him.

When Pharaoh's army saw the small party advancing toward them, they stood and began humming from deep in their throats. The sound became a low growl, and as it grew louder, vibrated like the roar of a lion!

Still on his horse, Pharaoh dismounted when Horemheb arrived to hand him the rope. "Make him prostrate himself before us," Amenhotep ordered. The interpreter explained and with a look of defiance Ikhey knelt, then laid face down in the dirt. Amenhotep walked forward and placed his foot on the neck of the Nubian as a great shout went up from his army.

"Ho-tep! Ho-tep!" they yelled until the ground shook.

Horemheb couldn't move. He stared down transfixed by what he saw on Ikhey's neck. "It's the same mark as my prisoner's," he whispered to himself. "By the Breath of Horus."

"Let the king stand," Pharaoh commanded, remounting his stallion and turning the animal around.

General Minnakf gave orders to his men that all Nubians were to be taken prisoner and brought back to the fort. As Pharaoh led the Nubian king behind his horse, more cheers greeted him from the ranks. It took them about an hour to reach the river. Once there, they stopped to regroup and to drink its refreshing water.

A water skin had been offered the captured king, but he refused it. Horemheb ordered a cordon of warriors be placed around the Nubian to keep anyone from trying to injure the fallen ruler. General Minnakf guaranteed Pharaoh the prisoner would arrive in Thebes alive.

"What did the Nubian say when he threw down his spear?" Pharaoh asked Horemheb as he rode beside the king.

"I think he thought only of his warriors, Majesty. He wanted to know if *you* were a man of your word."

"And how did *you* respond?"

"I assured him that you are a man of honor like your father, may his name be remembered, Great One. I told him our kings keep their word."

"And it will be so. His men will live as slaves, Captain. I have heard that is what he said when you defeated his champion. You became *his* slaves."

"Yes, Majesty, so it is only fitting for it to end this way. It is Maat—a balance."

"Rightfully so," General Minnakf grumbled as he stared at their ebony-skinned enemy.

The sun had moved from its zenith, and by mid-afternoon they reached the fort. The streets of Swentet filled with jubilant inhabitants cheering their conquering warriors. Pharaoh went on board his galley to bathe and put on clean clothes.

A meal had been prepared, but before they ate, Horemheb handed a report to general Minnakf who read it to his majesty. "We have taken seven hundred and twenty prisoners, Majesty. Three hundred and twelve severed enemy hands have also been gathered. The prisoners are under guard along the river until they can be moved."

"What about their king?" Amenhotep wanted to know.

"He refused to have his shoulder treated, Majesty," Horemheb answered. "He's removed his loincloth and covered his naked body with dust. He will not eat or drink, nor will he speak to anyone. I would say he is in mourning."

The next day Horemheb became concerned for the life of the Nubian king. He decided to bring the physician to Pharaoh's cabin.

"Report," Pharaoh commanded.

"The guards thought the king had died, Majesty," Senemut began. "But he had only passed out. I've removed the arrowhead from his shoulder and sewn up the wound. Naturally, there's still a danger of infection."

"Keep him alive until our victory celebration," Pharaoh ordered. "Your life too may depend on it." They were on the main deck where the prisoner received treatment.

Senemut knew better than to equivocate with the king and simply replied, "If the gods will it, Majesty."

"Unfortunately for you," Pharaoh corrected him, "it is *we* who will it!"

Horemheb saluted as Senemut bowed and said, "Majesty." Dismissed by the wave of the king's hand, the aging physician followed the captain back to the main deck.

Late in the afternoon, Khamet and Horemheb sat outside their tent. After washing in the river they were enjoying a jar of beer, discussing how the battle had gone as soldiers often do. Khamet could tell his friend had become preoccupied with something but didn't ask about it. Standing, Horemheb walked over to where the Nubian woman had been kept.

"Untie the prisoner," he ordered the guards. "Leave us," he told them when they had done what he asked. Khamet protested, but his friend insisted. "Let me do this," he told Khamet, who nodded, shrugging his shoulders. When he had gone, Horemheb took his dagger from his arm and moved toward the Nubian. He crossed his arms and said, "The king has been captured, *Princess* Abar." He watched her reaction as she realized he knew her identity. "Your father is alive and here in Swentet."

"Then it is a sad day for my people, Egyptian," she said defiantly. "How did you discover my identity?"

"The mark on your neck finally gave you away," Horemheb explained. "When I saw it on your father's neck I knew you were not one of his wives. Shabaka told me the king's children wore such a mark, so I assumed who you were."

"May I see him?" she asked, politely, surprising the Egyptian.

"Well, you are Pharaoh's prisoner now, not mine. But I know the king and he will want to show the courtesy of one royal to another. King Ikhey's life has already been given in exchange so your people may live." He saw her shoulders relax, perhaps for the first time. *She knows it's over*, he thought. "I'll ask Pharaoh to assign you as my prisoner, Princess. I will say we can still learn much from each other."

She nodded, finally giving up. "May I see him after I've taken off this horrible piece of cloth and had time to bathe?"

"Yes, Highness," Horemheb answered. "But I must be at your side every moment."

"Men do not frighten me, Captain. Is it possible you desire to watch me because you're attracted to me?"

Horemheb grumbled something she couldn't hear. "Khamet," he shouted. His friend came over to see what he wanted. "Have the men bring several buckets of water for our prisoner, Princess Abar, daughter of the king of the Nubians."

"By the gods," Khamet exclaimed, he eyes growing bigger.

"I will stay with her at all times," Horemheb explained. "We cannot risk any further attempts to escape."

"As you say, Brother," Khamet replied, grinning. "Being the king's friend also has its privileges," he added. His men brought pieces of sailcloth to form a makeshift enclosure, allowing the woman privacy.

When the water arrived, Horemheb handed Abar a loofah sponge and sat inside the screen on a wooden bench. She didn't show any timidity in exposing her body as she washed. In fact he felt her sensuous movements were calculated to stimulate his senses. Horemheb's eyes beheld nothing but perfection. Using a linen towel to dry herself off, she took pride in lingering on her breasts longer than needed. Once dry, she picked up her small apron, placed it around her waist and slowly walked toward him.

Horemheb couldn't move. His body had responded to what he saw and he shifted on the bench with some difficulty. She stood next to him, reaching out and pulling his head to her. He loosened her leather covering, letting it fall to the ground. Reaching up, he gently touched her breasts making her tremble. Overcome by their passion, they lay down on the towel, engaging in an urgent, aggressive union. Afterward, as they waited for their breathing to return to normal, Princess Abar explored his body with her fingers, lingering over every scar.

"May I see my father now?" she whispered. Horemheb stood, looking around for his kilt. "Wait," the princess whispered. "I want to remember you as the gods made you one last time."

"A *last* time?" he asked puzzled. "Why must it be a last time, Highness?"

"This is a breach of our custom. My father will not allow it to happen again. He still thinks I'm a virgin." She grinned and added, "Of course he doesn't watch me every moment."

He hurriedly pulled on his kilt and handed her the leather apron. She let him tie up her hands again and lead her from the bathing area.

"Is everything all right, Brother?" Khamet asked, walking toward them. "Did you have time to bathe too, Commander?" The smirk on his face told Horemheb his friend knew what had happened.

"No, by Seth's backside! Bring the guards. We're escorting the princess to her father."

Horemheb led the princess along the river to where the Nubians were held prisoner. When Abar saw the king, she gasped. His feet were tied to a large pole, his hands tied together. He lay crumpled on the ground. His ashen color made him look like a corpse.

"Tata," she whispered, kneeling beside him, speaking Kenuzi. Horemheb could only watch as she tried to get her father's attention.

Ikhey didn't respond immediately until she knelt down and took his hand, rubbing it against her cheek. Tears came suddenly to the king's eyes, as he recognized her. She wiped them away and he spoke once more.

The princess translated. "He says the Egyptians told him I had been killed. He can't believe I'm here. He's also mourning the loss of my mother who died in the fighting."

When the king recognized Horemheb, he became agitated. His daughter helped him stand and he shook his fists at the Egyptian. Speaking angrily, he spat on the ground.

"What did he say?" Horemheb asked. "Don't be afraid: tell me everything."

She helped the king sit down on a small stool, then turned to face the captain. "He cursed you because your king has broken his word. He told my father if he surrendered his life would be the payment for the lives of our people. Why have we been enslaved?"

Horemheb nodded toward King Ikhey. "I stood there, Princess, when your father surrendered his spear. My king told him if he surrendered, then your people would live—all that is true." He saw her face change as she took it all in. "Tell your father," he continued, "they were the same conditions he gave us when we were captured. If I defeated his champion, we would live—that is, be his slaves. Our Pharaoh is keeping *his* word. You will all be taken to Egypt and serve us. Only the king will die."

Princess Abar translated his words and the king stood once more. He spoke less violently and his daughter explained what he said. "He says you have brought him his daughter, and for that he is grateful. Perhaps in Egypt she will marry and have a child to carry on his name."

The princess looked into Horemheb's eyes. He saw in them the same frantic concern about the king's last words. He wondered if she realized what could happen. His mind began to race in a thousand directions. Seeing the guards were not close enough to hear he said "What will happen if the gods favor you with a child, Princess? Our encounter will be made public and my life ruined." Not daring to look at her father, he whispered, "By the gods! What have we done?"

CHAPTER NINE

INTRIGUE

It took the army a week to travel back to the capital. Word of their progress reached the capital five days before their arrival. Thebans filled the streets ready to cheer and praise their victorious Pharaoh.

"They've come to see the conquered Nubians," Ramose told his friend.

"Well they won't be disappointed," Horemheb declared.

A loud murmur spread through the crowd amid the cheers for Pharaoh and his family. To everyone's amazement, a Nubian princess rode in a golden palanquin behind Pharaoh's entourage. Hundreds of captured prisoners marched behind her, their hands bound in chains. For an instant, her eyes met Horemheb's and she nodded. He acknowledged her with a smile.

Ramose saw the exchange and asked, "Who is she?"

Horemheb grinned. "She is Princess Abar, Star of the Morning, daughter of King Ikhey, Ruler of Nubia."

"I only joked about the women of Abu keeping you happy," his friend laughed. "I never thought the women of our enemy would be so beautiful."

Horemheb only smiled and asked about the victory celebration.

Ramose said, "Pharaoh Amenhotep has chosen to honor his triumph in ten days. As Vizier of Thebes I am in charge. Priests of the major temples will take part, with a place of honor accorded the priests of Ra." A troubled look covered his face as he paused.

"What is it?" Horemheb asked.

"They will officiate at a new altar built for the Aten. You've seen it, Harm, the god's symbol shows the sun-god's many hands reaching down to bless the people."

"Yes of course, but what about the priests of Amun?"

"They have not been included by Pharaoh's orders," Ramose murmured.

"That'll mean trouble," Horemheb said. "But I don't have time for that now. I want to visit Prince Thutmose. Can you arrange for Khui and me to see him?"

"Of course, Brother, but you won't like what you find. I'll arrange it for the morning."

"What do you mean, 'Mose?"

You'll see in the morning," his friend replied, leading him away from the procession.

With his general's permission and the royal family's acquiescence, Captain Khui met Horemheb and led him down the long corridor in the palace. Leaving Khui outside, Horemheb entered Thutmose's room. Sitting on each side of the prince's bed were Princesses Sitamun and Iset. They had brought him fragrant lotus flowers and sweet cakes. Excusing himself quickly, Horemheb backed out of the room, not wanting to intrude.

A few minutes later the two women came out. "It was kind of you to come, Captain," Sitamun said, smiling. "'Mose is most anxious to hear about the battle."

"Don't tire him," Iset said kindly. "He's not good at judging when he's exhausted."

Horemheb bowed politely. "I won't stay long," he said. The princesses smiled and returned to their apartments. Horemheb opened the door and smiled at the prince who lay propped up in bed. At first glance, the room didn't look like a royal chamber at all. It contained a simple bed and two chairs. He moved to the foot of the bed, and waited for the prince to give him permission to sit. What he saw shocked him. Thutmose looked emaciated. His face had a sickly color and his eyes had lost their fire. His cheeks were beginning to sink in. The prince could hardly wave his hand, indicating for Horemheb to sit.

"I hear you are the one who persuaded the Nubian king to surrender," the prince declared.

Horemheb cleared his throat, trying to control his emotions. "No, Highness. Your father sent the ultimatum forcing the king to surrender. I only accepted his spear."

"Aha! But you see," the prince said with a grin, "he would not have surrendered it to just anyone! I knew it! You escaped from him, and then returned as conqueror!" His coughing suddenly worsened brought on by the exertion. "One day you will be *my* general of the armies, my friend. We will retire old Minnakf, and I want a warrior like you at my side!"

"It would be my highest honor to serve you, Highness. I am yours to command!"

"Not yet," a voice said entering the room. Thutmose's youngest brother, Prince Amenhotep, approached the bed and said, "He must be Pharaoh first, Captain. You should know that, 'Mose."

Horemheb knelt and saluted, simply saying, "Highness." He moved away from Thutmose's bed, about to take his leave, but Amenhotep stopped him.

"I did not mean to interrupt, Captain," the prince declared. "I only wanted to see how my brother is feeling today."

"Do not get any ideas, 'Tep," Thutmose grinned. "Do not let my appearance fool you. I will *still* be Pharaoh before you!" In spite of the prince's grin, Horemheb sensed the tension behind his words.

Lord Senemut entered, frowning when he saw his patient's visitors. "Away with you, Captain," he said, waving the soldier toward the door.

Horemheb turned back toward the prince and said with a grin, "If you ever have another princess to rescue, Great Prince, call on me!" Thutmose chuckled, causing him to cough again. Senemut pushed both men out the door.

"What's wrong with him, Highness?" Horemheb whispered. "He looks terrible." They continued talking as they made their way down the hallway.

"Not even that old charlatan knows what's wrong," Prince Amenhotep answered with a sigh. "We've tested all his food in case someone had been poisoning him—that is what it looks like." He stopped walking and turned to face

Horemheb. "Whatever it is, it's moved into his lungs. He can't breathe, as you saw. We thought he would die before Father sailed for Nubia."

"I don't know how to say this, Highness," Horemheb said, "but what about that snake, Mena? You know, Queen Tiye's spy. Surely he wouldn't dare act on his own, would he? The prince is her son after all."

"No, Captain, she loves him too much. She wouldn't do anything against him," Amenhotep assured him.

"Are there any other physicians you can call, my Lord?" Horemheb asked.

"Yes, but none of them wants to lose his life, Captain. You know what happens to healers who allow their royal patients to die. It's an old decree."

"Yes my Lord, but will you permit me to bring a Greek healer to examine him? I'm worried about him too. Does your father not see his condition?"

Amenhotep said, "His only response is 'He is in the hands of the gods.' That is Father's answer to everything. He prays for them to save his son, and that is all," the prince added. Amenhotep turned and continued walking. "Bring your physician to me."

"We'll come this evening, Highness, but where should we meet?"

"Come to my garden at sunset. You know where it is—just off the palace veranda. If anyone asks where you are going, say you are bringing a friend to meet me. Do not say anything else."

"Of course, Highness, and thank you," Horemheb saluted quickly, and then hurried away.

Aristarchus lived in Thebes for two years. Egyptian physicians were skeptical of his methods at first, but the Greek proved himself to be a good healer. His colleagues often consulted him about the types of treatment and medicines that were used by healers in countries around the Great Sea.

"You must be mad, Captain," Aristarchus said when Horemheb told him what he wanted.

"We can pay you any fee, my Lord. Please come. We fear the prince will die. Something is seriously wrong, and no one knows what it is." Horemheb explained.

"You insult me, Horemheb, if you think I would come only for the money."

"Forgive me my friend, but you must come."

INTRIGUE

Aristarchus sighed and said, "All right, but tell me again what you saw. It will help me choose what medicines to bring. And that's also a problem, Captain. Won't people see what I'm carrying and know that I am a physician?"

Horemheb thought for a moment. "First, change your appearance. Leave your blue-bordered robe at home. Wear Egyptian clothes. Secondly, take only what instruments and potions you need in leather pockets hidden on your person. It may seem dramatic, but we can't leave any evidence of your visit. If anything does happen to the prince, the palace staff might remember our visit!"

"I understand. I'll prepare what I need and meet you here a little before sunset."

"Agreed, my friend."

That evening, with the healer's medicines and instruments secured under his clothing, Aristarchus went with Horemheb to Prince Amenhotep's garden. He met them and Horemheb introduced the Greek, who prostrated himself before the young royal.

Insisting he stand, the prince said, "When we go, act as normal as possible. The servants must not suspect anything unusual."

Fortunately, only a nurse sat in the room beside Thutmose's bed when they arrived. Amenhotep motioned for her to leave and she obeyed at once.

"By Zeus' breath!" the healer exclaimed when he saw the sick man's face. Surprised to see his brother again so soon, Thutmose listened as Amenhotep introduced the Greek to him.

"This physician, 'Mose, has practiced in Thebes for two years. He is highly respected by our physicians. Horemheb and I ask your permission to let him examine you." He saw the frown on his brother's face and added, 'Mose. Please, for my sake? Please?" Thutmose smiled. His younger sibling sounded as he had so many times when they were children; especially when he wanted something very badly. "But don't tell Senemut," he added.

Thutmose laughed. "All right, all right. If it will bring me some peace." He opened his robe and said, "Proceed physician."

"Highness, with your permission," Aristarchus began, placing his head down so that his ear touched the prince's chest. "Take a deep breath, please," he asked, and the young man did so, but it made him cough violently. Aristarchus sniffed the young man's breath, then, taking the prince's hand he felt his pulse, followed by a close examination of the fingernails of both hands.

"Once again, Highness, forgive me," and he looked closely at each eye, lifting the eyelids, top and bottom. "Open your mouth, please," and he examined the tongue and the inside of the mouth. Aristarchus helped the Prince remove his robe completely. What he saw made the older man gasp. There were enormous bruises on the young man's side and upper abdomen.

"What is it?" Thutmose asked as the Greek helped him put his robe back on.

"When did you first notice those bruises, Highness?"

"About a month ago,"

"I see, thank you. I'm sorry to have caused you any discomfort."

"But what have you found?" Thutmose demanded.

"Something is attacking your liver, my Lord. The whites of your eyes are turning yellow—a sure sign. The yellowing is hard to see in bronze mirrors, but it is easy to see close up." He paused, and took something out of his cloak. "If you permit me, I'll give you a powder to help the pain and let you sleep."

"You mustn't be seen taking this medicine, Highness," the physician warned. "People will think we are trying to harm you. But I assure you it is simply the powder from the red poppy to take away the pain."

Amenhotep said, "It is true, Brother. Our mother has used it many times for the pain in her knees."

"Indeed," the Greek nodded. "His Highness must rest now, gentlemen."

Horemheb grinned at his friend. "Soon you'll be up and around chasing servant girls again, Great Prince. Horus give you strength and healing."

His younger brother said, "Good night, 'Mose. Remember it is *you* who must become Pharaoh! I only want to study religion; you know that. Please get better." He took his brother's hand for a moment and squeezed it as a gesture of affection.

"Good night, 'Tep," Thutmose replied. "Do not worry."

Once the three men returned to the garden, the prince saw the concern on the Greek's face.

"What is it Aristarchus?" Horemheb demanded. "Tell us what you've found!"

"You were right, Horemheb." Turning to the prince, he said, "Forgive me, Highness, but your brother *is* dying. Someone has been poisoning him for a long time. I can see that in the half-moons of his nails, and his breath reeks of it. He will probably die in a matter of weeks."

Amenhotep had to sit down. "No," he exclaimed angrily, his eyes filling with tears. "Why didn't Senemut see it?"

"The elderly physician's eyesight may be failing, Highness. I don't know, but there are large bruises over his liver and the organ is ceasing to function," Aristarchus explained. "His robe covers them, so perhaps Senemut didn't want to undress the prince completely. I can't explain it."

INTRIGUE

"How has it been done?" Horemheb pressed; his anger growing with the healer's every word.

"In his food, Captain, or his wine. He's losing his sense of taste, I can see that by the color of his tongue. If I had only examined him a month ago, I could have stopped what will become his slow and painful demise. I'm so sorry, dear friends." He walked over and sat down on a bench some distance from them.

"I cannot tell our Father," the prince groaned. "His big victory celebration is in a few days. This news will ruin everything, and he'll blame me!" Seeing Horemheb's troubled look, he added, "I know my brother thinks highly of you, Horemheb. What should I do?"

Horemheb paced back and forth then said quietly, "We must think first about your brother, Highness. These coming weeks must be special for him. Make him as happy and as comfortable as you can. Surround him with pleasant things—beautiful young ladies, his favorite songs, friends and family. I don't think we should tell the family the truth. In fact I advise against it. There's nothing any of us can do now." He stopped, waiting for the prince to respond, but when he didn't, he continued. "I'll make finding his killer my priority, Highness. Who could possibly do this?"

"He doesn't have any enemies," Amenhotep mumbled. "Not one. And I know that sounds impossible—but everyone likes him."

Horemheb said in a kind voice, "Apparently not everyone, my Prince. I'll begin by asking Lord Aperel and his son Ramose. They know the court better than anyone."

"Ramose is a true friend," Amenhotep said. "He'll keep any discoveries to himself. I'll invite him for supper tonight, and he'll not refuse. You will come too, Captain, of course."

"I would be honored Highness. I only regret the reason for our supper." Moving slow, Horemheb and the physician left the room with their heads down.

That evening, when his two guests were seated at the prince's table, the servants brought in food and beer then left the residence, dismissed for the evening.

"Something's going on," Ramose said, forgetting his place. "Pardon, Highness, I spoke out of turn."

Amenhotep nodded. "Horemheb and I wanted you here, my friend, to discuss an important matter. I'll let him explain. I don't want to talk about it." The explanation of Thutmose's illness alarmed Ramose.

"By the gods, no!" he exclaimed. "And your father doesn't know?" The prince shook his head. They were silent a moment until Ramose turned toward

83

the prince. "I *have* seen something, Highness, but never thought any more about it until now. Nebamun visits your brother two or three times a week. You know him. He's the priest of Amun who has the birthmark on his forehead. I've seen him bringing Thutmose fresh fruit from the temple gardens."

"How long has this been going on?" Horemheb asked, already certain of the answer.

"About a month now," Ramose told them.

"By Seth's bowels!" Horemheb exploded.

"Watch your language in my palace," a deep voice said behind them. Pharaoh entered the room and his son started to stand while the others made obeisance. The king waved them back to their seats.

"What is this, 'Tep? Some nefarious gathering to overthrow your father?" He grinned, and laughed when he saw their faces.

"Ramose and I wanted to hear more about the Nubian campaign Father," the prince lied. "Maybe you'll take me with you next time."

Ramose added to the untruths. "We were learning more about the great elephants on Abu, Majesty. How magnificent they must be."

"Ah," Pharaoh replied. "Yes, I've been to Abu before. I understand in some places across the Great Sea, men ride them! Can you imagine?"

"No—such a thing would be impossible, Great One," Horemheb reasoned. "I would like to see the man who could control such a beast."

"As would I," the king replied. "But don't let me disturb you. I only wanted to say good night."

The prince waited until his father had gone, then took several deep breaths. "Arrest this priest, Horemheb," he commanded quietly. "I want him torn apart."

"All in good time, Prince. First we must lay a trap for him. Does he come to the palace on certain days?"

"I believe so," Ramose replied, "but I'll check with Hapu, the king's steward. He'll know. If I remember correctly, he should come again tomorrow."

"Excellent." Horemheb said. Go now and ask someone in the temple of Amun about him. Make it seem casual. Let them know the crown prince is hoping he'll come again."

Ramose nodded and quickly left the apartment.

"We have to catch this murderer!" Young Amenhotep cried out in frustration.

"You will, Highness. This is what you will do. He must see you with your brother. He'll think nothing of it. Then you will step out into the hall—and that will be our signal. He could be armed, Prince, so don't take any chances."

"I'll have my dagger on me tomorrow, Captain, you can be sure of that. I wouldn't enter a room with a cobra and not be prepared!" Amenhotep brought out some wine as they waited for Ramose to return. He shared stories with Horemheb about his brother when they were children growing up in the palace. The panic they caused when they brought a small baby crocodile into Thutmose's room and lost it somehow in their bedchamber.

When Ramose came back he looked pleased. "The priest will come tomorrow," he said. "He usually arrives by mid-morning."

"Good. Now try to get some rest, Highness," Horemheb suggested. "We'll be back in the morning. Ramose and I will wait for this killer near your brother's room."

The two visitors said goodnight and left the royal apartment. Out in the hallway Horemheb said, "I pray Horus delivers him into our hands."

"As do I," Ramose breathed, jamming a fist in his hand.

CHAPTER TEN

CAUGHT

The next morning, when Thutmose's friends arrived at his room, Prince Amenhotep met them.

"He is still sleeping," he told them. "Senemut left instructions my brother cannot be disturbed. Khui has also been ordered to move his guards away."

"Let us hide first, Highness," Horemheb whispered.

He and Ramose walked to a small alcove about twenty paces from the prince's chamber. Ramose closed a curtain part way to conceal them. As they waited in silence, both frantically tried to think how they would get the assassin out of the palace once caught.

"I'm going in now," Prince Amenhotep told them. Horemheb peered around the curtain and watched as the prince entered his brother's room.

Horemheb lowered his voice. "Now we wait. Hapu, the palace steward, has reassigned the servants so no one should disturb us." A while later they heard the sandaled footsteps of someone approaching. Looking through the space in the curtain, they saw a bald priest carrying a basket of fruit open Thutmose's door. He went inside and they heard him greeting the two brothers.

A moment later, Amenhotep came out and nodded to his friends. They hurried toward him and Horemheb whispered, "I'm sorry, Highness, but you must stay out here."

"Never," Amenhotep said. Pushing Horemheb out of the way, he opened the door. They found the priest standing by the head of the bed reciting prayers. When he saw the three men his eyes showed surprise, then panic. Pulling a dagger from his robe he raised his arm to stab Thutmose, but Horemheb leapt at him knocking the weapon to the floor. Grabbing the assassin, he and Ramose dragged the priest out into the hall. He continued to struggle until Horemheb punched him in the jaw, knocking him out. Hurrying back to the alcove, he retrieved the rope they had brought and tied the man's hands.

"Ramose and I will walk him out, Highness. People will think he's drunk or sick." He suddenly changed his mind. "No, that won't work. We can't take him by the guard post. They'll know something's wrong. Allow us to put him in your apartment."

"Of course," Amenhotep said. "Let me first tell my brother what has happened. I won't say anything about the poisoning, only that we stopped an attempt on his life. Wait for me there." His two friends lifted the assassin and, each taking an arm, dragged him to the apartment. Fortunately they met no one in the hallway.

When the prince returned he said, "'Mose couldn't believe what just happened. He wants to thank you for what you did, although because of his medicine, he can't speak very well." He sank into a chair. Tears welled up in his eyes. "His tomb isn't finished yet." He couldn't go on.

Ramose said, "Who would have thought he would need it so soon?"

It took Horemheb a moment to realize what his friend had said. Royal families built their final resting places in the Valley of the Kings, west of the river. The living dwelt across the Nile, to the east. This custom had been followed for hundreds of years.

"His tomb will be finished, my Prince," Horemheb said, hoping he hadn't been too familiar with the young man. "I'll personally see to it. Hundreds of men will be sent to complete it during the days of mourning." It took seventy days to prepare a body in the House of the Dead. Perhaps that would be enough

CAUGHT

time to decorate and finish the tomb. "We'll encourage your father to see that it's completed."

The prince nodded, and then sat down on a soft divan. "At our age, Horemheb, who thinks about tombs? There must be more to life than this. This is why I want to study our religions. There has to be an answer somewhere, and I mean to find it." The prince's anger flared up again, and he jumped up and went over and kicked the unconscious man. "Get him out of here."

"How, my Lord?" Ramose asked.

"Ramose, you must go back to the court," Horemheb said. "You mustn't be involved with this in any way. Go now." His friend nodded and bowed his head to the prince as he left.

Horemheb continued. "I'll walk our unconscious killer out of here, Highness, just as if he simply passed out. I can ask a guard to help me get him back to my barracks. I'll just say he's an old friend. There'll be no need to interrogate him. We already know the priests of Amun are plotting your father's downfall." Prince Amenhotep nodded. "Do you know how to find the tavern of the Leopard's Tail, Highness? There is a small dock there and I'll wait for you when the moon is overhead. Dress accordingly, my Lord. Can you get past the Royal Guard?"

Prince Amenhotep nodded. "Leave that to me. The guards are used to us sneaking out of the palace for a variety of rendezvous. Do not worry, I will not be followed."

"Good, then I'll take this son of Seth out of here. Good night, Highness."

Later that night, three figures made their way through the darkness to the river. Confiscating a small skiff, they rowed a short distance from shore. Following the riverbank they found a spot where the sound of crocodiles could be heard. If anyone happened to be watching, he would have seen the dinghy returning with only two figures in it. After tying it up, they disappeared into the darkness. The only sounds from the river came from the servants of Hapi enjoying a midnight treat.

Princess Abar sent Horemheb's Nubian scout to him with a message. "Her Highness requests a meeting with you, my Lord."

Horemheb frowned. "Very well, where shall we meet?"

"At Lord Ramose's villa, my Lord. Tomorrow evening. If that meets with your approval?" Horemheb nodded, and the messenger left. Making his way to the palace, Horemheb went looking for Ramose. The chamberlain told him he might still be in the council chamber.

Thanking the nobleman, he walked down the corridor leading to the council room. Looking inside he found Ramose sitting alone.

"You look as if you've the weight of the kingdom on your shoulders, brother. Can it be as bad as that?" Horemheb asked.

"I do, Harm," Ramose laughed, and got up to greet his friend. "What brings you here?"

"A certain Nubian princess," he answered with a grin.

"I thought so. I saw how you two looked at each other at the celebration. Is she someone special?"

"None of your business, Mose. Do you know what this meeting is about?"

"Well, she wanted to meet with me and I agreed." He looked at his friend more closely. "Why is Ikhey's daughter interested in you, Harm?"

"We had a brief encounter, my friend. Our passions got the better of us. She is a beautiful woman."

Ramose grinned. "She is that. You should have seen my wife's face when the princess came to our villa." Horemheb smiled, imagining Benefer's reaction.

"Well, what does she want?" Horemheb said.

"I don't know, Harm. She said it is of a personal nature. Because I am your friend, I should make the arrangements. That's all I know."

"Very well." Knowing he could trust his friend he asked, "Can she make trouble for me?"

"Women can always make trouble, brother. You know that."

"She can't possibly be with child," Horemheb reasoned, shaking his head, perturbed.

Ramose didn't show any surprise. "In any case, the person who must not learn of it is his Majesty. He is going to execute her father before the court, as you know. That means she will be queen and heir to Ikhey's kingdom. Egypt needs Nubia's gold. Pharaoh will want to insist the way to the gold mines must remain open. The princess is the key to that."

Horemheb shook his head and didn't speak for a moment. Then he exclaimed, "What have I done?"

"What have you done?" said a voice behind them. Pharaoh had entered the chamber while they were talking and had heard their last words. Horemheb knelt at once, and Ramose bowed his head, the accepted obeisance for a member of the king's council.

"I may have offended the Nubian princess, Great One. I did not mean to do so."

With growing concern in his voice, Amenhotep asked, "How so?"

"It is embarrassing, Majesty," the captain began. "We were both attracted to each other, and well. . ."

Pharaoh frowned, then raised his hand, indicating Horemheb could stand. "Go on."

"That's all, Great King. Now she's asked to meet me at Ramose's villa. He has been telling me about her invitation."

"Well," Pharaoh began, "you must go, my friend. If you are to lead my army one day, then we must make sure Nubia becomes our ally. If you are her friend or lover, perhaps she'll think twice before attacking us." He walked over to the chair he used during the council and sat down. "As protector of the morals of the kingdom I cannot say I approve. But she is a charming and beautiful woman, Harm. Even I can see that."

Ramose smiled. "Harm's rather thick-headed when it comes to women, Majesty. He always has been." Horemheb scowled at his friend, making Pharaoh chuckle.

"I give you this order, Captain," Pharaoh said. "You will meet with her and see that she becomes Egypt's ally. She is about to lose her father, whom we know to be an honorable and brave man. You should prepare her for that day."

Putting his fist across his chest Horemheb saluted. "As you command, Majesty." Pharaoh raised his hand in response, stood and left the council chamber.

"Thank the gods, Harm," Ramose said, relieved.

"I wish he'd stop doing that," Horemheb said. "He's always coming up behind us."

Princess Abar liked being in Thebes. She enjoyed all of the attention she had been given. She ate the finest food and given the best clothing by the queen's own ladies-in-waiting. She rode now in a carrying chair, escorted by four Egyptian guards assigned for her protection. The bearers of the palanquin were black slaves from Punt, but she could not speak their language. They stopped and lowered the chair in front of Lord Ramose's villa. The guardsmen escorted her into the Vizier's garden where Ramose and Benefer came out to greet her. Bowing politely, Benefer invited her to be seated near the small pool at the center of the beautifully designed oasis.

The princess smiled. "You treat an enemy with kindness."

"That all our enemies were as elegant and as beautiful as you, your Highness," Ramose responded. That made her smile even more. She wore a long pleated white linen gown, which contrasted brilliantly with her skin. A golden necklace adorned her neck and Lady Benefer complimented her on it.

Abar said, "It is a gift from Pharaoh to honor my succession to my father's throne." Benefer smiled when she noticed the Nubian wore no sandals. The young woman also refused to wear a wig as Egyptian custom demanded.

A servant rushed in and said, "He's here."

"Show him in," Ramose said. The servant nodded and went to bring in their friend.

"Welcome, brother," Ramose said greeting him. "There is someone here to meet you." Horemheb smiled, greeting his friends, and then, turned to face their guest.

"Your Highness, it is good to see you again," he said. His speech sounded too formal.

"Captain," she replied, nodding. Her heart beat faster just being near him again.

Lady Benefer smiled at him. "We'll leave you two. If you need refreshment, the servants will bring whatever you require."

Horemheb nodded and sat down on a bench opposite the princess as their hosts left the garden. An awkward silence fell between them, neither knowing what to say. Abar realized he wanted her to speak first.

"Do you still find me attractive, Captain?" she asked.

"You ask that of a man who has been enchanted by your charms, my Lady. You are the sorceress who has beguiled me. Of course I am unable to see all the beauty I beheld when we first met."

She laughed. "I see. So then nothing's changed. I too feel strangely compelled to be near you. You must be a formidable magician yourself, Man of the Spear."

Horemheb laughed and then suddenly became serious. She noticed it at once.

"You know what is going to happen don't you, Princess?" He asked in a soft voice.

"You mean my father's execution?"

"Yes, Highness. I wish you did not have to be there."

"No," she protested. "I must be there. He wants me there. That is how a king should die; honorably, in front of his enemies." Her voice trembled as she spoke.

"Will you stand beside me on the day?"

"Yes, Highness, if Pharaoh allows it. It would be an honor."

She looked him in the eye. "If I become with child, will you marry me and be our king?"

She saw the surprise on his face before he looked away. Her heart sank, and she wanted to run out of the garden.

Horemheb, however, stood and walked over to her. Taking her hands he lifted her up. "It would be the greatest honor, Highness. If the gods will it, then we must let it be so."

She embraced him, and they held on to each other for a very long time. He kissed her passionately as a swallow's song filled the air.

Pharaoh's victory celebration became part of his Sed Festival. Such manifestations of joy were held to commemorate the continued rule of the king. His success as ruler became a reason to rejoice. On the last day of the Festival, the royal guards brought out King Ikhey and Princess Abar. Led before Pharaoh, they were made to kneel before the conqueror of Nubia.

Horemheb looked at his friend. "What is he going to do?"

"Ikhey's life must be forfeited so his people may live."

Pharaoh stepped forward and extended his hand to the princess. She stood, and he escorted her onto the dais behind him. He motioned for Horemheb to come forward. The captain walked up the steps to stand beside her.

General Minnakf followed, carrying the king's sword. The crowd, which had been shouting obscenities and insults at the vanquished king, immediately fell silent. Amenhotep stepped down from his throne, temporarily placed on a large wooden platform, and walked toward the Nubian. He stopped to allow the general to join him. The officer held the king's sword out with both hands and Pharaoh placed his hands on it, then nodded.

"May your gods welcome you, King Ikhey," Pharaoh exclaimed. He turned and walked back to his throne. Standing in front of it he nodded to Minnakf, who raised the weapon and yelled as if in battle. In one swift stroke, he severed the king's head. The crowd cheered, clapped and danced for joy. Horemheb glanced at Princess Abar, but she showed no emotion. Instead she looked straight ahead. Horemheb felt her fingernails digging so deeply into his arm, he almost cried out.

Pharaoh Amenhotep shouted, "Long live Queen Abar, Queen of Nubia, and friend of Pharaoh."

The courtiers cheered and applauded as Horemheb escorted her down to where Pharaoh awaited the future queen. Offering her arm to the king, Pharaoh took it and walked forward to face the crowd who applauded ever louder. Queen Tiye came down the steps and stood beside them as everyone celebrated a new day of peace with Nubia.

As Pharaoh and his queen walked back to their thrones, Horemheb escorted Abar to her place. While the king's warriors rushed up to remove the king's remains, he whispered so only she could hear. "Your father's body will be embalmed and treated with the greatest respect. He will be returned to his people with you when you sail up to the first waterfall. You can give him an honorable burial."

She had difficulty speaking and could only say, "My people are grateful for that."

Lord Herihor, the king's chamberlain, raised his staff and brought it down hard three times. The jubilant crowd had difficulty settling down so he tapped once again as Pharaoh stood.

The chamberlain raised his voice so all could hear. "General Minnakf, step forward."

The proud veteran walked forward, knelt in front of the king and saluted. Pharaoh raised his hand, and the general stood, awaiting the king's pleasure.

Pharaoh spoke in a clear, loud voice. "For leading our armies at our side beyond the first whitewater rapids, and for defeating the People of the Bow, we honor you with this Gold of Victory. It is well deserved."

The chamberlain opened the box and the king placed the gold necklace around his general's neck. The king turned the elderly warrior around so the crowd could applaud him. The loudest cheers came from the general's men standing around the courtyard.

"You deserved that more than he," Ramose said. He had been standing behind his friend, so he mumbled it so only Horemheb could hear.

"He is the head of the army, brother. Pharaoh has done well. Besides, it's Maat." Ramose nodded but continued to mumble under his breath.

"Captain," one of Horemheb's men interrupted. "Lord Senemut, the physician is calling for you and Lord Ramose."

Both men knew immediately what had happened. A sudden sorrow gripped them as they left Pharaoh's happy celebration.

"I pray the gods were merciful to the prince," Ramose said.

Horemheb's face fell. In a sad voice he said, "As do I."

Both knew that Thutmose the Fourth's Ka had already left his mortal remains and flown into the glories of the afterlife.

CHAPTER ELEVEN

UNEXPECTED CHOICES

Seventy days later, when the days of mourning had been completed, Horemheb took part in his friend's funeral. Thutmose's embalmed remains were placed on board the royal galley, The *Radiance of the Aten*. As a friend of the crown prince, Horemheb felt honored yet saddened to stand by the sarcophagus while the ship sailed across the river. Thutmose's brother, now crown prince, stood on the other side, both men finding it difficult to be there. The songs chanted by the musicians were joyful, celebrating Thutmose's passage into a new life, but the two men were not pleased with the way his *old* life had ended.

When they first came on board, Amenhotep said bitterly, "I am glad Senemut the physician paid with his life for his actions."

Horemheb nodded in agreement.

The prince added, "I refused to allow the priests of Amun to take part in the funeral procession."

"How did you convince your father?" Horemheb asked.

"I told him that they never liked my brother, and I believed they prayed for his death. Father only nodded and said, 'As do I, my Son.'" He saw the look of concern on his friend's face. "However, I did not go so far as to reveal that a priest of Amun had, in fact, killed him. I do not know if you were there, Harm, when father spoke of this. He said that the priests of Amun have had too much prominence in the kingdom."

"Yes, Highness, I remember. He addressed the whole court. He said that the god Ra had revealed to him that the Light of the Sun alone would be worshipped during these dark days." The prince nodded, and Horemheb added, "He also reminded them that his throne name means *The Lord of Truth is Ra.* I'm not sure everyone understood what he meant."

The prince's face changed. "I know. He meant that the worship of the sun is to have priority in the royal family. Father has yet to decide what to do with the priests of Amun."

Horemheb became uneasy hearing such blasphemy, but didn't respond.

As the galley sailed westward, Sitamun and Iset, Thutmose's sisters, stood beside Queen Tiye, the Great Royal Wife. Pharaoh's daughters had been elevated to the position of royal wives, a custom Horemheb found distasteful. In doing so, Amenhotep followed in the tradition of previous kings.

Prince Smenkhare, the other remaining son, stood beside his father. Horemheb noticed the stark contrast between the two. The prince, tall and thin, had become quite muscular from his military training. The king, on the other hand, had put on a lot of weight, becoming grossly obese.

After the bearers placed the sarcophagus on the deck, Queen Tiye went immediately to the royal cabin. Amenhotep remained beside his father.

Ramose joined his friend Horemheb. "She's taken her son's death very hard," he said. "They were very close."

Horemheb looked around at the nobles on deck. "Pharaoh's foreign wives are not here, Mose."

"This is for family, brother. Even though they are Pharaoh's legal wives, the rest of the family consider them outsiders."

Horemheb looked up to the top of the mast where a yellow pennant fluttered in the breeze. He could barely make out the writing on it. Pointing, he read, "The Dazzling Sun Disk? What is that? It's unusual isn't it? Amenhotep's name means 'Amun is Pleased.' Instead he honors the Aten, I don't understand."

Ramose shook his head. "He is Pharaoh, brother, and worships whom he pleases. However, I agree that this is an insult to Amun, and the priests will not be pleased."

Horemheb nodded. "The priests of Amun are very influential. Pharaoh will be making some powerful enemies."

"Not to mention Maat being thrown out of balance," Ramose said.

When they reached the western shore, the priests were there to meet Pharaoh and his family. Palm branches and flower petals brought from Thebes covered the path to the tomb. Pharaoh's servants went ashore first, where the gold-covered carrying chairs for Amenhotep and his family awaited. Musicians began the processional once everyone found their place.

Hundreds of courtiers and king's council members lined the path. They had crossed the river in an assortment of ships, along with important leaders of Thebes. Lord Rahotep, the high priest of Ra, led the procession. After him came hundreds of priests carrying incense and offerings for the gods. Some recited prayers while others chanted sacred songs. Servants followed, carrying items the dead prince would need in his afterlife, such as clothing, combs, jewelry and furniture. Members of the king's family came next in their covered carrying chairs.

Horemheb had to smile as the next group entered the procession. Four servants carried a beautifully carved small sarcophagus of limestone. Inside lay Ta-miu, the prince's favorite cat.

"Ta-miu comes before his mother?" Horemheb whispered.

"Quiet," Ramose hissed back.

Queen Tiye followed, carried in her chair ahead of her son's body. The great stone sarcophagus had been placed on a wooden sled pulled by eight white oxen. Earlier, Horemheb had been pleased to see carved on it Thutmose's rescue of Princess Tadukhepa from the Cave of the Hawk near Ugarit. It seemed so long ago now. The princess had been held captive by a group of bandits asking for two wagonloads of gold. The carving showed Thutmose lifting her to safety onto his chariot. He thought his friend would have liked that.

Prince Amenhotep walked behind his brother's coffin, as did Prince Smenkhare, still angry he had not been named crown prince. The most important mourner, Pharaoh Amenhotep, came last.

The high priest and two other officiates entered the tomb ahead of the royal family. Everything had to be in place. Waiting outside with the other courtiers, Horemheb and Ramose stood in the shade on one side of the entrance. Prince Amenhotep came out later and stood with them, leaving his parents inside.

"'Mose would have been pleased with his tomb," the prince said reflectively. "I did not think it would be finished in time without you, Horemheb."

The captain grinned. "Then you admit I am also a prophet, Highness. I knew the king's artisans were good workers, my Lord. I too think your brother would be pleased."

"I am grateful," the prince said.

As they waited for the king to come out, Ramose pointed to a nearby tomb. "Whose tomb is that over there?"

"That is Yuya's tomb," Amenhotep said. "He is the father of Queen Tiye, and I guess he is my grandfather, although I never met him. They allowed him to build his tomb in the Valley of the Kings. His son Ay has been an influential advisor in father's court." He lowered his voice and whispered so only they could hear. "Some say he is part Asiatic."

Horemheb frowned because such an admission could bring disgrace on a family.

They talked a while longer until their majesties came out for the sealing of the tomb. More singing and clapping ensued, and then in reverse order the Lord of Egypt led everyone back to the ship. Horemheb noticed that Pharaoh went directly into his cabin, followed by the new royal physician. Later, when the ship sailed, he asked the prince about it.

"It is his teeth," the younger man replied. "As he has aged, his teeth have given him a great deal of trouble and pain. I am sorry for him. He eats very little."

"Yet he's not getting any thinner," Ramose pointed out.

"It's our bread that caused it, Highness. Too much bread," Horemheb said. "Sand gets blown into the dough when it's kneaded and that grinds down our teeth. I say we should drink more beer and eat less bread." That made the prince smile, and then he had difficulty keeping a mournful face.

A large crowd in Thebes waited for the king's ship to dock. They sang and waved branches as the royal party disembarked. The green branches reminded them of the afterlife, and their happy songs were put to melodies sung for centuries.

A shout rang out when the crowd saw the new heir to the throne in his chariot. He followed his father, but Horemheb could tell by Amenhotep's face he felt uneasy.

"No Nubian king has ever had a coffin as magnificent as this," Queen Abar said. Horemheb stood at her side on the deck of the *Wings of Horus,* carrying her majesty home. She ran her hands along the polished sarcophagus, admiring all the painted images of her father's life.

"You must build him a tomb worthy to hold it, Majesty," Horemheb said.

"One of Pharaoh's architects, Lord Bek, gave me the plans for one. You will see it the next time you come south."

"It will make me glad, my Lady. I liked your father, even though he tried to kill me twice. As a warrior, he believed in honor and serving his people."

"He respected you, Horemheb," she said. "He admired your courage when you faced Shabaka, the king's champion."

"Shabaka," Horemheb repeated with a smile. "A great name for a great warrior."

The guardsmen on board were from Horemheb's company. They were assigned to escort the new queen. Horemheb tried to be careful, keeping his distance from Abar's cabin. He hoped to avoid any appearance of impropriety in front of his men and crew. The journey to Swentet would take four days, giving the couple plenty of time to talk about the future.

On the morning of the second day, one of his men approached him. "What is it Sergeant?" Horemheb asked.

"The Queen is very beautiful, Captain."

"Yes she is, Kasiya. Isis has blessed her."

The man cleared his throat nervously. "We think you should know, Sir."

"Know what, Soldier?"

Kasiya cleared his throat again and said, "The men wanted you to know that we saw you slipping into her cabin last night. We're pleased for you, Captain—and very jealous."

Horemheb couldn't help but laugh. "So I'm not fooling anyone. I should thank you for telling me, but I'm more inclined to wring your neck for it." He paused a moment, then said, "Queen Abar is a great lady and deserves our respect."

"Yes, Sir. We have the greatest respect for you both."

"Carry on," his commander ordered, dismissing him with a grin.

That evening as he lay in Abar's arms he told her they had been found out. She laughed with him. "I'm glad," she said. "Did you tell them you might become my king?" He nuzzled up closer to her, oblivious to what she just said.

"I will be there waiting for you, my love," she continued, kissing him on the cheek. "I'll meet you at the fort by the first whitewater."

Horemheb suddenly sat up and looked at her intently. "What? What are you saying?" he said. It finally struck him, and he added, "But you said I should only come if you are with child."

"And so I am," she said, kissing him again.

Horemheb leapt from the bed with excitement. "By the gods!" he yelled, running out on deck to tell someone. A roar of laughter greeted him as the men pointed to his obvious lack of a kilt.

Several months later, Prince Amenhotep responded to his father's summons. Walking slowly to his parents' apartments, he knew it had to be important.

"Marriage?" the prince exclaimed, when the king told him why he'd been called. At first he thought they had lost their senses. "I am not ready for marriage."

"Of course you are," Lady Tiye contradicted him. "What you want or do not want is of no importance. It is what you father wants, and you will obey."

Her son looked at her with alarm. "But Mother. I am not interested in anyone."

"Ah," Pharaoh spoke up. "We have taken care of that my Son. She has already been chosen for you. It is the will of the gods."

Amenhotep knew better than to argue. Once his father's mind had been made up he wouldn't change. "Who is she, if I may ask?"

"The Lady Nefertiti," Queen Tiye said. "A beautiful young woman."

Her son's voice now had an icy tone to it. "I'm sure she will make a good daughter-in-law, Mother, and will give you fine sons." He turned and walked toward the door.

"You have not been dismissed, "Pharaoh growled.

"Oh but I have, Father. You have dismissed me every day of my life. Do what you will," Amenhotep shouted, slamming the door behind him. He stood with his back to it, hoping to hear his parent's reaction.

Angered by such disrespect, Lady Tiye said, "Order him back."

"I told you the boy had a mind of his own, Tiye. You are turning him against us."

"Nonsense," she shot back. "He knows better than to defy you."

"Their marriage will take place," the king said. "Bring her in and prepare her. It is my command."

"So shall it be done, Majesty," Tiye replied formally.

Amenhotep could hear his father walking out onto the large veranda. Stepping into the shadows the prince watched as his mother opened the door and came out into the hallway. He could hear her mumbling. "Thutmose should have married her. I will not make that mistake with this son."

When she had gone, the prince slipped away without being seen.

The next evening, the Crown Prince invited Ramose and Horemheb to his apartment. After a pleasant supper, they took extra jars of beer out into the garden so the servants couldn't overhear them.

Suddenly, the prince had the look on his face of a man condemned to death. "I am to be married," he said.

"Congratulations, Highness," Ramose said. "It's about time."

"Ha." Horemheb said. "Who are you to talk, you old hyena? You'll never get married—no woman would have you." That made the prince laugh.

"Who is the lucky one, Highness?' Horemheb asked, "If you don't mind us asking."

"The Lady Nefertiti. She is the adopted daughter of Lady Tey."

Surprised, Ramose said, "Nefertiti? Hadn't she been promised to your brother—or so we were told."

The prince ignored the question and posed one of his own. "What can you tell me about her?"

"My men say, Highness, that she is the most beautiful woman at court, and I agree," Horemheb said. "I've only seen her a few times, but she takes my breath away. She has the longest neck which her head rests on perfectly, like a lotus flower on its stem."

"I know a little of her background," Ramose said. Speaking in his usual didactic monotone he continued. "She's the adopted daughter of Ay, one of your father's advisors. Her name means *The Beautiful One has come*' and it's well chosen—as this Old Man With the Spear has told you."

They both laughed at Horemheb's expense.

"She has a sister Mutnojme and we know she is not of royal blood. Her mother died early in her life and Ay's wife raised her."

The prince looked surprised. "How is it that you know all this?"

"It's my business to know what goes on at court. But I swear only good things are said about her."

"Pharaoh has the greatest respect for Lord Ay, her father, Highness," Horemheb added. "General Minnakf says he served Pharaoh's father as a good military commander."

Amenhotep let out a long sigh. "But I do not have time to settle down. Our Father Ra, the god himself is leading me in a new direction. I cannot be involved in such mundane arrangements as marriage."

Horemheb smiled. "You won't find it so mundane on your wedding night, my Prince."

Ramose laughed, but the prince did not.

Hoping to please him, Ramose said, "The Lord Chamberlain told me she is well-educated and has a sharp mind. She is very devout and has been a priestess in the Temple of the Aten." That captured the prince's attention.

"If that is so, I must meet her as soon as possible. Can you arrange it, Mose?"

"Perhaps in the morning, Highness? Here in your garden?"

"Agreed. Now let us enjoy more beer," the prince suggested. As they drank together, Horemheb saw the smile on Ramose's face.

When compared to the countries around them, marriage in Egypt remained less formal for the common folk. For the royal family, however, anticipation of such an event provided celebrations for their subjects. A banquet planned by Queen Tiye brought her son and his bride-to-be before the court for the first time. When the royal couple entered the banquet hall, the courtiers gasped in awe at the sight of Nefertiti.

Horemheb whispered. "Look how regally she walks, Mose. That golden necklace accentuates her beautiful neck."

"Quiet," Ramose hissed under his breath. "Such thoughts are not proper. Besides," he said, "my eyes are on Lady Benefer, one of her attendants. She's the one over there, third from the end." He nodded toward the four women walking behind Nefertiti.

Horemheb looked at the young woman in question and his eyes grew larger. He hadn't noticed her before, but immediately felt envious of his old friend. "She's very pleasant," he observed.

"Aha," Ramose mumbled. "Hands off. She's mine, if she'll have me."

UNEXPECTED CHOICES

A month later, Horemheb found himself about to become the only single man left in his small circle of friends. He felt a sudden desire to sail for Nubia.

Princess Nefertiti sensed this. One evening when Horemheb had been invited to the palace for an evening meal, she arranged a surprise for him. Introducing a young woman sitting beside her at the table she said, "This is Amenia, my childhood friend."

Horemheb bowed his head to her across the table.

The next day he had forgotten all of the previous night's conversation, except the kind words Amenia had spoken to him. Like Prince Amenhotep, Horemheb had no intention of marrying. Even the possibility of becoming King of Nubia couldn't deter him from his higher ambition in the army. He hadn't told Abar, but he didn't want to be tied down. However, as much as he tried that day, he couldn't get Amenia out of his mind.

A month later, however, Pharaoh Amenhotep the Third, Son of Ra, and Blessed of Horus, died in his sleep. His Ka flew up on the wings of Horus into the morning sky. Horemheb could not have imagined that his beloved Egypt would not be the same again for a very long time.

CHAPTER TWELVE

LOVE AND MARRIAGE

Amenhotep, now the fourth pharaoh to bear that name and ruler of the Two Lands, stood at the edge of the palace veranda with his friend Horemheb. He stared across the river to the Valley of the Kings where his father lay buried. From their vantage point overlooking the great river, they could see the entrances to the royal tombs buried deep in a large hill, chosen because it resembled the mound of creation; a shape also copied by the many pyramids built to honor Egypt's rulers.

Amenhotep walked over to a granite bench and sat down. He had been very melancholic during these weeks. No one, including Nefertiti, had been able to discover what troubled him.

Horemheb broke the silence. "You are still in shock, Majesty, as are your people. First, your brother the Crown Prince died, and now the father of us all is gone. Our hearts go out to you."

"I am grateful. Father left me a good council of advisors, and I have my grandfather and Ramose, my new Vizier. I include you, too, my most trusted friend, and this encourages me."

Horemheb bowed his head, but chose to change the subject. For the rest of the evening the two friends shared stories and dreams for the future.

The next day, at the conclusion of Pharaoh's first council meeting, the king ordered Horemheb and Ramose to remain in the chamber.

Dismissing his guards, the king motioned for them to sit down. "The Queen Mother is being difficult about my coronation, brothers. She insists I marry Nefertiti before the ceremony and I agreed to it." He smiled at them sheepishly. "I cannot help but be taken with such a goddess. Every time she smiles at me I grow weak all over." His friends grinned, pleased the king had found someone to love.

"Mother," he continued, "is trying to restrict those who will be in the wedding ceremony. Contrary to her wishes I have chosen you two to stand with me and my bride." He then leaned on the table toward them. His voice softened. "I did not say anything at the time of Father's death, but knowing what we do about my brother's murder, I believe the priests of Amun killed him too." He watched their reaction. "How they could have succeeded is a mystery because there is no evidence of poison. Still, I don't trust the priests of Amun or the royal physicians."

"Rightfully so, Majesty," Horemheb said. "We must all be vigilant." He paused a moment then said, "About your marriage, Great One, Ramose and I will be honored to stand with you at your wedding."

Ramose nodded. "It is true, your Majesty. I know I shouldn't address you so until your coronation, but permit me to say, you are Pharaoh. Remember that. Not even a queen or queen mother can dictate to the king."

Amenhotep shook his head. "That may be the law, my friend, but I would be a fool to ignore my mother." He paused before going on. "There is something else. I want you, Horemheb, to take charge of the Palace Guard. Choose an officer to command them. Handpick every man. Select only those you would trust with your own life, then I will know that my family and I will be safe."

"As you command, Majesty," Horemheb said. "But what about the present guardsmen? What's to become of them?"

Amenhotep nodded. "Yes, I have given that some thought. It is by our will the Royal Guards serve where Pharaoh pleases. It pleases me now to send them

LOVE AND MARRIAGE

as reinforcements to our garrison at Swentet. Queen Abar of Nubia must be reminded that we are serious about protecting our borders."

Horemheb cleared his throat, unsure of how to phrase what he wanted to say. "Very good, Majesty. I know the law forbids us to tell you what to do, but I would suggest sending only the guards who have no families. Transfer the others into the army." He knew he had violated protocol and expected the king's displeasure.

"Agreed," the king answered, surprising him. "Let them be assigned to the Valley of the Kings. They can help guard the tombs of the Pharaohs. It is disgraceful the way their final resting places are broken into. The guards can put a stop to it."

Horemheb grinned. "An inspired idea, Majesty. Only you could have thought of such a move."

Amenhotep laughed. "Oh, I do not know, Captain. I am sure you would have tried to."

Over the next few weeks, Horemheb chose Captain Khamet, his old army friend, to become Captain of the Royal Guards. He would be Pharaoh's personal guard and protector. Amenhotep accepted him at once, knowing of his bravery in the Nubian campaign. Lord Ay, Pharaoh's future father-in-law, however, protested the changes.

Shortly after the appointment, Horemheb received two disgruntled visitors at his barracks. "Why did Pharaoh choose you, a mere captain, to make these decisions?" Ay challenged.

"It isn't right," General Minnakf said.

"All I know, my Lords, is that these are Pharaoh's orders and it is not for me to question them." He knew that the two men had been hoping to name one of their own aides to the position. Neither of them responded to his comment. Evidently, they too knew the king had already made up his mind.

Ay changed the subject. "Now, what about the wedding ceremony of my step-daughter? Will the Guards be ready?"

Although annoyed by the question, Horemheb remained calm, not wanting to offend the retired officer. "All will be ready General," he said. "We have even checked the background of every priest in the Temple of Ra."

"Excellent," General Minnakf said.

"Temple of Ra," Ay repeated. He turned and stepped closer. He poked his finger in Horemheb's chest. "Pharaohs are married in the Temple of Amun. Who has dared change it?"

Knowing he had to respond, Horemheb spoke as courteously as he could. "Pharaoh has chosen to honor his god, my Lords. He feels Ra has spoken to him directly and is guiding him to pay homage to the Sun—the Giver of Life. His architects have already designed a temple to the Aten to be built in the Karnak complex."

"An unwise decision," Ay grumbled. "The priests of Amun will be offended by it as will their god." Murmuring, the two older men stormed out of Horemheb's quarters, grumbling about what they learned.

Khamet came in just at that moment and sat down on his friend's bed. "My feet are killing me," he complained. "Did you know that High Priest of Ra acts like an old drill sergeant? He barks more orders than any I ever had." His friend laughed, nodding his head. Khamet said, "I saw those two old vultures leaving. What did they want?"

Horemheb told him and called for his orderly to bring them some beer. When they had their fill, Horemheb said, "I'm worried about security in that temple, Kham. There will be too many priests and courtiers for us to protect Pharaoh. If we could move the wedding to the throne room there would be no problems. I don't like having it in the temple."

"But Harm, there'll be guards at their side at all times, you know that."

Horemheb scrunched his forehead. "All it takes is one well-aimed arrow. I don't have to remind you of that. We'll bring the high priest to the Throne Room and he can bless them there. There will be no ceremony in the temple."

"Amenhotep may not agree brother, or the priests. I wouldn't want to be the one to tell him."

"I can convince Pharaoh," Horemheb said.

Khamet didn't think his friend sounded very sure.

Three weeks later, the marriage ceremony did take place in the Throne Room. Pharaoh allowed the ceremony to be held there, attended by chosen members of his court. Lord Ranofer, High Priest of Ra stood on the steps just below the thrones. He faced the assembly and waited for the royals to enter. Garlands of fresh flowers filled the room, and the guests wore their finest attire.

Lord Sen-nefer, the mayor of Thebes, stood in a prominent place near the front. On the ceiling were magnificent color paintings depicting the life of

Amenhotep III, the new king's father. The walls were covered with bas-reliefs of the royal family offering gifts to the gods. One near the thrones pictured Prince Amenhotep as a small boy.

Lord Ineni, the new Chamberlain, tapped his staff loudly on the granite floor, calling for silence. A small chorus of priests entered, chanting as they walked slowly toward the steps. They took their position to the left of the thrones.

A fanfare of trumpets announced the Queen Mother's entrance and the people made obeisance, palms turned toward her as she passed. Upon reaching the steps, she walked to a third throne brought in for her. Queen Tiye wore a pure-white linen robe, pleated to the floor. Her golden necklaces caught the morning sunlight filtering through the narrow windows. Lord Ineni tapped the polished floor again signaling for the courtiers to stand.

Priestly voices sang the *Hymn to the Sun* and all heads turned to behold a vision of beauty entering the great room. Princess Nefertiti, wearing a brilliant turquoise gown, walked slowly forward as courtiers bowed toward her. No one raised their palms as she had not yet become royal. At the steps, she bowed respectfully to the queen mother, then moved to the center in front of the first step and turned to face the assembly.

Lord Ineni tapped again, more loudly than before, and boomed in a loud voice, "Behold Pharaoh Amenhotep. Son of our Glorious Father, may his name be remembered. Son of Ra-Horakhty, Ruler of the Two Lands and beloved of the gods." Drums rolled as Pharaoh walked into the Great Hall. Everyone fell prostrate before him, not daring to look as their living god walked among them.

Horemheb smiled as he knelt and placed his fist across his heart. Ramose made obeisance on the floor next to him. Amenhotep walked majestically, as if born to be king. He kept his back straight, and his eyes focused on his future queen. When he reached the steps, he bowed to his mother who nodded approvingly. Pharaoh wore his white linen kilt and a gold necklace bearing the image of his god covered his bare chest. He turned, took Nefertiti's hand, and together they faced the court, which greeted them with loud applause.

The High Priest moved to face the couple. He recited simple words used by Egyptians from all walks of life, rich and poor. "You promise this day to share the good times and hard times side by side. You give your hands and hearts as pledges of faith and love." Placing a golden rope around their hands he added, "This symbolizes a circle without end, just as your love is eternal. He lifted his voice. "This cord, made from the metal of the gods, is an incorruptible substance, reminding you of your commitments to each other which will never fail."

An assisting priest carried a bowl of incense to the king who gave it to Lord Ranofer. A small fire stood on an altar to the right of the thrones, and another priest took the sacred frankincense and offered it to the god. A collective sigh of happiness filled the room as its pleasant fragrance penetrated the hall.

The Chamberlain declared in a loud voice, "Bow before their Majesties, Pharaoh Amenhotep, Father of the Two Lands and Queen Nefertiti, Our Mother and Guardian of Kemet's children. May the gods be praised." The audience bowed low once more, and when given permission to stand, they cheered as the newlyweds walked together down the middle of the throne room and out of the hall.

"Is that it?" Horemheb asked. He sounded disappointed.

Ramose laughed. "There would have been more prayers and incantations if we had been in the Temple. Didn't you find it long enough?" he chuckled.

At the great feast following the ceremony, Horemheb sat with Captain Khamet and his guards. He chose to sit with them so as not to be reminded of his lack of nobility. He vowed that would change one day.

"It's good to see you again, Captain," someone said behind him. Horemheb turned around but didn't recognize the younger man. "You don't remember, do you? I'm Maya, Amenia's brother."

"Of course," Horemheb lied. "How is my Lady?"

"She sent me to find you. She's waiting by the pool in the king's garden." He turned to leave, but said, "A word of warning, Captain. I know my sister, and I can tell when she's about to lay a trap." Laughing, he walked away.

Horemheb smiled. He had known many women in his life, including the beautiful Queen of Nubia, but no romance had lasted more than a few days. He had become skilled in breaking off such relationships.

Ramose approached him with Lady Benefer on his arm. "A jar of beer for your thoughts, brother."

"Good evening, my Lady," Horemheb responded, ignoring his friend. "Why in the name of the gods would you allow yourself to be seen with this deranged politician?"

The young woman laughed. "Be kind, Captain. I've come to warn you. You're about to be captured, Harm."

"Never, my Lady," Horemheb said. "I've yet to meet the woman who could do it." That made his two friends laugh even harder.

Ramose spoke in a more quiet voice. "Will you come to Father's villa in the morning, Harm?"

"Of course, right after I've met with Khamet."

"Good, now have a pleasant evening. Oh, and beware of snares." Ramose then gave him an exaggerated and badly executed soldier's salute.

Horemheb walked with a determined air toward pharaoh's formal garden and found Maya's sister sitting on the edge of the small pool. She ran her fingers along the surface, teasing the silver fish below.

"Careful my Lady," he warned. "You could lose a finger." She smiled and turned to face him.

"It's good to see you again, Captain." Bowing her head politely she stood to greet him. He encouraged her to sit once again and he joined her.

"I've been warned about you, Lady Amenia. Not once but twice."

Her lips formed the beginning of a smile. "About me? Who would do such a thing? Can I know the names of my accusers?"

"Well, your own flesh and blood for one," he answered with the expression of a cat playing with a mouse. "The other, the king's Vizier."

She laughed. "I'm not afraid of Maya or Mose. I swear you have nothing to fear from me, Great Warrior. I am but a weak woman." He grinned and saw her grinning back.

In that moment, he really looked at her. Since their meeting at Pharaoh's dinner a month ago, his memories of her had dimmed. Amenia's beauty charmed him. Her eyelids were tinted with green malachite eye shadow accenting her eyes, and he felt a thrill when she looked at him. He preferred the way her golden-brown hair curled tightly about her head. He didn't approve of the exaggerated wigs worn by most noblewomen. She had a slim figure, yet her breasts were well rounded and appealing.

"I came to ask you for a favor," she said. She leaned closer and looked him deep in his eyes. It made him nervous. "I know I have no right, but 'Mose told me to ask."

"What is it, Amenia? Tell me."

"My father is concerned for my brother's future," she began. "We know you are esteemed by our new Pharaoh, and Father has asked me to see if you would use your influence to recommend a position for him."

"Me?" Horemheb replied, more as an exclamation than a question. He thought for a moment. Amenhotep might listen to such a request. "I'm only a lowly officer, my Lady, who is blessed to have the king's confidence. I'll see what I can do, but I don't know your brother very well. Perhaps you can send him to me and we can go hunting. I can learn a lot about a man while out in the fields."

"Thank you Captain, my family will be grateful." He could tell by her voice that she meant it. "You see, there's no reason for anyone to warn you about me."

"Not true, my Lady. You have already trapped me here," he said pointing to his heart. "Your beauty and kind words are like arrows piercing my heart. While I am here with you, my pulse quickens and my nerves tremble. What have you done to me?"

She laughed. "Do all your women believe such fantasies?" She realized she had said the wrong thing and quickly added, "But I too am in a trap, Captain. Here, take my hand and feel the beating of my heart." He took it gently and placed his fingers on her breast. He inhaled quickly as he felt the rapid pulse. Then without thinking, he took her hand, bent down, and kissed her palm, making her blush.

"I must go," she whispered. "May I see you again?"

"Pray the gods it will be so," he said as she left the garden.

The early morning sunlight streamed through a foggy mist on the marshland. Horemheb watched as Maya released his arrow.

"Well aimed," Horemheb told his hunting companion. It surprised him because most noblemen were not good marksmen. Maya, however, had already brought down an antelope and bagged two geese.

"I always thought I would become a warrior, but my father knocked that notion out of my head—literally."

"Well, from what I've seen this morning, you would have been a good one," Horemheb said. He and five of his men had sailed from the city and found a grassy area along the river, home to all kinds of game. Returning in the small felucca, they encountered a herd of hippos not happy to see them.

Horemheb shouted to the man at the tiller. "Steer clear, Ibi. Hapi's creatures are so unpredictable they could easily damage or overturn the boat."

"I want your men to keep the venison and geese, Captain," Maya said. The soldiers on board heard him and cheered. "I've enjoyed today."

"You're not getting off that easy," Horemheb said. "We have to drink to the gods with the best beer in Thebes." Another cheer from his men echoed across the water causing ducks to take flight.

During the following weeks, Maya became a regular visitor to the officers' quarters and he and Horemheb became friends. "When are you going to marry my sister?" Maya suddenly asked him one afternoon.

"I will not marry anyone until Pharaoh makes me a noble." He felt the same way about marrying Queen Abar. He wanted to be her equal. "I had hoped his father, may his name be remembered, would have done so after the Nubian campaign. Now I'll have to wait for his son to make it happen." He paused, unsure whether to go on. "It's true. I'm eager to marry Amenia, but only as a nobleman. Tell her for me to be patient."

"It may be too late," Maya said. "Father has welcomed the attention of two other suitors: Kenamon, the son of a wealthy land owner, and Makaya, a cousin of ours from Memphis."

"By Seth's bowels," Horemheb swore. "I thought Amenia would be different. I believed she liked me as a person, not for my wealth or position."

"It's not Amenia," Maya tried to explain. "It's Father. Amenia loves you. She's told me so many times, but she's afraid to go against his wishes."

"Your father's the king's Treasurer, isn't he?"

"Yes, the Overseer of the King's Treasury," Maya said, being precise.

"Then I will go to the king. Only he can prevent your father from going through with it. I just pray it is not already too late."

Maya shook his head. "My dear mother used to say, nothing is impossible where love is concerned. You'll find a way, brother, I believe it."

The next day, a messenger from Pharaoh commanded Horemheb's presence. When he arrived, the steward ushered him into the king's apartment. Amenhotep walked toward him and he knelt in a salute.

"I am here, Majesty."

"I pray that the Aten give you strength my Brother," Pharaoh began. "Walk with me," and he led his friend out onto the veranda. Amenhotep said, "We have received sad news from Nubia. There has been an uprising among Queen Abar's people. She and many of her followers are dead. I thought you should hear it from me. A new king has taken over the capital at Meroe. I am so sorry."

Horemheb had to sit down, and Pharaoh allowed it. "I should have been at her side, Majesty. She wanted me to go with her because she carried my child."

"By the gods," Amenhotep gasped, forgetting himself.

CHAPTER THIRTEEN

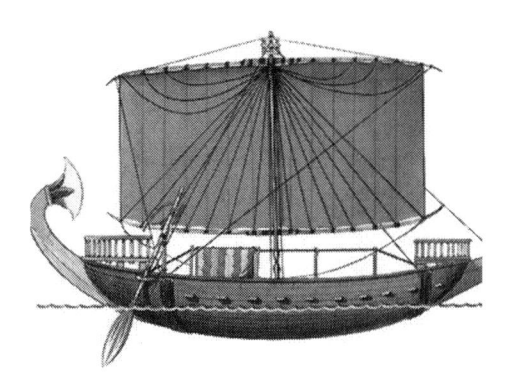

MYSTERIOUS JOURNEY

Pharaoh chose a shady spot on the veranda and sat down. Shocked by his friend's revelation he looked at Horemheb. "When would you have told me, Harm?"

"As soon as I'd heard from her, Majesty. She told me she would send word when she wanted me to come and we would meet at the first whitewater rapids. I would not have gone without your permission and blessing, Great Pharaoh."

The king nodded but didn't immediately respond. "It would have been good to have you as king and my ally in Nubia. I know how you felt about her, and I am sorry she is gone."

"Thank you, Majesty, it is kind of you to tell me."

Lady Nefertiti walked onto the veranda and approached Horemheb. He quickly knelt before her and saluted. She motioned for him to stand and then put her hand on his shoulder. "We are so sorry to learn of Abar's death." She motioned for him to be seated.

"It wasn't just her, Beloved," Pharaoh said. "She carried his child."

"Oh," Nefertiti said. It sounded like a sigh. "May Isis be with them." Silence permeated the air and no one spoke for a while.

Then, Pharaoh stood and began pacing. "I fear this will mean more trouble in the south. Egypt is going to need you and Khamet once again, my friend."

"I am yours to command, Pharaoh."

"Yes, but keep this sad news to yourself for now," the king said. "We have just celebrated a great victory over Nubia. Our subjects do not need to know there could be more trouble ahead."

"Of course, Majesty."

Horemheb turned to go, but the future queen said, "Maybe the gods meant you to marry Amenia all along. Keep your heart open for their guidance, Captain."

"Highness," Horemheb bowed his head politely. "Horus will decide for me."

"I pray it will be so," she responded.

The coronation of Amenhotep took place a month after his wedding. At the solemn ceremony, Lord Ranofer, High Priest of Ra presided. The priest of Aten assisted him, which caused tongues to wag. Lord Ramose and Captain Horemheb stood beside Prince Smenkhare, the king's only living brother. This, too, provoked more unpleasant remarks by the courtiers.

"Such impertinence," Lord Harkhaf grumbled loud enough for people to hear. He and the chamberlain stood behind Horemheb and Ramose, who couldn't help but hear them. "Who does this Horemheb think he is?"

The chamberlain spoke up. "He is who Pharaoh says he is." The courtier stopped talking.

Horemheb knew the affronts to the priests of Amun troubled the court. The king's very name *'Amun is pleased'* bore homage to Amun and the worship of a god that had continued for hundreds of years. The courtiers could not understand what had happened.

"Quiet. Here she comes," Ramose whispered to his friends.

Following a fanfare of trumpets, Nefertiti entered. The courtiers' anxieties diminished slightly when they saw her. They fell prostrate on the floor, but many dared look to see her finely pleated gown of gold.

"She looks like a goddess," Horemheb said. The very devout believed they would all receive a golden body in the afterlife. The soon-to-be queen seemed to embody that hope. Her beautiful face and long neck drew envious looks from every woman in the great hall. She, however, kept her eyes fixed to the front, walking regally, with her head high. Upon reaching the steps, she turned to wait for her husband.

The Queen Mother entered separately and stood beside the chamberlain who motioned for the court to stand. No extra throne awaited her this time. Horemheb was pleased her son determined to demonstrate there would be only one ruler in the land.

A much louder and longer fanfare announced Pharaoh's entrance as the courtiers fell prostrate once again. He walked slowly toward his queen, and when he reached her, extended his arm to help her up the steps. She smiled at him with affection. During the weeks since their wedding, those at court had seen the young couple's looks and gestures to each other. They clearly loved each other very much. Once seated on their thrones, the chamberlain tapped three times on the floor giving the courtiers permission to stand.

Surprisingly, the high priest of Aten walked forward carrying Nefertiti's crown. It would normally have been the high priest of Amun's honor to do so. Pharaoh stood, took the crown, and placed it on his queen's head. Cheers and clapping echoed around the room, lasting until the chamberlain tapped the floor again.

"Behold Nefertiti," Lord Ineni shouted. "Mother of the Two Lands, Beloved of Pharaoh, Priestess of Aten, and Daughter of Light." The courtiers' shouted her name over and over again.

Lord Ay stepped forward carrying the double crown of the Two Lands, which he handed to Lord Ranofer. A silence gripped the Throne Room. The high priest held the red and white crown high for a moment so everyone could see it. It gave the king's subjects time to reflect on the days before the people of the north and south had become one. The double crown symbolized that union.

"In Aten's name," Ranofer said in a loud voice, placing the crown on Amenhotep's head. The trumpets sounded and the people once again cheered and clapped their hands.

"Behold Pharaoh," Lord Ineni declared, "Ruler of the Two Lands, Son of Amenhotep the Third, may his name be remembered."

"*Ba-kher*. May it be so," the courtiers responded.

The Chamberlain continued, "Son of Ra and the Aten, Giver of the True Light." The people clapped again, but less enthusiastically. The king turned and bowed to his mother, acknowledging the passage of power to himself.

"She's not going to bow her head," Ramose whispered. "Look how long she's taking." But eventually Queen Tiye bowed her head to her son. Ramose and many others let out a sigh of relief.

When the chamberlain tapped the polished floor again, the courtiers divided, leaving a large aisle between them. A short cadence of drums announced their majesties' readiness to receive gifts. First to approach the thrones were ambassadors from neighboring countries. Important courtiers and members of the king's council followed them. When their majesties left the hall, they received their guests at a banquet prepared in the palace garden. Feasting and music would continue through the night.

Ramose and Benefer decided their marriage would be a private affair. Only family and friends were invited. Both had been devastated by the death of their friend's Nubian queen. They did all they could to include Horemheb in their social gatherings. Their friend stood now with the groom while the priests of Amun blessed the young nobleman and his beloved. Lady Amenia stood with the bride, and Horemheb thought her to be a vision of beauty and grace.

Horemheb reminded his friend. "Of all men you are the most blessed, brother. Benefer is a beautiful woman who will make you a fine companion."

"Thank you, Harm," Ramose used his childhood friend's old nickname. "I only wish you and Amenia would consider marriage too. You both need someone."

"It is in the hands of the gods, so it could happen," Horemheb said. "First I must help her brother."

Pharaoh received Horemheb cordially in the royal apartment. "If Maya is as trustworthy as his father, Captain, I will be pleased," Amenhotep said. "I grant your proposal." He paused and spoke again. "I also have an order for you, my friend. You and Ramose will accompany me tomorrow afternoon. Be at my galley at midday. I will tell you where we're going once on board."

"As you command, Majesty," the officer replied. "I am grateful for Maya's sake."

"Remember, Horemheb. I am all knowing. I know you are grateful for your own sake. You have an eye on his sister, the Lady Amenia."

Horemheb laughed. "That too, Great One, but I don't stand a chance. My origins are too poor for such a lady, even though I have feelings for her."

"You were not poor brother, just humble, and the gods favor the humble. You were raised as a true Egyptian. Your father worked with his hands, and I call that blessed."

"Your words are kind, Majesty. He did love to work, but Amenia is of noble blood. That is just the way it is. That's Maat—the true balance of things."

Amenhotep became cryptic. "Hmm, I understand." Horemheb saluted and left the king's apartment.

The next day as Horemheb drove his chariot to the ship, Ramose stood beside him. "What happened to your honeymoon, Mose?" Horemheb chuckled.

"Seth's foul breath," the new groom swore. "Why has he summoned us, do you know?"

"He wouldn't say. Couldn't the courtiers tell you anything about our destination?"

"Nothing," Ramose said.

When they reached the galley, Captain Khamet met them at the gangway. They dismounted and one of Horemheb's men drove his chariot back to the barracks. "Come aboard," he said. "His majesty will be here any moment." One hundred of the new Royal Guards lined up in front of the great ship awaiting the king's arrival.

"Who's the nobleman?" Ramose asked, pointing to a distinguished-looking man already on deck.

"I asked him the same question," Khamet told them, "but he replied 'His Majesty will speak for me.'"

A cacophony of trumpets announced the approach of the king's chariot. The fifty guardsmen on horseback surrounding him quickly dismounted and knelt on one knee. Amenhotep stepped down and handed the reins to his charioteer. Everyone on the ship made obeisance before pharaoh—their palms held toward him. Pharaoh walked up on deck and greeted his two friends. He gave the captain of the vessel a wave of his hand and *The Light of Aten's Glory* came to life.

"Cast off all lines," the first mate shouted.

"Ready the sail," the captain ordered. Thirty sailors pulled on the lines, lowering the great rectangular sail from the long spar at the top of the mast. The three passengers followed Amenhotep to a raised portion of the deck outside his cabin.

"Gentlemen," the king began, "allow us to introduce Lord Bek. He is our Chief Architect and Designer. It is he who will show us what the god Aten has revealed to us. When we arrive at our destination, you will understand what the god wants us to do."

Lord Bek seemed as perplexed as the other two men but kept quiet. Ramose hoped when they were alone he might tell them more.

"We should be there by late afternoon," Amenhotep told them. "We are going to meditate and seek further guidance. See that we are not disturbed."

"Majesty," the men replied, bowing their heads politely as the king entered his luxurious cabin.

"The captain will know where we're headed," Horemheb said. "I'll go see what I can find out."

"I see Pharaoh chose you for this voyage, Captain Henenu," Horemheb said, greeting the older man. "As the senior officer of Pharaoh's fleet you know the great river like the lines on your hands. We will have a smooth journey."

The ship's captain acknowledged the soldier's presence at the helm. "Captain Horemheb. Why are we here? What's going on?"

"It's a mystery my Lord," Horemheb said. "We were hoping you could tell us where we are headed."

"That's just it," the mariner responded. "No one knows but his majesty, and he told me he had to await his god's instructions."

"He's a Pharaoh of mysteries," the younger man murmured.

The ship's captain nodded. "Yes he is."

Harm walked back to his friends. "Even the captain of the ship doesn't know where we're going," he reported. "We're sailing without a destination."

"Pharaoh has not been acting like himself lately," Ramose said. "Lord Ineni has spoken to me privately about him. He is concerned Amenhotep might not be well."

Lord Bek spoke up. "It's obvious I'm to design something for him, but it can't be a tomb, we're sailing away from the Valley of the Kings. Of course we could be going to the necropolis at Abydos, but I'm at a loss to understand it."

"This requires patience, something I'm not very good at," Horemheb growled.

Ramose laughed. "I can certainly attest to that."

For the rest of the afternoon the men walked around the deck speaking with the sailors. That evening, Amenhotep appeared cheerful and chose to take his meal with his friends in front of his cabin. Fish caught that day sizzled on small iron braziers, and vegetables brought with them that morning were steam cooked. Fruit provided dessert and they had their choice of wine or beer. Pharaoh chose the finest wine, while the others chose beer.

When they had eaten, Pharaoh declared, "Tonight, before the sun sets, we'll go ashore and meditate on the glory of the Aten. We will pray throughout the night and ask the god to reveal his truths to us and my people."

"But Majesty," Ramose said, "we've anchored at an isolated spot. There's no dock or settlement here."

"True, Mose, but we will go ashore in the small boat to listen for the Aten's voice. "Order our pavilion brought with us, and summon the guards to surround our camp."

"As you command, Great One," Horemheb said. Puzzled, he scratched his head.

"Good. Then prepare to disembark," the king ordered and everyone hurried to obey. Guardsmen brought the great tent up from the hold, and two skiffs were lowered to carry it and several chairs ashore. Horemheb and Khamet organized the guards who placed the tent on a level plain before returning to the ship. A human barrier of guards stood in a square around it, each two cubits apart.

"All is ready, Majesty," Captain Khamet informed the king.

"Excellent. Let us go, Captain. I have an encounter with my god." Amenhotep followed the Captain of the Guard to the small dinghy.

Watching from the railing Horemheb said, "There he goes. By the gods, look at him. He's sitting beside a commoner. Extraordinary."

"Why is that so extraordinary?" Ramose asked. "He sits with you all the time." That provoked a scowl on his friend's face, but he didn't respond.

Once ashore, the guards gathered branches of dead scrub trees and started a large fire. Others gathered enough to last through the night. The men were not pleased they would have to stand in place all night, but orders were orders. They saluted when Amenhotep arrived and walked to his tent where a simple cot awaited him.

"I want blankets placed on the ground here, Captain," Pharaoh commanded, taking special note of the position of the sun.

Khamet called for his aide and gave him the king's instructions. The skiff went back to the ship to bring blankets as well as more waterskins.

Amenhotep invited the architect and his two friends into the pavilion. They hoped he would now give them the reason for their journey. Instead, he only perpetuated the mystery.

"We know you are concerned and may think we have taken leave of our senses," he said. "We understand, believe us, we do. But what is about to happen is a great and wonderful thing. For a year now the Aten has been speaking to us. We are not worthy of such revelations, but He has made us his instrument. The priests of Amun killed our brother; there can be doubt of that. They took Thutmose before his time and we are convinced they ended our beloved father's life as well."

Without thinking Horemheb blurted out, "We don't know that, Majesty."

"Peace, Horemheb," the king said. "It has been revealed to us that the worship of Amun must end. Our relationship to the gods is about to change, and that is why we are here. We must listen and hear the message of the god of light."

"Yes, Great One," Ramose said. He spoke before Horemheb could say anything else. "Only you are blessed to speak with the gods."

"Not so, Mose. You will see how that too will change," Amenhotep said. "We can all speak to the Aten and know His will. Just be patient."

Horemheb knew the architect found it troubling to be there. The nobleman frowned at Pharaoh's blasphemy against Amun and dared raise his voice. "If you permit, my Lord King. Will this involve some kind of building for this new religion you've discovered?"

"Yes, Lord Bek, but be patient, we beg you. What you will be asked to do will astonish the whole country. The god has chosen you." The architect bowed his head politely but Horemheb could see the man's hands shaking.

"We ask all of you men to remain prayerful through the night as we seek the Aten's purpose for our presence here. It will become clearer at sunrise." The men stood and left the tent, their puzzled expressions showing how they felt.

"Did we learn anything, brothers?" Khamet asked. They shook their heads. "We'll settle in for the night. You're welcome to sit with us."

Gathering near the fire, they shared their speculations, talking late into the night. The guardsmen were hungry, not having eaten supper, and that made them restless. They could hear Pharaoh intoning prayers and chanting songs of praise. The sound reverberated throughout the camp and bounced back from the side of the large ship anchored just off shore.

"We should take turns sleeping," Horemheb said. "One of us must be awake in case Pharaoh needs us." Using the blankets brought ashore, each of the king's guests laid out his bed on the ground. In the dark, a jackal laughed at the intruders, but one of Khamet's archers quickly silenced it. The moon had already set, so only the light of the distant stars shone down on them. Horemheb couldn't sleep. His mind raced with the information Amenhotep had given them. He felt completely unprepared to respond to any of it.

Several long hours later, as the horizon in the east grew bright, Amenhotep called for Horemheb to join him. "The god is coming," he announced just as the brilliant orb of the sun rose above the distant hills. Pharaoh prostrated himself before its bright light and began to recite from memory the Hymn to the Sun:

> *"Thy dawning is beautiful,*
> *In the horizon of the sky,*
> *O living Aten, Beginning of Life.*
> *When thou rises in the eastern horizon,*
> *Thou fillest every land,*
> *With thy beauty.*
> *Thou art beautiful,*
> *Great,*
> *Glittering,*
> *High above every land.*
> *Thy rays,*
> *They encompass the land,*
> *Even all that thou has made."*

Suddenly to everyone's horror, Pharaoh fell to the ground, shaking violently.

CHAPTER FOURTEEN

THE VALLEY OF THE WIND

Pharaoh made terrible gurgling sounds and couldn't speak. Horemheb saw this happen before in his home village.

"Khamet, give me a dagger quickly," he yelled.

The officer handed it to him but said, "Do him no harm or you die."

Horemheb ignored him and dashed to a scrub tree. He cut off a small branch, peeling off the bark as he ran back to the king. Placing the short baton between the king's teeth, he asked Ramose to help hold the king.

"Keep him steady. It's the holy sickness. Only those blessed by the gods are afflicted. It's a good sign," Horemheb shouted it so all the men could hear.

"He'll have us put to death for touching him, you fool," Ramose growled, "You put a stick in his mouth, by the gods."

"So he won't bite off his tongue, brother."

Then, just as quickly as it started, the king became still and began to breathe normally once again. His friends released him and he sat up. He took the crude baton out of his mouth and examined it closely.

"Someone has touched the royal person," were his first words. He saw the alarmed look on their faces and said, "And we are grateful. Who did this?" He held out the wooden baton.

"Horemheb, Majesty. He knew what to do immediately," Khamet said.

Pharaoh turned and smiled at the young man. "So, once more I am in your debt, my friend."

"I did it without thinking, Majesty, which always gets me into trouble."

"Tell your men not to worry, Khamet," the king said standing up. "Tell them their king is fine. The Aten has visited him, and he now knows our destination. Pack up all this and let us resume our journey. It isn't far."

A short time later, with the tent removed, all hands were back on board and Pharaoh gave the order to set sail.

"What is our destination, Majesty?" Henenu asked.

In a loud voice so everyone could hear, Pharaoh answered. "Akhetaten, the Horizon of the Aten."

The *Light of Aten's Glory* moved north toward the Great Sea, toward a place known only to the king and his god.

The ship had now been docked a short while. Horemheb and Ramose watched as Pharaoh and the architect walked up from the riverbank on a rise a hundred cubits from the river's edge, allowing them to see across to the hills beyond. The wind carried Pharaoh's conversation with Lord Bek.

"It is here you will build Aten's city," Amenhotep said. "You will design everything: the palace, villas for my nobles, and the temple to the god, represented by the sun disk in the center. It will remind us that His light is the center of all life."

"Yes, Majesty," Lord Bek replied with some hesitation. "This new city will be a living example of the Aten's importance to your glorious reign."

"Well said," the king replied, "but I would be more pleased if they remembered the Aten as the Giver of all Life and Light." Horemheb tried to see what the king could possibly be looking at, but couldn't. He saw only a vast expanse of sand and scrub.

He watched Pharaoh wave his arm and heard him say, "One day this will bring forth the reality of my vision." He turned to his architect. "You may ask why the god has chosen this spot, my Lord. It is because no temples of worship of the ancient gods were built here to contaminate this soil. It is pure and holy."

Lord Bek nodded. "You are a Seer, my Lord, to have received the vision described to me."

"Exactly," Amenhotep answered in a louder voice. "I will call it Akhetaten—*the Horizon of the Aten*—in honor of my god."

Horemheb shook his head. The horizon had become an obsession of the king's, first as a symbol in Egyptian writing, then as the place where his god would touch the earth.

Ramose said, "Do you know what this means, Harm? Pharaoh is going to move his capital here. He will no longer rule from Thebes."

"What?" Horemheb said. "Surely not. Thebes is the heart of Egypt, the soul of the Two Lands. He wouldn't do such a thing."

"He's the Divine Son of Ra and can do whatever he wants, brother. But…" and Ramose paused a long time before adding, "…his nobles, courtiers, and the priests of other religions especially Amun, will be opposed to such a move."

Horemheb shook his head in anger. "That will mean civil unrest and trouble. The generals and the army will not accept it."

Ramose walked over to a large outcropping of rock and sat down. "That won't be true of Lord Ay. He's the king's father-in-law now, and I don't think he would dare oppose him."

"Aren't we getting ahead of ourselves, Mose?" his friend said. "We don't know if it is the king's intent to move the capital. Right now, he desires more than anything to please his god. There's nothing wrong with that, in fact, it's commendable."

"Well-spoken, you two," Pharaoh said in a pleasant voice. "I could not have summed it up better myself."

Embarrassed that he had overheard them, they tried to excuse themselves for speaking so disrespectfully, but the king would have none of it.

"No, no, I am serious. You have spoken the truth, and Aten is the father of truth."

"Is that right, Great One? Does Aten wish your capital to be here?" Horemheb asked, hoping he wouldn't anger the king.

Amenhotep smiled. "I will seek further guidance. That is all any of us can do." They followed him as he walked back toward the architect, who bowed his head politely to Pharaoh.

"Majesty, perhaps you could leave a few warriors with me," Bek said. "They could hunt for food and provide protection. I need to stay here to measure the land and draw up the plans for your city. Markers will be placed first, then I can calculate how best to turn your vision into reality. Another ship could return with my tools and more parchment. In a month perhaps, I can deliver your designs, Majesty. You have made it clear what you want, and the plans will reflect your vision."

"Let it be so," Amenhotep said. "Horemheb will see that your tools and whatever else you need are sent." Extending his arm in a sweeping gesture he asked, "What has this region been called in the past?"

Horemheb said, "One of the guards told me it is known simply as 'The Valley of the Wind,' Majesty. May I suggest that a royal banner be placed on this high spot so it can be seen from the river?"

"Granted. See to it at once."

Horemheb bowed his head and saluted.

The *Light of Aten's Glory* sailed at midday leaving the architect and ten archers. The ship's captain left his extra rope so the architect could begin measuring the land.

Pharaoh and his friends stood at the railing, watching the royal pennant fluttering on the small hill. "Lord Bek is a good man," Pharaoh said.

"He has a big task before him, my King," Ramose said. "I believe that Bek designed my father's beautiful tomb in the valley."

On an impulse Horemheb spoke up. "Whatever we can do to help you with the new city, you have but to command."

His words made Pharaoh grin. "Your remark is interesting, Captain. I am naming you the military commander of Akhetaten. You will work closely with Lord Ay of course, but you'll report directly to me, not to him…is that understood?"

Horemheb replied, trying to be amusing. "Yes, Great One. The Aten has reached me."

"I believe he has, Captain, but do not make light of my beliefs," Amenhotep warned.

The captain knew he had overstepped the line and nodded to show he understood.

The journey back to Thebes took longer because of the opposing current. Horemheb liked standing in the stern, helping the rudder men who had to be relieved every one hundred strokes of the oars. Keeping the large rudder-oars on course took all one's strength. The ship's crew of rowers below deck manned the long oars. With their strength and a good wind, the great galley sailed closer to home.

Riders from the villages they passed rode ahead with the news of Pharaoh's return, so a large crowd greeted them at Thebes. His golden chariot stood ready with the palace guardsmen there to escort him home. When the people saw him come out on deck as the *Glory* prepared to dock, they chanted his name, "Amen…hotep. Amen…hotep."

Pharaoh walked off the ship bringing loud shouts and clapping from the crowd as he stepped into his chariot. Holding his head high and his back straight as a reed, he rode off toward the palace.

"We've been gone three days, brother," Ramose grumbled, "but it seems like three weeks." Horemheb laughed and then Ramose said in a more serious tone. "I wish the king would give you permission to marry that woman of yours. I'm tired of looking at your sad face."

"Go away," Horemheb said.

They parted ways when Ramose's servant arrived with his master's chariot. A guardsman waited for Horemheb and handed him the reins to Shu, his stallion. Patting the horse's neck he spoke to it. "One day I'll come home to a loving wife, Shu. You'll see." He climbed up and rode toward to the barracks.

A week later, Horemheb entered the king's Council Chamber, summoned along with the rest of the king's advisors. General Minnakf and Ay were already there as well as the queen. Other nobles, namely the chamberlain, the Keeper of the King's Treasury were also there, along with the high priest of Ra.

Horemheb knelt in front of Pharaoh when he reached the front of the room, placing his fist over his heart.

"Horemheb, Son of Kheruef, Captain in the King's Army, member of the King's Council, stand forth and hear the word of your Pharaoh."

The officer stood and faced their majesties.

"As a friend of Pharaoh you have saved the lives of father and son. You have been honored with the Gold of Valor and there is no higher honor." The king paused, then added, "Except for establishing a tie of blood, and I do that today in front of these nobles and my Queen. From this moment, Horemheb, you are Pharaoh's brother of blood. This makes your blood royal and noble."

A wide grin spread across the soldier's face as he realized the meaning of the king's words. He looked at Nefertiti, who smiled an all-knowing smile. The king stepped away from his chair and placed his hands on the officer's shoulders. "Marry her, Brother," the king said. "Nothing stands in your way."

"May the Aten bless you Great One for what you have done. Know that I will not forget." He tried to kneel again but the king insisted he stand.

"Come, friends, Greet my new brother, Horemheb, Man of the Spear," Amenhotep said. "He has our trust and loyalty."

The councilors walked forward and congratulated the officer for his elevated standing at court. Just then, Amenhotep's half-brother Smenkhare, entered the council chamber, the frown on his face an ominous portent of trouble.

The opposite happened, however. The prince approached the king and bowed his head respectfully. "I understand we have a new brother, Majesty. May I congratulate him as well?" Turning to Horemheb he said under his breath, "Come to my villa this evening. I will congratulate you there." Horemheb saluted the prince, but did not respond as the courtiers continued to congratulate him.

Turning to the king, Smenkhare laughed. "He is much better looking than either of us, Brother."

"Watch yourself, Khare. Now that we are Pharaoh, it is unwise to insult us," the king reminded him. The prince bowed a little too politely by bending almost to his knees, and then walked over to stand next to Queen Nefertiti.

Later, when Horemheb and Ramose were alone, his friend said, "By making you his brother, Harm, Pharaoh has made Smenkhare your enemy. They don't need an extra heir to the throne. Smenkhare is already the official one. Be careful at his villa. I wouldn't be surprised if he tried to poison you or even try something more violent."

Horemheb grunted and ignored his remarks.

That evening at the prince's home, built on a beautiful hill overlooking the river, the household steward greeted Horemheb and provided servants to wash the guest's feet and hands.

"Ah, there you are, Brother," the prince greeted him, stressing in a louder voice the captain's new royal relationship.

Horemheb went onto one knee and saluted him. "I'm here as you commanded, Highness."

Smenkhare waved his hand. "Come, come, no need for such formalities now that you're part of the family."

"If you please, Highness, I am very uncomfortable with this. I am well aware of my lack of noble blood."

"Be calm, Horemheb, I bear you no ill will. It is I who will succeed my brother. The gods have ordained it. You are no threat to me."

"Then I am pleased, Highness. You know as well as I that Pharaoh has done this only so I can marry the Lady Amenia."

"And a beautiful woman she is, too. Congratulations," the prince said. "You are also a brave man. First you saved my brother Thutmose, and now Hotep. Our family is in your debt." He watched the soldier's face for any sign of disapproval, and then added, "I too would like to call you friend."

"I only did my duty, Highness. Horus enabled me to do it."

"Quiet. We don't speak that name openly any more in Thebes, Captain. My brother no longer believes in the gods of his ancestors." The prince said it with a great deal of sarcasm.

"Forgive me, Highness," Horemheb said. "I will honor Pharaoh's beliefs but can't deny the god who has blessed me all these years. I vow to do my best to honor the king's new religion."

"Between us," Smenkhare said quietly, "I join you in honoring Horus, Amun and all the other gods. This sudden obsession with the sun disk is really a personal thing between my brother and Nefer. I don't think it is intended for the common people, just his family."

"Then with all due respect, why is he going to build his city downriver?" Horemheb said.

The prince paused, but didn't answer. "Would you like a beer?" The soldier nodded and followed the prince to the garden. A servant brought their jars and they sat in the moonlight.

"I believe this new city is to be a demonstration of his power. He wants to show the priests of Amun, and by them the people, that it is he who rules the kingdom, not them. It is something my father spoke about—this worship of the Aten—but he would never have dared do what my brother is planning."

Horemheb took a long swallow of beer then wiped his mouth. "He will bring the wrath of the gods on us all, Highness. If he persecutes the followers of

Amun he will start a rebellion that the army and all his guards may not be able to stop."

Smenkhare nodded. "Agreed. But you are now military overseer of his new city, I hear. It will be up to you to maintain Maat, the eternal balance of things, my friend."

Horemheb nodded. "I felt awkward, Highness, because of my new relationship to the king. But now what you said earlier pleases me."

Smenkhare grinned. "If Pharaoh has a son that will put both of us out of contention. You should know that. Even so, as his real blood kin, I would have precedence over you no matter what."

"Good," Horemheb remarked. "Then I too would like us to be friends."

"That's better," Smenkhare answered. "More beer?"

***

"Lord Bek has returned," Ramose told Horemheb. "Pharaoh has summoned us both to his Council Chamber."

"It's only been three weeks," Horemheb observed. "Can he have finished so soon?"

When they entered the chamber, Pharaoh said, "Look. Come and see this." He pointed to a model of his new city. On the table were also Bek's line drawings of every building. The three-dimensional model brought them to life. "Behold Akhetaten—the Horizon of the Aten. It is exactly as I saw it in the Valley of the Wind."

Horemheb looked at Ramose and could see on his friend's face the same concern that must be on his own. He felt as if his stomach had fallen to the floor. *Pharaoh plans to move the capital. There's nothing any of us can do.*

CHAPTER FIFTEEN

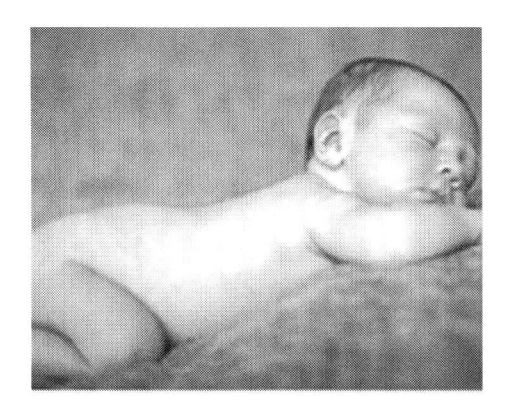

TUTANKHATEN

"It is truly amazing, Majesty," Horemheb said. He moved closer to the model city and asked Lord Bek several questions, but saved the most important one for last. Looking at the floor plans of the buildings he frowned. "Where are the soldiers' barracks and guard posts, my Lord?"

Bek became embarrassed. "They are not on the priority list of buildings, Lord Horemheb. Bek's reply acknowledged the Captain's new social standing.

Pharaoh spoke. "And rightfully so, Captain. This is to be a city of peace not war."

"But Majesty, if you and your family are to live there, you must be protected. Please, Great One, you need the guards."

Ramose now risked the king's anger by agreeing. "He's right, Majesty. Your lives above all must be protected."

Pharaoh scowled, thought a moment and said, "Can you modify the city to provide our protection, Lord Bek, but keep the city center as it is now?"

"Of course, Majesty," Bek said. "It will take some time, but we can begin construction of the city center immediately. I'll prepare a list of builders for your approval."

"Good," Pharaoh said. "Do so at once. We will show these plans to our council this afternoon. We are very pleased with you, Architect, very pleased indeed." Lord Bek bowed, and then left the chamber.

Ramose felt nervous about what he would say next. "Majesty, do you think it wise to tell your advisors the truth about the city? It might be best not to mention that you will be moving the court away from Thebes. Instead, let them understand this is to be a building project to honor your god. That too is true, is it not?"

"Mose is right, Great One," Horemheb blurted out. "They must be prepared."

Pharaoh sat down on his chair and crossed his arms. Horemheb clenched his teeth because the king only did it when displeased. "I know you both mean well, but I am not pleased by your remarks. Am I Pharaoh or am I not?"

"May we sit, Majesty?" Horemheb asked. The king motioned for them to do so. "You are our king above all, Majesty, and you hold in your hands the power of life and death. We just feel that if changes are made too abruptly there will be bloodshed, and your god might not be pleased."

Ramose gasped when he heard his friend's words. He spoke up, "You've already begun building the beautiful temple for the Aten here at Karnak, Majesty," Ramose said. "The people will see its importance to you. Therefore, this new city will be an extension of the temple. You are building the city to honor the worship of the Aten."

"Enough," Amenhotep said. "I will consider what you have said, but I will decide the Aten's will on my own." He took a moment to calm himself. "I am glad you like the city."

Captain Khamet entered the chamber and awaited acknowledgment.

"What is it Captain?" Pharaoh said.

"It is the Queen who summons you, Majesty. She said to tell you it is urgent."

"Am I now at the beck and call of a woman?" the king shouted.

The Captain of the Guard became flustered. "She said she would have me thrown to the crocodiles if I did not return with you, Great One." That made Pharaoh laugh and he followed the officer out the door.

Horemheb walked over to study the model of Akhetaten once more. "It *is* beautiful, though. You have to give that to Lord Bek. He's created a masterpiece."

"But at what future cost of blood and sweat, brother?" Ramose said.

Just then, the door burst open and Pharaoh rushed back in out of breath, and with the widest smile his friends ever saw.

"It's Nefertiti!" he shouted. "She's with child again! May the Aten be praised."

"And you too, Great One. I think you are also responsible," Horemheb laughed.

"Congratulations Great Father of the Land!" Ramose said. He joined in the laughter, both men happy for the king.

"This time it will be a boy—I just know it," Amenhotep bragged. "He will be the Son of the Aten."

Several months later, a large middle-aged woman held the newborn in her arms. Queen Nefertiti's distant cousin served as the baby's wet nurse. She lovingly wrapped the baby in linen cloth to keep his arms and legs immobile. At two days old, he still looked very red. His mother's delivery proved difficult, but she now rested peacefully in her bedchamber. She could hear the midwives fussing in the other room.

"Hold him carefully, Maia," the midwife said. "He's the future of Egypt."

"Quiet you old cow," Maia hissed. "Do you think this is the first baby I've nursed, Tener?"

"No, but he's the first heir to the throne; I know that," Tener shot back.

"Quiet, you troublesome old ravens," the queen commanded sitting up in bed. "Your constant bickering annoys me. Now bring him to me."

The midwives found it difficult to believe her majesty just gave birth. She had been bathed and wanted her face made up to look her best. She wore eye shadow and a touch of red pomegranate on her lips.

"I want to see his fingers and toes," Nefertiti insisted. "Why is he so wrapped up?"

Tener answered. "Lord Kh'a insisted, Majesty. You'll see every inch of him soon enough."

"Unwrap him," the queen ordered. Maia began removing the linen cloth until his little arms and hands were free.

"There now, he'll grab onto your fingers if you touch his hands," Maia said.

The queen did so. She laughed as the infant's fingers gripped hers. After several minutes the wet nurse wrapped the linen back around him and his mother seemed content. The baby became hungry and started to cry. The nurse took him and placed his mouth to her breast. When he fell asleep, Tener put him in the crib beside his mother who closed her eyes. The women slipped out onto the veranda outside the queen's chamber and began speaking in whispers.

"Kh'a said the boy will never be able to use his left foot. It's twisted; anyone can see that," Tener lamented.

"What about the little split in the palate of his mouth?" Maia asked. "One of his uncles has that too. I understand it runs in the family."

"Has Pharaoh discovered this?"

Maia shook her head. "No, and he's blinded by the fact he has a son. I don't think he's noticed the cleft in the boy's mouth. The child will have trouble speaking at first. It's so sad; they're such a beautiful couple. It will hit them hard when they realize how difficult the boy's life will be," Tener said.

"Pharaoh's new god doesn't seem to have blessed this baby," Maia whispered.

Horemheb waited patiently as Pharaoh finished praying. They were in the new temple of the Aten in Karnak's eastern court, accompanied by twenty guardsmen.

Pharaoh Amenhotep seemed moody all the way there. His only words were to ask Horemheb to stay with him in the sacred sanctuary. The beautifully carved papyrus-shaped columns cast dark shadows onto the polished granite floor. Sunlight streaming into the temple illuminated the bas-relief of the Aten on the far wall. Each carved ray coming from the sun ended in a long outstretched hand reaching to the earth.

Pharaoh's face looked troubled as he prayed. Horemheb could only catch a word here and there. He drew closer, recognizing a few of the words the king often recited:

> *Creator of the germ in woman*
> *Maker of seed in man,*
> *Giving life to the son in the boy of his mother,*
> *Soothing him that he may not weep,*
> *Nurse even in the womb.*
> *Giver of breath to animate every one that he maketh.*

TUTANKHATEN

When he cometh forth from the body...
On the day of his birth,
Thou openest his mouth in speech,
Thou suppliest his necessities.

As he offered incense to his god, Pharaoh slowly backed away from the image of the sun disk.

"What is bothering you, Great One?" Horemheb asked. In a kind voice he added, "Is there anything I can do?"

"It's a family matter, Captain," Amenhotep said. "It's between Nefer and me. The glorious birth of our son has also brought problems."

"I see, Majesty. You know you can ask anything of me, just say the word."

"I'm grateful Brother," the king said, "but Nefer doesn't know about our son."

"Know what, Great One? Is something wrong with him?" He whispered so the guardsmen couldn't hear.

Pharaoh replied in a low voice, "The baby's wrapped in linen as are all newborns, so she's not seen his feet yet—only his arms and hands."

Horemheb swallowed hard, afraid of what the king might say.

Pharaoh leaned against one of the columns for support before answering.

"His left foot is turned and Lord Kh'a said he'll never walk right. Apparently we have this abnormality in my family—the Thutmosid family that is. Even I will not be able to spare him being teased and mocked by everyone."

"Give him time, Majesty. He's only just been born." Horemheb said. He paused trying to think how to change the subject. "How will he be named?"

Amenhotep shook his head. "Somehow the name I have chosen isn't fitting now that he has this infirmity."

"What name did you choose?"

"He will be called Tutankhaten—the *living image of the Aten*," the king answered. "But if the Aten is pure, and perfect, how can I name a boy with an imperfect foot in honor of him?"

Horemheb waited another moment before responding. "I am but a soldier I know, but permit me to say, Majesty, that it is his Ka that is the living image of your god, isn't that so? His Ka is pure and good. There is nothing impure about that."

The king's eyes widened in surprise as he listened to his friend's words. "You're right of course, you son of a stonemason. Bless you, Horemheb. The

Aten has shown me through your words the truth of it. Now you see why I included you as one of my advisors." They laughed and the king said, "Come, I want to show you my son."

A short time later, they surprised Maia when Pharaoh entered the nursery. She fell to the floor before him. Motioning for her to stand he said, "I've come to see my son, Maia, bring him."

"Shh, Majesty," Tener hushed him as she came out of the queen's room. "Nefer is asleep." She went back and lifted the baby out of the crib. "Let's go into the front room." She walked holding the baby, the men trailing behind. When she handed the boy to his father, the king insisted she remove the wrapping.

"No, Majesty. It is not good to do so," Tener said.

"Obey me," Amenhotep said. The nurse trembled as she unwrapped his son. Carefully placing her hand behind his head, she handed him to Pharaoh.

Horemheb approached the king who held his son as if he would break. Tutankhaten continued sleeping as the king rocked him back and forth.

"Prince Tutankhaten, meet your uncle Horemheb," the king whispered.

"Such a strong-looking warrior, Majesty." He laughed, moving closer for a better look. "I'm honored to be one of his uncles."

"Here is the reason for my concern, brother," the king said. He showed his friend the baby's malformed left foot.

The soldier groaned. "Oh. May the gods bless him."

"You mean the Aten of course," Pharaoh said. He smiled as he suddenly held him out. "Here, hold him."

"But." Horemheb started to protest. The king put the baby into his arms. Pharaoh's guardian suddenly felt very protective of the little life he held.

"Please Majesty," Nurse Maia pleaded. "Let me return him to his crib." Pharaoh nodded as Horemheb handed him back. The king walked into the queen's room and laid him in the crib. Going out onto the veranda the two men sat down on granite benches. Horemheb still marveled that he could sit in the king's presence. He stretched out his legs, as did his majesty.

"I'll be able to tell Nefer about our son now, and reassure her he will be all right, thanks to you."

"I promise by all that is holy, my King, that I will dedicate my life to protecting him. With no offense to the Aten, I swear it by Horus, my protector."

"My son's Ka has touched you, Horemheb. Of that I am certain. I know we can trust you with our lives."

"What about his sisters? What do they say?" Horemheb asked.

"They have only been allowed to hold him, but they are very happy."

"Has your brother Smenkhare been to see him?"

"Not yet, but he will. First, I wanted to be ready to show Egypt the heir to the throne. I did not feel that I could face my people. You have changed my mind. For that, I am grateful. The people deserve to see their prince the Aten has given us."

Lord Ay, the queen's father, sensed something might be wrong. He could not see his grandson. When he asked to visit his daughter, Pharaoh told him she needed rest after the difficult delivery.

"Something is not right. I just feel it," he told his wife.

"I'm sure there's nothing to worry about, Husband," Lady Tiy said. "Just give Nefer some time."

"That's not enough. Pharaoh wouldn't even let you be with her," Ay grumbled. He decided to do something about it. He sent one of his aides to find out where the royal midwife lived.

That evening Ay paid Tener a visit. The woman became frightened when she saw such an important man at her door. She let him in, then bowed to the ground.

"I want the truth, Tener," Ay insisted. "You know who I am and that I would not do anything to hurt my daughter."

"Yes, my Lord."

"Then tell me what is wrong with my grandson."

The woman hesitated, fearful of violating her trust with the royal family. But she also felt obligated to tell the grandfather the truth. "He has a deformed foot, my Lord. His left foot is bent inward, may the gods help him."

Ay sat down abruptly upon hearing the tragic news. He made the sign against the evil eye, putting his thumb between his third and fourth fingers. The gods were angry with Amenhotep because of his neglect of the god Amun. Now he must pay, or so the elderly man reasoned.

"The poor child," Ay said. He referred to Nefertiti, not his grandson. "Apart from his foot is he all right? Everything in place as it should be? Fingers and toes and all his other bits?"

"Yes my Lord. . ."

"Well?" Ay insisted.

"He also has a small cleft in the roof of his mouth—but it is very small."

"Gods." Ay swore. "This is what comes of marrying cousins. It is displeasing to the gods; everyone knows that." He fumed and then stopped, looking at Tener closely. "Is this why we have not been allowed to see the child?"

Tener nodded. "Even Nefer doesn't know, my Lord. Pharaoh has tried to spare her this tragedy until she is stronger."

"Indeed. I see. You have done well. When I speak to his majesty about this I'll not tell him how I learned of it—that will spare you."

The woman abruptly fell on the floor in front of him. "Mercy, my Lord," she said. He saw the fear on Tener's face and his cruel smile reminded her that her life would be forfeit if Pharaoh discovered what she had done.

CHAPTER SIXTEEN

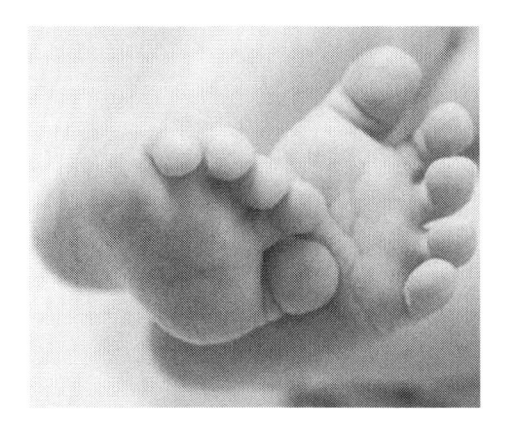

IMPERFECTIONS

When Horemheb told Ramose about the baby's foot his friend didn't know how to react. "The poor prince," he said.

Horemheb saw the alarm on his friend's face. "Other than that, Mose, he's a healthy looking boy."

Ramose made the sign against the evil eye and sighed. "The little boy will not be able to run and play with other children. It'll be sad to watch. I don't think we've ever had a Pharaoh who couldn't walk."

"He'll be able to walk, brother. He'll just need a cane. One of the boys in my village had such a foot, but he could fight as well as the others. He used a cane to get around, so don't feel sorry for him yet."

Ramose nodded. "Well, he is a prince after all and will receive the best help in the land." He said it more to reassure himself than his friend. Then his face lit up. "You can teach him to use the spear like you, Harm. It will make him look princely and strong." Ramose smiled when he remembered giving Horemheb a new spear after the Nubians took the other. He thought Harm looked lost without one. He presented it to him when Horemheb took over the Royal Guards.

A servant brought beer and they didn't talk for a while as they attempted to drink away the sadness they felt for the little prince. When their jars were empty, Ramose spoke up.

"After such tragic news, perhaps this will cheer you up. I know you're going to like this. Benefer is with child, Harm. I only learned of it this morning."

"What? Aha. Happy news indeed," Horemheb shouted. He pounded his friend on the back, almost knocking him over.

"Easy," Ramose cried out. "At least let me live to see my son born."

"This calls for a real celebration. Jumping up, Horemheb asked the servants for more beer. "You and Benefer must be my guests at the *Golden Ibis* tonight. We'll have a great feast."

Ramose knew he couldn't decline.

That evening, he and his wife met Harm at the inn. To their surprise, Lady Amenia also joined them. After a leisurely meal, Ramose posed the question he and Benefer had been dying to ask all evening. "Now, what about your happy wedding day, Harm? Have you thought about it?"

Horemheb nodded. "I'll let my lady tell you."

Amenia smiled. "It will be at the conclusion of the Festival of Ra near the end of this month. Pharaoh himself might honor us by attending the ceremony. You two will be there of course, as our closest friends."

"At long last," Ramose said. He reached over and patted his friend on the back. "This truly is a great day for us all."

When Nefertiti finally saw her baby's imperfections, she wept for a week. No one could console her and she refused all visitors except her mother. Not even Lady Tiy could bring her daughter out of her despair. The Captain of the Royal Guards became the only exception. Horemheb could visit the family when he pleased.

"Will you tell me more about this boy from your village?" Nefertiti asked one afternoon. She invited him to sit with her in the front room.

"Oh, the boy's name is Sinuhe, Majesty. Everyone liked him. He had many friends and could play kickball better than any of us."

Nefertiti sat on the divan across from him. "Kickball?" she marveled. "You mean with his deformed foot he could beat the other boys?"

"Of course, Queen Nefer. And he could wrestle, beating even the biggest of them. You see, Majesty, his strength came from in here," he pointed to his chest. "From his heart." Horemheb watched as the queen began to relax and smile. "His father never let him use his foot as an excuse for anything. He had to do his chores at home like the other children. His parents told him over and over again not to let anyone take advantage of him."

Nefer spoke in a soft voice. "Maybe his parents could teach us a thing or two."

"Perhaps, but I could help too, my Lady, that is, if you'd let me. When he gets bigger, I can teach him how to use a warrior's spear. It's good to learn how to keep your balance and defend yourself in a fight."

"And what happened to this Sinuhe? Nefertiti asked. "Where is he now?"

"I saw him when Ramose and I went back to my village, Majesty. He's now a wealthy scribe and has a large house and family. His four sons manage the farm and have trained to be scribes as well. The family is well respected in the region."

The queen stood and walked over to Harm. "You have brightened my day, Captain, something I did not think possible. Now, this evening my husband and I would like you to bring Amenia to the palace with you for supper. I want her to tell me all about this great wedding she is planning."

"Thank you, Majesty," Horemheb said. "Remember, she and I will want to practice holding the little prince, if you allow it. Who knows? The gods might honor us someday." He grinned and bowed his head.

"Agreed," Nefertiti said. "That is if you can get him away from his father." She grinned and added, "The little one needs to see other happy faces." She clapped her hands and one of her servants entered with a small wooden cage. "Pharaoh and I have a present for you, Harm. We know how you loved his brother Thutmose, may his name be remembered, and so we decided to give you one of Ti miou's kittens."

Horemheb took the cage and looked inside. "I am touched, Queen Nefer."

"It's a male," she told him.

"He's beautiful. Look at that spotted coat." The dazzling green eyes of the kitten looked out at him and meowed pitifully. "Thank you, Majesty."

She smiled at him. "May the Aten go with you."

Horemheb saluted with his fist across his chest and left the apartment.

As he left and walked down the long hallway, Horemheb didn't notice someone hiding in the shadows. Queen Tiye's servant managed to listen to every word from the veranda and could hardly wait to tell his mistress everything. Like a venomous cobra, he disappeared into the lower regions of the palace.

On his wedding day, Horemheb held Amenia's hand as they walked into the great temple of Horus. The tall columns inside always made him feel he had entered one of the forests of trees he had seen on the island of Abu. His heart beat faster as he realized that after this moment, the woman at his side would be his forever. He kept glancing at her, not believing she had actually agreed to be his wife. Almost as tall as he, her slender figure and narrow waist were perfect. She wore a light blue, tightly pleated gown that fell from her shoulders to the floor. A gold necklace, decorated with dozens of polished green malachite stones, covered her full breasts.

"You are beautiful," he whispered.

"Quiet." Ramose hissed. He walked behind Horemheb and didn't want to be embarrassed. "Do you want to offend the priests?"

Lady Benefer smiled when Horemheb turned to look at his friends. The groom dressed as he always did, with one exception. He wore the large Gold of Valor necklace over his bare chest. Soldiers did not wear the wigs expected of the nobility, but preferred the traditional nemes head covering, as did Ramose. His sandals made little noise as he walked toward the altar.

Horemheb knew Pharaoh would not come to the wedding since his majesty no longer believed in the old gods. However, his closest friends were there, including Captain Khamet and the Lord Chamberlain. They stood waiting near the statue of the great Falcon, a representation of the god Horus. A small choir of priests chanted hymns to their god as Lord Re'hotep, the high priest, motioned for the bride and groom to step forward.

The ceremony didn't last long. As they exchanged vows, the priests intoned hymns again. The high priest made offerings from the couple to the god who had watched over Horemheb since his birth.

As their friends were congratulating them, a commotion started outside the temple. When they exited the building, hundreds of the palace guards rushed up the steps and stood at attention. A crowd began to gather and the thunder of chariots rumbled in their direction.

"It's Pharaoh," someone shouted.

Amenhotep arrived driving his own chariot. He reined in his horses at the bottom of the temple steps. The instant he stepped out, the guards went down on one knee in salute, and the people fell prostrate before him. Amenhotep motioned for everyone to stand and he waited for Horemheb and his bride to come down to him.

Pharaoh smiled. "Such a good looking couple." He motioned for them to remain standing. "Forgive us for not entering the temple."

"Majesty, you do us a great honor in greeting us on this happy day," Horemheb said.

"I've come to invite you and your friends to a banquet this evening in the royal gardens. We wish to honor your union." He saw that he had pleased the couple and that made him smile even more. "I am on my way to the docks to meet Lord Bek. He has news of my new city and I cannot wait. May the Aten bless you. We will await you this evening."

The wedding party bowed as the king stepped into his chariot and raced away—his guards ran after him, vainly trying to keep up. Fortunately, it wasn't far to the docks.

"I can't believe what just happened." Horemheb exclaimed. He and the wedding party were astonished by Pharaoh's unexpected appearance.

That evening when Horemheb and his wife arrived at the palace, his majesty's courtiers greeted them warmly. To their surprise, Prince Smenkhare came forward to congratulate them first.

"May the gods bless you and give you many children," he said.

"Kind words, Highness, and we thank you," Horemheb replied.

Smenkhare bowed his head to Amenia. "You have never looked more beautiful, my Lady."

Blushing, Amenia bowed her head. "From such a handsome prince, my Lord, that is a pleasing compliment. Ramose and Benefer came over to welcome them next.

At that moment, Pharaoh and the Queen approached them. Horemheb knelt and Amenia made obeisance. Smenkhare bowed his head to his brother.

Pharaoh motioned for them to stand. Nefertiti took the bride by the arm and led her around the garden to greet all the guests.

"You have chosen wisely, Horemheb," Amenhotep said. He turned to watch the ladies depart. "Not only is she wise, but exceedingly pleasant to look at."

Smenkhare sensed his brother wished to speak with Horemheb in private so he excused himself and joined the other guests.

Ramose spoke up. "It's amazing such a country boy would be able to attract such a beauty." Horemheb struck his friend on the shoulder, hard enough to make him wince.

"I'm sorry," Ramose laughed, rubbing it vigorously.

The king turned to Ramose and his wife, and they knew they should move along.

"I'm going to make an important announcement in court tomorrow, Harm, and I want you and Mose to be there," Amenhotep said.

"Majesty," Horemheb replied. It would have been useless to remind the king he would still be enjoying newly wedded bliss.

Pharaoh grinned, knowing full well where Horemheb would be. "Are you prepared for this night?" the king asked with a twinkle in his eye.

"I've been ready for three years, Great One," Horemheb said. "I feel honored Amenia has agreed to be with me. I love everything about her, although I'm not sure her family feels the same about me."

Pharaoh laughed. "Ha. You may have a problem there. Lord Akhom can be difficult, but you'll win him over. You're my Brother now and that raises your social standing at court. Just remind him of it when he becomes obstreperous."

"I will," Horemheb said. Then, speaking he spoke in a softer voice. "Majesty, your wedding gift is beyond generous and is undeserved. We don't know how to thank you."

"Well, I can't have a brother of mine living in the barracks, now can I?" the king said. "Amenia should be happy in your new villa while you're off in our new city. Lord Bek sent men to see that your house was built correctly."

"Yes, Brother, if I may call you that," Horemheb replied.

"Yes of course, but not in Smenkhare's presence. It will only start him off again about who is to succeed me. He doesn't like to remember that I have a son now."

"How is my nephew?" Horemheb asked.

"His wet nurse tells me he is gaining weight and is very happy. He knows me and gurgles when he sees my face," the king bragged.

Laughing, Horemheb turned to the king. "It could also mean he has gas, Majesty." He saw that his words made the usually dour monarch laugh as well. "I can't wait to go riding with him some day, if the Aten wills it."

"Nor can I, my friend," Pharaoh said. "You must help me do all we can to make him strong and healthy. His bad foot will be problem enough, but I want him to be robust and live to be a good ruler."

"May it be so, Great Egypt. May the Aten hear your words."

"It will be so," the king declared.

When the last guests of the banquet had gone, the bride and groom were finally alone in their bedchamber. Their servants had placed flower petals on the bed and around the room. The newlyweds found themselves in what began as an awkward moment. Even though Horemheb had been with other women, Amenia had become the love of his life. He didn't want to do anything wrong.

Amenia, became shy and timid and didn't know why. She suddenly felt vulnerable. "Turn around, Husband," she admonished as she undressed. He did as she asked, but still managed to steal a glance or two.

Holding her thin nightgown over her breasts she complained, "There are too many lamps in here." Her husband blew them all out but one. He sat back down on the edge of their bed still dressed in his kilt.

"What is good for the goose is good for the gander, Harm," she said. He stood facing her as he removed his only piece of clothing. Sitting back on the bed, he smoothed out the linen sheet for her and waited.

"I will put out the lamp," she whispered, her voice affected by what she had seen.

"No," her husband said. "I have waited too long to see your true beauty, my Love. Please don't hide yourself from me, not on this of all nights."

Her face flushed as she placed her gown on one of the chairs and turned to face him before getting into bed. Horemheb, pleased by what he saw, extended his hand to her. She took it and he drew her to him in a loving embrace. She sighed with contentment as they lay together for a long time.

"One would never think you to be a gentle man, Horemheb," she whispered in his ear. "That makes me love you even more." They kissed passionately and were soon lost in the rapture of their union. Not only did the warrior and brother to pharaoh prove to be gentle, but he pleased his new bride in ways she had never dreamed possible.

The next morning they slept late. Suddenly, Horemheb sat up. He remembered the king's summons. Dressing quickly, he left his bride sound asleep.

"What's this all about?" Ramose whispered to his friend. The courtiers huddled in the Throne Room, anxiously awaiting the entrance of his majesty.

"He told me it would be something important. That's all I know," Horemheb said.

Suddenly the Royal Guards entered and formed an aisle down the center of the great hall for his majesty's arrival. The Chamberlain, Lord Ineni, stepped forward at the front of the great hall and tapped his long staff.

"Bow to the Divine God Pharaoh Amenhotep, the Great House of Egypt, the All-Seeing. Ruler of the Two Lands." The courtiers fell prostrate before the throne.

The Chamberlain tapped the polished floor again. "Bow to Queen Nefertiti, Daughter of Isis, Mother of the Crown Prince, and Mother of Egypt." The courters remained on the floor as Pharaoh and the queen walked toward their thrones. A sudden murmur passed through the crowd as some dared look up. Queen Nefertiti walked beside Pharaoh, holding a baby in her arms.

The courtiers, pleased to see the royal family together in this way, began to cheer them. The chamberlain tapped again to restore order, but even he had to smile. When their majesties sat upon their thrones, the king raised his hand, permitting the courtiers to stand.

"We are pleased to present to our people the Crown Prince."

The Queen stood and held the baby high so the court could see him. Everyone prostrated themselves once more to the son and heir until Ineni tapped on the floor, allowing them to stand.

"His name is Tutankhaten," Pharaoh continued. "That is to say, *the Living Image of the Aten.*"

Taken by surprise, instead of a cheer, the courtiers filled the hall with angry whispers. Horemheb saw the danger immediately and began to applaud, as did Ramose and the Chamberlain. Then, the whole court realized what they should do and joined in.

"Hail, Tutankhaten," they shouted. "Living Image of the Aten."

CHAPTER SEVENTEEN

DANGEROUS DECREE

The courtiers, stunned by the announcement of the Crown Prince's name, began to speak in whispers.

Raising his hand for silence, Pharaoh continued. "Your Queen's name is changing too, my people. She has been Nefertiti, 'the beautiful one has come.' Now her name will be Neferneferuaten-Nefertiti meaning 'The Aten is Radiant because the Beautiful One has come.'"

The courtiers couldn't believe what they were hearing. They continued to murmur, looking at one another with consternation.

Pharaoh sensed it and stood, making the courtiers fall prostrate on the floor. He made them stay there longer than before, and then continued. "You may stand," he said, waiting for them to do so. "And I, your Great House and Ruler of the Two Lands, what name has my god revealed to me?" He paused, not expecting an answer. "He has proclaimed that I will henceforth be called Akhenaten, that is to say, 'The Living Spirit of the Aten.'"

Lord Ineni, the only one with enough sense to quickly respond, shouted, "Hail Akhenaten—Pharaoh and ruler of Upper and Lower Egypt. The Living Spirit of the Aten."

The courtiers hesitated, and then shouted, "Hail, Akhenaten."

"Hail, Neferneferuaten-Nefertiti," the Chamberlain continued, "Queen of both lands." The people shouted her name.

The courtiers shouted the little prince's name as the Queen held him up again, "Hail Crown Prince Tutankhaten, son of Akhenaten and heir to the throne."

But Pharaoh had more to say. He put his hands on his hips like an angry schoolmaster. "The name of the god Amun is henceforth forbidden to be spoken in this Hall, the Palace or in our presence." He paused, pleased to see fear on the faces of his subjects. "It is the Aten, the manifestation of the God of Light who will be worshipped by your king and his family."

He turned to the Chamberlain and said, "Bring forth the scribe."

Ineni motioned for the scribe to stand and bring the scroll on which he had written Pharaoh's words. Akhenaten looked at it, nodded and gave the scribe permission to pour wax on the document into which Pharaoh pressed his ring.

The Chamberlain shouted, "It has been written, now let it be done."

The court shouted, "*Bah-ker*, so be it."

The queen stood beside Pharaoh and the courtiers made obeisance once more as the royal family left the great hall in absolute silence.

Lord Ay waited until their majesties had gone. "This is madness. He can't forbid his subjects from using Amun's name—it's blasphemy."

"Be careful what you say, my Lord," Horemheb warned. "I am Pharaoh's friend and brother." He said it in a quiet voice so they wouldn't be overheard. "But I am also your friend, General. We must work this out somehow."

"Bah," Ay said. "He is making enemies of half the country, Captain. Now he is changing their names. What's that about? Pharaohs do not change their names."

Horemheb frowned. "Everything you say, my Lord, is true. But he is Pharaoh and must do what the gods tell him. We've always accepted that."

"But does he intend to kill or imprison all the priests of Amun? That's what he'll have to do in the end. Their numbers are too many to count."

"He hasn't told us what his plans are, Lord Ay. He must wait for the Aten to tell him," Horemheb said. He paused for a few moments, trying to decide how to say his next words. "I wouldn't oppose him in the Council if I were you, my Lord, even if he is your son-in-law. Don't make the error of assuming he is weak. He will surprise you."

Ay looked at his young friend closely. "I'm sure you're right, Captain. I appreciate your warning." When the older man moved away, Horemheb saluted him and Lord Ay nodded.

Ramose moved closer, not wanting to be a part of his friend's encounter with the former head of the army. "How did he react?"

"Not well, and I'm sure he spoke for everyone in the hall who thinks as he does," Horemheb said. "I advised caution, but that is something these men have in short supply."

"What does Akhenaten plan to do with the priests of Amun, Harm?"

"He hasn't told anyone, Mose, but I'm trying to think of a way to ask him without getting my head cut off."

Panic filled the temple of the god Amun. Lord Nakhte, the high priest shouted, "Pack up the images of Amun immediately. Call all the servants and brother priests to save the sacred vessels. Everything must be moved out of Thebes." Dozens of priests were already beginning to move out the holy objects.

The high priest turned to his aide. "My house too, Panhesy," he said. "My family will sail south tonight—probably to Edfu. We can anchor in the river until morning." He stopped to catch his breath. "We'll also need our guards to go with us. The king may send soldiers to arrest us at any moment."

"He wouldn't dare, brother."

"Oh no? I can still see the fear on the faces of our friends at court who hurried to tell me what the king has proclaimed."

"We have also sent temple guards to Memphis and Awen, my Lord," Panhesy told him. "They left as soon as you gave the order."

A crew of carpenters entered the building and began crating the statues and other sacred objects.

To Nakhte's surprise it had been Lord Horemheb who had ridden to tell him of Pharaoh's decree condemning the worship of Amun. His warning would mean that thousands of priests could escape to their home villages and farms.

"I will remember this, my Lord," Nakhte vowed to Horemheb, "and so will my priests. I know Horus is blessing you, but we will pray Amun's blessings on you as well."

"I am grateful, Servant of Amun," Horemheb replied. Nakhte watched as the officer remounted his horse and headed back to the palace.

When Pharaoh learned of Horemheb's actions he summoned him to the palace. The king made him sit in the atrium and wait. Horemheb stared at the beautiful, well-designed room. It allowed the sun to highlight bas-reliefs on the walls depicting the exploits of past dynasties. His heart, however, beat with fear and dread, while his head filled with thoughts.

"He's not pleased with you," a female voice said from the shadows. Queen Nefer came toward him holding her son who had fallen asleep with his head on her shoulder.

"I knew he wouldn't be, Majesty," Horemheb replied. He said it with more confidence than he felt.

The queen seated herself on one of the divans and rocked the baby on her shoulder. "Then why did you do it?" she said. "It is disloyal and not worthy of you."

He bowed his head, hesitant to respond. It would be better if he could tell Pharaoh his reasons.

"Answer the Queen," Akhenaten said, walking across the tiled floor toward him.

Horemheb stood, then knelt in front of his majesty. "I did not mean to be disloyal, Great One," he began. "I thought it best for all the inhabitants of Thebes if the priests left. It will avoid any conflicts with your guards. As you say, the Aten is a giver of peace as well as light. I thought he might abhor any violence. I'm sorry you are displeased."

Akhenaten walked to his wife and gently rubbed his little son's head before helping her stand. "Come," he said to his adopted brother. The royal family walked into their apartment and Pharaoh indicated for Horemheb to follow him out onto the veranda.

"You have displeased us, Brother," Pharaoh said. "It is our wish now that you leave Thebes and take up your position in our new city. We have every confidence in your friend Captain Khamet to manage the Palace Guards and supervise our personal safety without you. Take Amenia and see to the construction of a new home in Aten's Horizon."

Pharaoh chose to sit on a bench near the edge of the veranda. Horemheb had not been invited to sit, a sign of his friend's displeasure. Queen Nefer came out and joined them, taking a place on the bench beside her husband.

"We will miss you, my Lord," she whispered. "Little Tutankhaten has learned to recognize your face, and smiles when you are near him. He may forget you now."

"Then I am truly desolate, my Queen," Horemheb said. His voice became the proof of his sadness. Turning to Pharaoh he cleared his throat. "I will do as you command, my Brother and friend. I implore you to forgive my actions. Know that in my heart I could never be disloyal. I sought only the peace of your land."

Pharaoh didn't look at him but dismissed him. "You may withdraw."

"Majesties," Horemheb replied as he saluted with his fist to his chest.

As he left the apartments, a hand grabbed his arm and pulled him inside an alcove in the hallway. Lord Ineni put his finger over his lips in warning. Pointing to a door further along the corridor, he led Horemheb to the chamberlain's office. Once inside he invited him to sit down.

The elderly man looked at Horemheb carefully. "Tell me your fate, my son. I knew Akhenaten would not be pleased."

"It seems my wife and I are exiled to the new city, my friend. He could have had me executed, so for this punishment I am grateful. Horus still watches over me." He paused a moment, not having had the time to let it all sink in. "I'm to take my wife and begin building my house in Lord Bek's city. I'll miss you and Ramose. I pray you both will not be swallowed up in Pharaoh's revolution."

"Over the years, my boy, I have learned to anticipate Pharaoh's desires and whims. I must admit I saw this coming. I will do as he commands. His desire to return to the worship of the sun has been done before by others, without much success. We people of the Black Land like to worship our own gods. This new religion may be doomed before anyone understands it. We must walk very carefully."

"And may the gods protect you and Mose, my Lord. Watch over him and Benefer, will you? I don't know if his majesty will allow me to see them before we go."

"I promise you I will as best I can. Although Ramose has a quick mind and strong sense of survival like his father. I may need him to watch over me."

Horemheb laughed and Lord Ineni joined him.

Three days later, one of the king's ships waited to carry Horemheb, Amenia and their belongings to Pharaoh's city. She remained inconsolable with all that happened, refusing to talk to her husband. Leaving friends and family and above all, the beautiful villa Pharaoh had given them, broke her heart. Her father had given her ten servants to accompany her, but she remained miserable. She hadn't spoken a word since her husband told her the news, and she remained in the cabin for the entire journey. When they arrived, she waited patiently for her carrying chair to take her to their temporary home at the military barracks.

A young sergeant met them at the dock and introduced himself. "I am Paneb, my Lord." He saluted the brother of Pharaoh by kneeling on one knee.

"Thank you, Sergeant," Horemheb replied. "Lady Amenia and I are pleased you are here. My horse and chariot are in the hold. Order your men to help the sailors bring them ashore."

"Of course." Turning to another, Paneb gave the instructions. Four of Amenia's servants lifted her carrying chair, and one of the sergeant's men went with them to show the way.

Horemheb asked that they saddle his horse, and he sent his chariot to the military camp. When ready, he climbed up onto Shu, and started to follow his wife's bearers.

"Please my Lord, before you go, there is something you should see," Paneb called to him.

"Is it urgent?" Horemheb asked with some irritation.

"You will agree with me once you've seen, my Lord," the sergeant said. He climbed up onto his own horse. Horemheb nodded and Paneb led him to a small civic building near the center of the growing city. Dismounting, the soldier led him inside to a room where someone lay on the floor covered by a sheet. Blood had soaked through the center of the cloth.

"Look my Lord," Paneb said. His nerves made his hands shake as he removed the covering. Horemheb gasped, fell onto his knees and stared into the empty eyes of Lord Bek, Pharaoh's architect.

Horemheb waited until the shock of seeing Lord Bek lying dead in front of him passed. "Who could have done this?"

"This isn't all, my Lord. There's something else you should see," Paneb said. Horemheb followed him into an adjoining room. On the floor lay the body of another man, this one dressed in workman's clothes.

"This is a priest of Amun who has been working as an artist for several months. He stabbed the architect when he came to inspect his work. As he killed Bek, he shouted 'For Amun's glory.' You can see the tattoo all priests of Amun receive on his left thigh."

Horemheb shook his head vigorously. "No, no, no. His majesty will not be pleased, Sergeant. He liked Lord Bek. It is from his genius that this great city has been born." He paused. "It is our guards who will be made to pay for allowing this crime to happen." The younger man's face fell at Horemheb's words. "Who is your officer?"

"Captain Khawy, Sir."

"Why did he not come to meet me?" As soon as he asked he knew the answer. "Never mind my friend, I understand. I'll ask him myself." He knew that the officer would fall on his own sword rather than wait for Pharaoh's wrath.

"Yes, my Lord." Paneb led Horemheb to a small house near the river.

Captain Khawy heard their horses coming and came out to greet them. He went down on one knee and saluted Pharaoh's brother. "Greetings, Lord Horemheb."

"I salute you, Captain, with a heavy heart. Let's go inside and you can tell me about it." The men entered the simple mud-brick dwelling. When the officer finished telling the nobleman what he knew about the assassination, he shrugged his shoulders and could only look down at the floor.

"Don't trouble yourself, Khawy. You will still have an honorable death. A soldier can't ask for more than that. I will see that your body is properly prepared and guards will accompany you on your final journey. Where is your home?"

"A small village near Abydos, my Lord. Not far."

"Your comrades will go with your coffin and will see that you are buried among your family tombs. They only need to know that you died doing your duty—which in a real sense is the truth."

"I am grateful, my Lord. I only regret I couldn't protect Pharaoh's friend." He paused, then added, "All our workmen are thoroughly checked and evaluated for their loyalty to his majesty. This son of Seth somehow got through in spite of all that."

"You could not have saved him, Captain," Horemheb said. "We'll have to tighten our controls that much more. We'll leave you now to prepare yourself and write your final words to your family." The officer nodded and walked with them to the door.

As Horemheb got back on his horse he said to Paneb, "Assemble the guards, Sergeant, then come and get me. I'll speak to them about what has happened and what we must do next."

"Yes, my Lord." Paneb saluted and rode off toward the barracks.

Horemheb rode to his temporary home and wondered how he could console his wife. The mud-brick house, while large enough for them, in no way compared to the magnificent villa left behind.

Approaching her, he took her by the hand and led her outside to a shady spot by the river. "You'll help design your new villa, my Love," he told her, knowing his words could not ease her pain. "Every stone, every room will have your touch. The workmen will begin tomorrow and I will suspend all work on Pharaoh's city until your villa is done and you are happy again."

She smiled for the first time in many days. "Do you promise?"

He nodded and she embraced him, happy he would try to please her. Later, he helped organize the servants, telling them where to place the furniture and the crates containing all their belongings. When the sun had reached its zenith, Paneb came for him, and he left to address the Royal Guards.

Horemheb said all he could to encourage his men, telling them how much his majesty counted on them to build his glorious city. When he finished he paused a moment. "Captain Khawy, stand forward." The officer stepped out and stood front and center as he saluted.

"We honor you today for your faithfulness to duty and to your king." His men, pleased by Horemheb's words, pounded on their shields with their swords. The sound became so loud the workmen on the new buildings stopped to see where it came from.

"Your commander will give his life today in Pharaoh's service and we honor him," he said. The guards stomped their feet as they often did on the battlefield and the vibration made the ground tremble.

"Tomorrow, men, you will have a new officer and new orders. May Horus bless our Pharaoh, and help us complete his dream." The men shouted Pharaoh's new name in response, and Horemheb turned and told Khawy to dismiss them.

He knew he had broken the royal decree by using the name of the god who protected him all his life. He hadn't done it to displease Pharaoh, but to please the god Horus, honored by all the pharaohs before him.

CHAPTER EIGHTEEN

"CITY OF THE HORIZON"

Five years passed, and on the thirteenth day of the eighth month, in the fifth year of his reign, Pharaoh arrived at his completed city.

Horemheb stood with his wife on the polished white limestone dock, watching the king's galley arrive at the beautifully designed landing. Thousands of workers lined up to greet the royal family. The city's guards, under the leadership now of Captain Paneb, came to attention. *The Light of the Aten's Glory* eased into the dock and her lines made fast. Her standards and battle honors were streaming out in a fluttery blaze of rainbow colors. The great ship of state lay safe at her berth.

"Furl the sail," the captain of the galley shouted. The symbol of the Aten, sewn with gold thread, billowed in the center of the sailcloth. The sailors pulled on the lines of the great rectangular sail, lifting it to the top spar and tying it off.

Several kingfishers hovered in the air like jewels of lapis lazuli, then darted down to hit the water in a flash of spray and then rose again with a silver sliver quivering in their long bills.

The laughter of a child watching them caught Horemheb's attention. He recognized the boy standing in front of Pharaoh and smiled.

Young Tutankhaten stood straight and tall so he could see everything. Next to him stood his mother, the Beautiful One. Queen Nefer looked radiant as the morning sunlight beamed its approval on the royal family. Behind the king stood his brother, Prince Smenkhare and half-sister Princess Meritaten, who had also changed her name to please Pharaoh. Smenkhare refused to change his.

A ship filled with musicians had arrived the day before and they stood ready to greet the king. Trumpeters blasted a fanfare as soon as the gangway touched the shore. Pharaoh's horses and chariots had also arrived beforehand, as had the golden carrying chairs.

Lord Ineni, whom Horemheb had not seen at first, stepped to the gangway and shouted, "Behold Akhenaten, Ruler of the Two Lands, and Son of the Aten. Bow before him and be made worthy of his presence."

Akhenaten walked forward and stood at the gangway. The guardsmen knelt and saluted him as everyone else on the landing fell on their faces. The chariots for Pharaoh and his brother arrived, and Akhenaten immediately stepped into his.

To Horemheb's surprise, the little Crown Prince climbed up onto his father's chariot beside him.

Pharaoh gave the signal for everyone to stand and cheers broke out as the people shouted his name. Prince Smenkhare's chariot followed, while the royal women waited for their palanquins.

Akhenaten followed the priests who led the procession toward the great temple in the city center. The streets had been paved with limestone ferried downriver from ancient quarries at Abydos. Crowds of people lined the length of the center boulevard, cheering the royal family.

Horemheb felt disappointment that the king had not chosen to greet him or his wife. "It is the excitement of this glorious moment. Pharaoh needs to focus his attention on the temple and the city. His crowning achievement is finished and he wants to enjoy his dream come to life."

As the priests of the Aten approached the temple, they began chanting words Horemheb had heard many times before. This time, however, they included Akhenaten's name, as well as his queen's:

> *"You are in my heart,*
> *There is no other who knows you,*
> *Only your son, Neferkheprure,*
> > *Sole-one-of-Ra,*
> > *Whom you have taught your ways and your might…*
> *The king who lives by Maat,*
> *The Lord of the Two Lands,*
> *Neferkheprure, Sole-one-of-Ra,*
> *The Son of Ra who lives by Maat.*
> *The Lord of Crowns,*
> *Akhenaten, great in his lifetime,*
> *And the great Queen whom he loves,*
> *The Lord of the Two Lands,*
> *Neferneferatenyu-Nefertiti, living forever."*

Even though Horemheb and his wife did not receive an invitation for the ceremony, Lord Meyre, High Priest of the Aten, told them what would take place.

"I don't understand it," Maya said. "We should have been invited to participate." Horemheb's brother in law and his wife stood beside him in the crowd. They had arrived a week earlier and were staying at Horemheb's villa.

"Maybe so, Maya, but in his eyes I'm still not in favor. It's the only explanation," Horemheb said.

Amenia grumbled. "After all you've done, he should make you his crown prince. Such disrespect."

"Careful Beloved, you know that all of these blocks of limestone have grown ears."

She frowned, but knew it to be true.

"We will wait for him to summon us," Horemheb said.

After the procession passed by, people moved closer to the temple, hoping to get a glimpse of the royals when they came out. Horemheb and his friends walked the short distance back to their villa at the edge of the Nile. Everyone admired their home. Amenia had worked with Maa'nakhtuf, Lord Bek's assistant, on its design. Now Chief Architect, he turned Amenia's villa into a work of art. Horemheb had only interfered with its construction when he thought it might be in danger of surpassing Pharaoh's palace.

Several hours later, as they sat in the shade of Amenia's beautiful garden, the architect appeared at their door. Horemheb met him and invited him to join them in the garden. Maa'nakhtuf seemed more quiet than usual and Horemheb had trouble trying to decipher the concern on his face.

After greeting Lady Amenia and her guests the architect blurted out, "We've been summoned, my Lord." His hands were shaking.

Amenia encouraged him to sit down.

He needed to take a deep breath. "Lord Ineni is most distressed and has ordered me to bring you to the king."

"I see," Horemheb replied. "When am I expected?"

"Immediately, my Lord. I'm to bring you right away."

Horemheb's heart skipped a beat. "Would you care for a drink before we go, my Lord?" Horemheb asked. The nobleman accepted willingly. After a relaxing jar of beer, they took their time walking to the new Audience Hall.

Bek had designed the magnificent structure, but Maa'nakhtuf built it. Every time he walked past it, Horemheb admired the beautiful sculpted and painted bas-reliefs depicting the glories of the sun.

When they entered, the old chamberlain smiled, nodded to them and struck the polished floor in the great hall with his staff.

"Your Majesties," he said in a loud voice. "Before you stand Maa'nakhtuf, Pharaoh's Architect and Builder of Akhetaten, and Horemheb, Brother of Akhenaten and Military Commander of the Horizon of the Aten."

The fact that the architect's name came first did not go unnoticed by Horemheb.

Pharaoh stood and motioned for the two men to approach the throne. The courtiers who filled the Hall had also moved to the city, and they stepped aside to let the two men pass. At the bottom step leading up to the thrones, Horemheb fell onto one knee and saluted his brother, while Maa'nakhtuf made obeisance on the floor.

"Rise, good Architect and Beloved Brother. You, Maa'nakhtuf have not only brought my dream to reality, but have even surpassed what we had hoped for." The king motioned for Ineni to approach.

The elderly man carried a cedar box Horemheb had seen before.

The king stood in front of the nobleman as Ineni opened the beautifully carved box.

"We place around your neck the Gold of Honor, a small token of our esteem for your work these past years. Our name is upon it and when people see it, they will treat you as Pharaoh is treated. I believe the Ka of Lord Bek, may his name be remembered, would be pleased."

"Even so," everyone chorused.

When the chamberlain finished closing the catch on the golden necklace, Pharaoh turned the architect to face the court and receive their applause. Then he approached Horemheb.

"And now for my adopted Brother. We honor him today for his organization of the workmen, artisans, and guards who have made this city possible. He already wears the Gold of Valor—the highest award for any soldier—so what honor shall we give?" Akhenaten turned and the Chamberlain opened a long cedar box. The king reached in and lifted out a magnificent sword, holding it up for all to see. "Our Brother is given this Sword of Honor by a grateful king and is hereby promoted to the rank of General of Pharaoh's Army of the North."

Receiving the weapon from his brother, Horemheb lifted it in front of his face as a salute to the king, then raised it high with his right arm as the members of the court cheered.

"I am honored, Brother. May the Aten bless you," Horemheb whispered.

"You have earned it and our trust once more," Pharaoh said. "You are the only one I could entrust with such a task and you have proved worthy."

As the two honored men moved back among the courtiers, the chamberlain tapped loudly once more and the king regained his throne. The little crown prince sat on his own throne to the right of his father. Behind them stood Prince Smenkhare and Princess Meritaten, reminders of the continuity of the royal line.

Lord Ineni's voice echoed around the great Hall. "Hear the words of Pharaoh, Son of the Aten and Father of the Two Lands."

Akhenaten spoke in a deep clear voice. "I declare today that this city in which we live belongs to the Aten, and only the ways of peace and light will rule all who live within its boundaries." The courtiers applauded again and the king stood, requiring everyone to bow in obeisance as the royal party left the hall.

Back in the old capital of Thebes, Ramose had not been happy ever since Horemheb moved to the new city. Having to remain in the old capital had become unbearable. Pharaoh had decided that his Vizier should remain to govern the city through the transition. Ramose, however, wanted to be in Akhetaten. Wherever Pharaoh lived became the center of all the action. Ramose only had disgruntled merchants to deal with, most complaining about the loss of business because of all the closed temples.

It's an insult," his wife reminded him. "Your friend Horemheb has been exiled down there for five years, and we are condemned to remain here. Are we to be marooned here forever?" His wife missed all her friends and relatives, and made her husband's life miserable.

"Enough," Ramose exclaimed. "There's nothing I can do about it."

"I know Prince Smenkhare could ask the king to make a change if you really wanted him to." His wife had reminded him of it for the hundredth time. "He told you he didn't want to live in the new city either. He loves Thebes too much."

She spoke the truth. Ramose had often heard the king's brother say privately that he would do anything to get out of moving to Pharaoh's city. Perhaps Benefer had a point.

That morning, when he arrived at the old palace, still his place of work, he found Lord Ay there to greet him. He stopped in front of him in the hallway.

"We must talk privately," Ay said.

The Vizier nodded and led the older man into his office. Once seated, they looked at each other for a few moments, taking time to collect their thoughts. Ramose had forgotten how sinister the older man's eyes looked. His eyebrows were very dark and when he arched them, his appearance became reptilian.

"I'm surprised to find you here, my friend," Ramose began. "I thought you were living in Akhetaten."

"That's true," the politician grumbled. "I came back yesterday." He sat up straight in his chair. "Listen Mose, there is a serious matter we need to discuss. We must consolidate the interests of the followers of Amun here in Thebes. Secretly of course."

"You are speaking treason, Lord Ay and you know it. I can't listen to such talk." Even though he protested, the man's words did not surprise him. Ramose's friends had warned him many times that Ay still held great power in Egypt.

"Maybe so," Ay said. "But you know I'm right."

"The nation is divided, that's a fact," Ramose said. "But what you propose could destroy it."

"Don't be such an alarmist, my boy," Ay said. "We must move slowly and carefully. I believe the first step is to move you to the new capital where you belong. I am asking you to suggest to my son-in-law to make me governor of Thebes. Now that he's made Horemheb a general, it can be done."

Ramose's heart beat faster. He liked the proposal but couldn't see how he dared ask Pharaoh to do it. "Pharaoh has put me here and I dare not go to him and tell him he made a mistake, my Lord."

"Not so, Lord Vizier. In the event of a national emergency you are allowed to go to Akhetaten. While there, perhaps the opportunity will present itself to talk about my proposal."

"But there's no such emergency."

Ay smiled. "Oh, but there is my friend. There has been another incursion by the Nubians across our southern border. The army must go, and you can take the king my written message telling him all about it. The king alone has the power to send troops."

To Ramose, this proposal seemed a perfect excuse to go to the Akhetaten. Could Ay's plan possibly succeed? "I will sail for the new city, my Lord."

Ay grinned. "You could even leave today. I'll bring my letter and dispatches from Swentet shortly."

After he left, Ramose suddenly felt that perhaps life hadn't passed him by after all. He knew a villa for him existed already. Maybe now he could rejoin his friends.

When Ay returned, he had a worried look on his face. "There's been trouble in the city," he began. "A group of about a hundred followers of Amun had been meeting secretly down by the docks. Pharaoh's soldiers attacked and his archers have killed them!" Ramose sat down abruptly, shocked by the news.

"Don't you see, Mose," Ay said urgently. "It is even more imperative now that a strong governor be put in charge of Thebes before there is more bloodshed."

"But who would have given such an order?" Ramose demanded.

"One of the guards told me the order came from Horemheb."

In Akhetaten, Pharaoh listened to Ramose's report in his council chamber. "Who could have done this?" Akhenaten asked.

"There are rumors, Great One, that our friend Horemheb has done this to please you," Ramose said.

"Send for him at once," Akhenaten shouted. "Bring him to my council chamber." Captain Khamet saluted and went to find the city commander. When he came back with the general, Pharaoh dismissed the council members so he could speak privately. "You will stay as well, my Lord Vizier."

"Majesty," Horemheb said bowing to the king when he entered the room. His eyes widened in surprise when he saw Ramose there.

Pharaoh said, "Repeat what you've told us." Ramose did so.

"It's a lie, Great Pharaoh," Horemheb said. He broke protocol by speaking before receiving the king's permission.

"Enough," the king said, raising his hand. "We cannot believe it either."

Horemheb went on. "It is *not* true, Majesty. Why would I do such a thing? My concern for the welfare of the followers of Amun is what caused your displeasure in the first place. Why would I now turn around and order them killed?"

Akhenaten motioned for his friends to sit down before continuing. "What you say, Harm, is a valid point, but it doesn't explain Ay's accusation. What does he have against you?"

Ramose spoke up. "I've thought about that too, Majesty. Ay and Horemheb are both loyal to you and have proven it in the past. He may be jealous of Horemheb's friendship with you, Great One. Someone in Thebes must have started the rumor."

"Well, to use the language of your false religion, Horemheb, we'll have to send in a falcon. It will seek out this cobra who is trying to spread disunity among my people."

Ramose looked at Horemheb, uncertain whether or not to present Ay's proposal. Finally, he went ahead. "Lord Ay asks to be made Governor of Thebes, Majesty. It would give him more authority and some control over the army, which as Vizier I do not have." He paused a moment and waited for his friends to consider his words. Then he added, "I must say I agree with him, Majesty. I think you should give it some serious thought that is if you're not offended by my suggestion."

Pharaoh sighed and waited a moment before responding. "Well I have, believe it or not, considered such a plan. I have already decided to send Horemheb to Thebes as Governor, and Mose, I believe that your place is there beside him. Ay will become Vizier here where I can use his advice and wisdom, and he is family after all." The king's decision surprised his friends.

"CITY OF THE HORIZON"

"Yes, Majesty," was all Ramose could say. His wife would be displeased. They both wanted to be in the new city. But his disappointment was quick lived, because Horemheb would be back.

"Excellent," Akhenaten said. Turning to Horemheb he asked, "Now, what will you do about the massacre, Governor?"

"I'll get to the bottom of this, I promise, Majesty. Do I have your permission to deal harshly with those responsible?"

"Let it be so," Akhenaten answered. "I want all violators punished severely. This kind of rebellion must be stopped." He pushed his ebony chair away from the table. "Now, for something more pleasant. This evening, I want both you and your wives to join us for supper."

"Thank you, Majesty," Horemheb said. "But are you sure you will be safe with such a murderous soldier at the table?"

Pharaoh frowned. "If not, I have enough guards to bring down an elephant!"

Later, under the cover of darkness, a palace guard left for Thebes by canoe. As Ay's informant, he would tell him all that had transpired in the king's council chamber. As he pulled hard on the paddle, fighting the current, a beam of moonlight fell on a small tattoo on his leg.

CHAPTER NINETEEN

FAMILY

The royal family welcomed their friends and enjoyed a pleasant informal evening meal. Horemheb became acquainted with all of pharaoh's children, together for the first time. He noticed that Prince Tutankhaten's slight limp had become imperceptible, at least by those who didn't already know of his problem. He appeared a happy boy who enjoyed questioning the guests about the army, Nubians and elephants.

When the meal ended, the prince said, "Come Uncle, let us play a game of jackals and hounds. I know you cannot beat me." Horemheb smiled at the precise language of the lad. The royal family's speech set it apart from the tongue of common Egyptians.

Horemheb laughed. "Lead on, brave one, but be ready to fall in defeat."

The boy moved quickly out onto the veranda where a cedar box held the game pieces. Some called it "the game of fifty-eight holes" because of the number of holes around the board. To win one had to get five carved jackals or hounds around those holes first. The game of chance depended entirely on which numbers came up on two knucklebones.

Horemheb decided to let the prince win, but after a few plays, realized the boy could beat him without any help. "No-o-o," he groaned.

Tutankhaten laughed at his uncle and ran to tell the king of his victory.

"Well done, my Son," Akhenaten said. "Now you can say that you are the only warrior to have beaten General Horemheb."

That pleased the prince and he laughed and clapped his hands. Horemheb noticed there were several small walking sticks around the room, probably placed there for the boy's use, but he never saw him use one. His left foot was not as turned in as Horemheb remembered, a good thing. Tutankhaten's older sisters, Meritaten, Meketaten and Ankhesenpaaten were beautiful girls, but the prince avoided them like the plague. Typical behavior for a five-year old boy.

Their guests were preparing to leave.

"We will miss you, my Lord Horemheb," the queen said. "It has been reassuring to have you living nearby." As she embraced Amenia and Benefer, all three women had tears in their eyes.

Amenia whispered, "I'll miss your little girls, Majesty." The queen squeezed her hand as she walked to the door.

"Perhaps you will have a little girl of your own before long," Nefer said.

Amenia replied in an equally soft voice. "May the Aten make it so." The couple held hands as he escorted her to the carrying chair.

A week after Horemheb's return to Thebes, Ramose came with important news. "The queen mother has died, may her name be remembered."

Horemheb and his wife recited, "*Bak-her.*"

"Here's a surprise," Ramose added. "She will not be buried in the Valley of the Kings, but in Akhenaten's tomb outside the new city."

Amenia grew troubled by the news. "That can't be so. She must be honored and buried beside Amenhotep, her husband."

Horemheb said nothing for a few moments. Then he surprised his friend. "Amenia and I have decided to be buried in our tomb at Saqqara."

Ramose frowned, somewhat shocked. "Saqqara? Buried beside the old Step Pyramid? Why there, brother? It's already beginning to fall apart."

"Well, we are not of royal blood and can't be buried in the Valley of the Kings. We felt a tomb in Saqqara is where we should enter the afterlife, if the gods will it so. Nefer's father gave me a piece of land there for our tomb and Lord Maa'nakhtuf drew up the plans."

In a quiet voice, Amenia seemed for a moment to be far away. "We have seen his drawings. It will be beautiful."

Ramose shook his head. "We're too young, all of us, to be thinking about tombs."

Horemheb said, "We can't know on which path the gods will lead us."

Ramose conceded with a nod. "True, but you believe your god Horus still has great plans for you. That's what you've been telling me for as long as I've known you."

Horemheb grinned. "And it's still true."

Seventy days later, when the embalming ended, Ramose and Horemheb joined the royal family for the entombment of the Queen Mother. They represented the people of Thebes. As they gathered at the hillside west of the new city, they watched her sarcophagus as oxen pulled it into Akhenaten's new tomb. Placed in a separate room, it would be sealed shut. It had been carved from a large block of alabaster taken from the quarries near Abydos and looked magnificent.

Pharaoh told them about it. "The translucence of the stone allows light to penetrate into the interior. The stone symbolizes the Aten's light entering our lives." Sculpted from a soft shade of pink stone, artists had etched on its surface important events in the queen mother's life.

Horemheb didn't approve of the ceremony and told Ramose so. "This is all so different. It is not the ceremony we know and practice. Listen to the songs of joy Akhenaten has chosen."

"You're right," Ramose said. "Even the streets have been garlanded with flowers and palm branches as if for a festival."

Prince Tutankhaten, pleased to see his uncle again, rode with Horemheb in his chariot during the funeral procession, while his sisters rode in their gold carrying chairs. The queen, however, stood next to Akhenaten in his chariot. The mourners bowed to the ground as the royals passed by. Akhenaten could never be considered the most handsome of men, but his queen never looked more beautiful. Pharaoh commissioned the artist Djhutmose to sculpt a bust of her, which had a prominent place in the royal residence. Those who saw it, felt as if Nefertiti could come to life at any moment.

When the burial ceremony ended and Pharaoh and his queen left, the courtiers stood around talking, awaiting transport back to the capital. Horemheb noticed a short, rather ugly man standing beside Lord Ay. The man's eyes were constantly in motion, darting back and forth.

"Who is that standing beside Lord Ay?"

Ramose leaned closer. "His name is Mena, Lady Tiye's informant." He said the man's name with obvious distaste. "People say he knows everything that happens at court. I'm sorry to see that he's become friendly with Ay."

"That's unfortunate," Horemheb said. "The chamberlain warned me about Ay some time ago. He said he hoped his evil influence would end when Queen Tiye entered the afterlife."

Thebes, the former capital, stood tall and majestic along the banks of the fast-moving Nile. Its lotus-capped columns reminded everyone who passed that they were the sentinels of the temples of Egypt's gods.

For Horemheb and his friends, life became enjoyable once again. His brother-in-law Maya, proved to be as good as his father in the management of the king's treasury. Lord Ay came to the old capital from time to time to learn of events in the city. However, two years after the burial of the queen mother he brought some disturbing news.

He sipped beer with Ramose and the governor one afternoon. "His majesty is not well, my friends. His brother has stepped in and is taking care of his everyday duties. If anything happens to Akhenaten, I'm not sure who will succeed him. Prince Smenkhare could become Pharaoh, or perhaps be the regent for the young Tutankhaten."

Horemheb shook his head. "Are you certain someone is not making him ill? It's happened before. His brother perhaps, or someone else?"

Ay sighed. "No, his sickness is not of the body, Harm, but of the mind. He is living in a different world and rambles on about the Aten being the only god. He no longer speaks to any of us, and the queen is beside herself, as you can imagine. He takes no interest in his son or any of his children—it's very sad."

Horemheb grumbled. "For the young prince especially. At his age he needs a strong father."

Ay nodded, and then continued. "There's unrest among the courtiers as well. Prince Smenkhare holds court for his brother, making decisions in Akhenaten's name. Fortunately, the king's council still functions, but we are like a body without its head." He paused to drink more beer, and then changed the subject. "Let me hear more pleasant things. How are the people of Thebes?"

"Well enough," Ramose said. "The followers of Amun have calmed down and many meet to worship in secret places. Akhenaten would not be pleased."

Ay smiled. "This is good. I can see the day when things will return to what they've always been. It's in the hands of Amun now."

Horemheb spoke with some sarcasm. "You mean the Aten will let it happen?"

"I fear that Akhenaten cannot see that his religion has faded like an evening sunset," Ay said. "The light of his god is dying. The people of his city no longer sing the god's praises. Worship of the Aten is practiced primarily by the royal family."

"This is something we all feared would happen when Pharaoh moved away from Thebes," Ramose said. He spoke with a genuine sadness in the way he said it.

"Yes, well you two must prepare Thebes for the day when the court returns. Believe me when I say it is going to happen, even if I have to move it here myself."

Horemheb and Ramose looked at each other and finished their beer. As they sat there watching the sun set behind the western hills, Horemheb saw in its fading color a portent of things to come.

A year later, Pharaoh Akhenaten, Son of the Aten, Ruler of the Two Lands died. His son had just turned eight years old. Smenkhare assumed the title of Pharaoh while Queen Neferneferuaten became Regent for the boy-prince. Lord Ay arranged it to preserve Akhenaten's succession.

One evening when the air had cooled, the two couples met in Ramose's garden. As the men enjoyed their beer, their wives sipped wine, having acquired the taste from the royal family.

Horemheb suddenly waved his hand in a great sweeping gesture. "Do you hear that, my friends? That is the sound of a great sigh of relief passing through the land. Persecutions have ended and the court of Pharaoh's brother is more relaxed."

"What of Lord Ay?" Benefer said.

Ramose chose to answer. "Some courtesans I've met say he's proven to be a good advisor to Smenkhare."

Horemheb growled, shaking his head. "Well, he would be, wouldn't he? He's getting closer to the throne. I would sleep better knowing his days of intrigue were over." His friends nodded. The night, lit by a half moon, became deadly silent.

The tranquility of the land did not last long. At the end of that year, the people of Akhenaten's city suffered a severe plague. Word reached Thebes that the royal family had not been spared. Even the Crown Prince had caught the sickness.

This news frightened Horemheb. "He's contracted these fevers before, but this time they say it's very severe. The physicians are unable to bring down his temperature." He looked at Amenia. "I must go to him."

She nodded. "May Horus save him."

Rushing to the dock, Horemheb commandeered a four-man canoe to speed him to the royal palace. Racing with the current, they rowed through the night. When he arrived the next day, he found everyone subdued and concerned, and he feared for the boy.

"Pharaoh Smenkhare has died, my Lord," the Chamberlain said, "may his name be remembered. Nothing could be done to save him. His fever worsened and he became delirious. He died in his sleep in the middle of the night."

Horemheb held up his hands in exasperation. "By the gods. And the Crown Prince?"

"His mother and physicians are keeping a vigil by his bed. Nefer is like a shadow, sitting there watching her son waste away."

Lowering his voice, Horemheb put his hand on the chamberlain's shoulder. "Take me to them."

For the next two days he sat with the queen, but Tutankhaten failed to improve. Then, very early the next day they awoke to the sound of the lad's voice.

"Uncle. What are you doing here?"

Nefer and Horemheb rubbed their eyes and began laughing.

"My Son," Nefer said over and over. She pulled Horemheb closer to the bed. "Feel his forehead Harm. It's cool. The fever's gone."

"Forgive me, my Queen," Horemheb said. He raised his voice in a shout. "Horus be praised." The boy laughed, then put his hand over his mouth. His mother smiled and simply shook her head.

For his crime of failing to save Pharaoh Smenkhare, the royal physician died that evening by the sword. During the seventy days Pharaoh's body lay in the House of the Dead, a gloomy darkness engulfed the City of the Sun. A new tomb had been hastily prepared near Akhenaten's. With the king's brother laid to rest, the people sacrificed to the old gods for saving them from the plague.

Prince Tutankhaten became the eleventh Pharaoh of the Eighteenth Dynasty. At the age of nine, he would receive the crown, and his mother named co-regent. His grandfather, Lord Ay, named himself Chief Advisor to Pharaoh.

When Ay met with Horemheb and Ramose at Smenkhare's funeral, he took them aside. "The coronation will be in Memphis. It is a former capital and is blessed by the gods."

Puzzled, Ramose scrunched his forehead. "Why not in Thebes, my Lord?"

"Because Memphis is the first step in restoring the old ways and old religion," Ay said. "I've thought about this for a long time and I think this is best. Gradually, we'll move Pharaoh and the court back to Thebes, but it must be done in measured steps. It should at least appear that we have a plan. The people of Egypt do not like abrupt changes. Bless the gods, neither do I."

Horemheb nodded. "It is a good plan, my Lord. Shall I go to Memphis and prepare his coronation, or do you choose to do so?"

"No, you must go. I will give you Pharaoh's written decree to take with you." Horemheb agreed, putting his fist across his chest in salute. The older man continued in a softer tone. "I know you love the prince as much as I, so let us agree to make him the best pharaoh we've ever served."

"We will make it so, Lord Ay," Horemheb said.

Preparations for the coronation took a month. Excitement grew as the people realized they would now have a pharaoh who would bring back the old traditions.

Sitting in their garden, Horemheb shared many of the plans for the big event. "The high priest of Ra will co-officiate with the high priest of the Aten. All gods and goddesses will be honored on the great day."

Amenia had moved to Memphis to be near her husband. Now in her sixth month of confinement, she found it difficult to move about.

"I've scheduled my work so I can be with you in the afternoons and evenings," Horemheb said. "Benefer arrives tomorrow." It pleased him to see how happy the news made her. "She's leaving the children with their grandparents."

Kissing him on the cheek she reached up and gently turned his face toward her. "You are a thoughtful husband," Amenia said.

A week later, in the middle of the night, a severe pain awakened Amenia. She screamed, rousing the household. The midwives and physician were sent for and Horemheb stayed with her until they came. Chased out, he could only pace back and forth in the garden. No one had time to report on his wife's condition, which worried him even more.

"It's too soon, Ramose," Horemheb said. His friend had come over from next door. Benefer came too and stayed by Amenia's bed. The men drank several jars of beer as they waited. Ramose tried to encourage his friend, but Horemheb couldn't sit still. He smiled in anticipation of the good news as Lord Senbi came out with the senior midwife. Horemheb held his breath.

The physician had trouble speaking. "We did all we could, General. The baby boy is stillborn. I'm so sorry." He paused not knowing how to continue. "Lady Amenia's Ka has also gone with him. The hemorrhaging became so severe she lost too much blood. May her name be remembered." The midwife repeated the last words, as did Ramose.

Horemheb collapsed on the limestone bench, too stunned to move or speak. The healer and midwife left him and returned to the villa, leaving the general alone with his friend. Ramose, too horrified to speak, sat down on the bench opposite him. He saw Horemheb's eyes fill with tears, while his face remained as rigid as granite.

Horemheb spoke above a whisper. "The love of my life is gone. My hope for a son went with her. It's as if I'd been struck a heavy blow to the head in battle. Horus, help me now." He looked up at the sky before going on. "Give my Love and son their golden bodies and keep them safe." He wanted to scream it as loudly as he could, but managed to control his anger.

A few moments later, Horemheb walked to the edge of the garden and began to sob, breaking his friend's heart.

CHAPTER TWENTY

WAR IN THE NORTH

The sculptured bust of Queen Nefertiti sat on a polished marble pedestal in the front room of the royal apartment. Tutankhaten, now ten, liked to look at it, thinking he could hear her breathing. It had been almost a year since the gods took her away from him, and he missed her terribly.

Pinhasy, the royal steward entered, interrupting the young king's thoughts. "Majesty, Lord Ay seeks an audience."

The young Pharaoh turned away from his mother. "Show him in."

Ay bowed his head. "Good afternoon, Great One." Family members did not have to make obeisance before the living god.

"Welcome, Grandfather." He invited the older man to sit on a divan in the front room. Tutankhaten smiled. "I am not very 'great' yet." He had been required to grow up quickly and learned to speak like an adult.

"That is one of the reasons I am here, my Son," Ay said. "We must ensure you remain on the throne and become great. You must marry."

"But I'm only ten, Grandfather. I am not ready."

"Nonsense," Ay said. "Pharaohs must have wives. Many of our Pharaohs married young. I have decided you will marry your sister Ankhesenpaaten, giving you even more of your father's power."

Tutankhaten wailed, "Ankhesen?" He could not be more horrified at the disgusting possibility of marrying his sister, whom he did not like.

Ay raised his voice, a serious break of protocol. "You will do as I say. I am Regent and have the power." His words caused the young king to fall silent.

He continued. "Now, your Majesty, there is something even more important than that. You must send General Horemheb to our northern border. The cursed Asiatics have invaded again."

This disturbed Tutankhaten. Horemheb had been like a father to him during the past year. The boy loved being with him.

"But he is my instructor, Grandfather. What about learning my military skills? Horseback riding, archery, and hand-to-hand combat? You told me those were important."

"This is more important, my Son."

Tutankhaten believed his grandfather loved him, but the boy chose to share his secrets and concerns with Horemheb. He already knew his friendship with Horemheb did not please his grandfather, but didn't understand why.

"Will he take me with him?" Tutankhaten said.

"No Pharaoh, your place is here. You can go with him when you've finished your training and have become a warrior."

The king remained quiet. Instinct warned him not to cross the line Ay had drawn for him.

"I will bring the general's orders for you to sign in the morning, Majesty." Then, without so much as a courteous farewell, Ay left the royal apartment.

The boy walked over to the bust of his mother. Affectionately placing his hand on it, he looked across the veranda to the river sparkling with sunlight on ripples created by a late afternoon breeze. He spoke to the sculpture in a tender voice. "I like being Pharaoh, Mother, but I don't like not having any power. I will change that one day."

It had been a year since the death of Horemheb's wife. Their tomb at Saqqara had finally been finished to the general's satisfaction. His friends told him her sarcophagus resembled a work of art. He also ordered a bust of her carved from alabaster while his memory of her face remained clearly etched in his mind. Visitors to his villa said the remarkable likeness of Amenia kept her presence alive.

Two months after her death, the Nubians attacked Fort Swentet. He volunteered to show the Nubians Egyptian strength once again. Fortunately for him, the battles he led took his thoughts away from home and focused them on an old enemy. For a warrior, fighting hand-to-hand felt reassuring. A soldier has only one purpose in life—to survive and defeat his opponent.

One evening when the day's skirmishes were over, his worried aide spoke to him. "General, tell me if I'm being disrespectful, but you took some foolish chances today. Twice you charged into the enemy without waiting for your men. Fortunately, Horus is always at your side—but you can't continue like that, Sir."

"Paramessu," Horemheb growled. "The gods have been with me my whole life. Do not fear for me—they are with me still."

His aide shook his head. "As you say, General."

The next morning, a messenger arrived by ship. When Paramessu handed the scroll to Horemheb he saw Ay's seal on it. After reading the message, the general handed it back.

"Lord Ay is sending us north in the king's name," he said. "We are to defend our northern forts from new incursions by the Hattai invaders. First he sends us south, now as far north as possible. I'm beginning to get the impression that Ay doesn't want us around." He chuckled, knowing the truth of his words.

"But we're not finished here, my Lord," Paramessu said.

"It's true, I know it. But the Third Regiment can do the cleaning up, Messu. We'll take our men north when the moon is full at the end of the week."

"At your command," Paramessu said. "I'm rather looking forward to meeting an Asiatic or two, whether Hattai, Mittani or Phoenician—all the same. They killed most of my mother's family ten years ago. This will be a much deserved revenge."

"They may not be as easy to defeat as you think," Horemheb said. "They're fierce fighters. Remember, they've conquered Egypt before."

Paramessu stood straight and stuck out his chin. "Yes, well they haven't felt my sword yet—so, this won't last long."

That made the general laugh.

At the end of the week, they hired fifty ships for the move north. It would also require a second voyage by the same ships to bring the rest of Horemheb's men. He liked the fact that another battalion would follow them in a week's time.

On board the *Wings of Horus*, Horemheb and his aides planned the tactics they might use in battle. This time the Egyptians were better prepared. They fought with iron swords and chariots, abandoning the soft copper and bronze used years before. The Egyptians were using curved swords like the Hittites, and bows made from a similar design.

Horemheb met with his officers in his cabin. "These battles men, will be won by strategy and cunning. They are equal to us in every way, and in fact they may actually have more chariots. We will choose our best scouts and send them ahead to make accurate maps of the land. They will be crucial to our planning."

That evening, as his men chose places to sleep, Horemheb walked to the bow and breathed in the pleasant fragrance of the river. It always reminded him of home and he closed his eyes for a moment. Leaning on the railing, he opened them and took it all in; the reflection of the evening sun bouncing on the glassy surface of the water, and the noises of the children along the shore who shouted and waved at the ship. Suddenly, a high-pitched screech made him look up. A majestic falcon soared gracefully in a circle above the ship.

"It's Horus," Paramessu shouted. He ran to the bow to make sure the general had seen the raptor. "A favorable omen."

"Indeed," Horemheb said. "Our god is watching over us." He said it loud enough for the rest of his men and ship's crew to hear. They looked up and cheered. Under his breath he breathed a silent prayer for the success of his mission.

He lowered his voice when he and Paramessu were alone. "Ay won't be able to refuse me more power if this northern campaign succeeds."

"You'll be a hero again, General, and harder to ignore."

Their ship docked first at Avaris, near Diametta on the coast of the Great Sea. From there, they would disembark and advance overland to the Egyptian outpost at Kadesh. Their horses were glad to be on land again and pranced around, stretching muscles cramped in the bowels of the ship.

"Line up the chariots quickly," Paramessu ordered. Other soldiers set up camp by the river. "Fill up your water skins and get the wagons ready to haul supplies."

Most of his men preferred sleeping ashore, but Horemheb wanted the luxury of one more night in a bed. The ship's master would sleep on deck with the rest of his crew. Paramessu chose to stay with his battalion leaders and Horemheb joined them for supper. The sun quickly disappeared, snuffed out like a candle without any afterglow in the sky. Clouds had blown in from the north, plunging the camp into almost total obscurity. Egyptians were not used to the sudden darkness.

Tossing and turning, Horemheb dreamed he saw his lost spear flying through the air toward him. Grabbing it, he plunged it deep into the chest of an Asiatic warrior whose face had somehow transformed into that of Lord Ay's.

In Thebes, at the end of the week, a royal wedding took place. Pharaoh Tutankhaten married his sister Ankhesenpaaten. His people enjoyed the feasting and celebrations. Several days later, the boy-king sat at the end of the council table and frowned.

"But why must they be moved, Grandfather?" he said. He chose to ignore the look of consternation on the elderly man's face.

"Your father's body, may his name be remembered Majesty, should be entombed in the Valley of the Kings with all the other rulers of the land. So should the bodies of your grandmother and mother as well. Allow me to have tombs built for them, and when you are ready, we will bring them to their rightful place of honor."

The eleven-year old remained silent for some time. "Make it so," he said. He refused to look at his Chief Advisor.

Ay turned to the council's scribe. "So let it be done." He then brought up several other subjects for the council to discuss concerning the replenishment of Pharaoh's granaries and repair of the annual flood gauges before dismissing the council. He stayed behind to talk to his grandson.

"I also ask your permission to begin the construction on our tombs, my Son, yours and mine. Yours, of course, will not be needed for a long time if the gods will it, but mine is more urgent."

Tutankhaten knew already that this was a clever ploy on the old man's part, and a deception. He had learned from his chamberlain that the elderly man had already begun construction on two royal tombs. *How long does he think he can keep the secret from me?*

Speaking now in a very formal tone, Tutankhaten said, "Of course, my Lord. As father to a great queen, my mother, and relative by blood to the pharaohs, your tomb must be in the Valley. Build it close to us if you choose."

Surprised by the boy's grasp of his proposal, what the boy said next astonished the elderly man. "Next year, after the blessing of the flooding of our beloved river, we are going to change our names, Grandfather. I want all those members of the court who have honored the Aten, to change their names as well. We will honor Amun once again. I saw this in a vision and believe the god has spoken to me."

"Amun be praised," Ay exclaimed. "An excellent decision, Majesty." Tutankhaten saw how much this new decision pleased his grandfather.

Far to the north, the *Wings of Horus* rocked gently to and fro in its berth. Warm breezes from the red desert blew across the deck, a sure sign the day would be hot. The sun had not yet risen as Paramessu stood outside Horemheb's cabin door and knocked.

"Go away," the general said. His aide rushed in anyway.

"There's a messenger here from the Mitanni, General. He came under a flag of truce and asks for you by name."

Horemheb rubbed his eyes vigorously, grabbing a sheet to cover himself. "Very well, I'll be out as soon as I get dressed." He waved Paramessu away. A few minutes later, Horemheb went on deck and stood at the railing, looking down at his troops.

"Captain Paramessu, call the commanders to meet here on deck right away, then bring the messenger up." Paramessu saluted and went to carry out the order.

Shortly after, Horemheb addressed his leaders. "I want us to hear the messenger at the same time. There will be no suspicions among you about this meeting." He signaled to those guarding the Mitanni. "Bring him here."

The young Asiatic, still in his teens as evidenced by a lack of beard or stubble on his face, stood at attention. Horemheb thought the young man very brave to have undertaken such a mission. After saluting the general, he spoke in halting Egyptian, making the general wish for Ramose, his old interpreter.

"I am Pamba, my Lord, and I come in peace. His Majesty King Shattiwaza greets you in the name of his departed brother, King Tushratta, may his name be remembered."

The mention of Tushratta's name brought back memories of Horemheb's first adventure in the north with Crown Prince Thutmose. He regretted the loss of Egypt's ally and the father of Princess Tadukhepa. It could change the future of relations between the two countries.

He said, "We regret the loss of Pharaoh's friend, King Tushratta. Go on."

"King Shattiwaza and his army await you on the plain near Kadesh, Lord General. I have been sent to lead you there." The messenger saluted once more, having completed his mission.

Horemheb spoke to his officers. "Does anyone speak Mitanni?"

One of the captains spoke up. "I speak a little, my Lord."

"Good, Renni. Take the messenger and give him food and drink." Speaking in a more quiet tone so only Renni could hear, he said, "Don't let him out of your sight. I don't want him to think he's our prisoner, but in a very real sense that is what he must be. He'll have seen too much by the time we reach his troops."

"Yes, my Lord Prince," Captain Renni said. He then told the young man to follow him.

Once they had gone, Horemheb took his officers into his cabin so they could talk privately. "The death of King Tushratta does not bode well for us. The marriage of his daughter to Pharaoh united us. Now, as you heard the messenger declare, his brother, King Shattiwaza awaits us on the plains of Kadesh." He paused for effect. "Does he wait to meet us as an enemy or friend? Our scouts must find the answer. Tell them what is at stake, Commanders. The Mitanni must not see them." His men nodded.

"We will put our archers at the front of the march—with another company of them to the rear."

The next morning, the ships sailed south for the rest of the army. The voyage would take them perhaps six days, depending on the current. Selected scouts left camp on horseback. They would leave their animals when they neared the Mitanni camp and continue on foot.

During the time they waited for the ship's return, the men packed their supply wagons, sharpened their weapons and engaged in mock combat.

"We're going to miss all this game," Paramessu said. "We've enjoyed roasted goose, duck and plenty of fresh fish—all broiled to perfection."

"I'm afraid our men will get too fat from it all," Horemheb said.

Paramessu laughed. "Why General, without a full stomach an army cannot march. Surely you know that."

"Bah." Horemheb growled. "From some of the stomachs I've seen, they won't be able to move." That made those around the campfire burst out laughing.

Back in the land across from Thebes in the Valley of the Kings, a dark entranceway simmered in the humid heat. Two bearers carried torches through the passage toward the interior of a new tomb. Several workmen held polished bronze mirrors at the entrance, reflecting the sun's rays into the newly carved future resting place of Pharaoh. Ay entered the large rooms cut into the limestone, pleased with their layout.

The elderly man spoke to the priest of Amun. "When will the artists begin the decorations, Semmi?"

"Not until the walls have been made ready, my Lord. They must be plastered, then dried for at least two weeks before they can begin."

"Now, take me to my tomb," Ay said. He turned and headed back toward the sunlight. What he found didn't please him. He entered another new tomb much smaller than pharaoh's. He found four chambers half the size of the king's, and he didn't like it. *This will not do.* He had seen Horemheb's modest tomb at Saqqara and even that appeared larger than this design.

"I've seen enough," he said. "Call for my bearers. I'll return at once." The priest hurried on ahead and Ay's golden carrying-chair waited for him when he came out. Back at the palace, he learned to his consternation that Pharaoh and his wife had decided to leave the new city of Akhenaten and move back into Pharaoh's old apartment in Thebes. The Chief Advisor would have to move out. It proved to be the end of a disagreeable day for Lord Ay.

Up north, when the ships returned with the rest of Horemheb's men, the army began its advance across the sand.

The ship's captain gave Horemheb's men an old Bedouin blessing: "May your water skins stay filled, and may there be cool breezes for your brow when you cross the desert sands."

They followed the well-worn road leading up toward Kadesh and the passage through the Negev. Water became crucial to their survival and the men slept during the heat of the day, hidden in shadowy crevices and rocky outcroppings. They could advance only at night. Four days later, they were halfway to their rendezvous when the scouts returned. Their leader hurried to Horemheb's camp to make his report.

The middle-aged scout saluted. "We bring bad news, General. We searched everywhere around the fortress and the ancient town, but didn't find the Mitanni! There's no army out there!"

CHAPTER TWENTY-ONE

PHARAOH TUTANKHAMUN

Horemheb stared out across the sandy plain. As far as he could see nothing moved. The army had reached the town of Tjaru and began to set up camp near its ancient walls. Even so, the general felt something amiss.

"Where are they?" he said.

Pamba, the young messenger, became frightened, certain the Egyptians would think he had led them into a trap. "They were here, my Lord. I swear before all our gods."

Horemheb squinted his eyes and thought he could see something moving. A small cloud of dust moved on the horizon. At first, it had the shape of a dust devil, but then gradually became a camel and rider. Horemheb sent out a small platoon to meet and escort the rider to camp. When he arrived, the man jabbed his heels into the camel's sides to make the animal kneel. As it folded its back legs and sat down, the rider jumped from the beast and stood at attention. He saluted those he assumed to be the officers in charge.

Horemheb stepped forward with Pamba behind him. When the dust-covered rider began to speak, Horemheb recognized his language as Hurrian, spoken by the Mittani nation.

"He says he has been sent by our general to greet you, my Lord," Pamba said. "Two days ago a great sandstorm forced our army to retreat into the mountains behind Tjaru." Pamba listened as the rider continued, and then interpreted for him. "They are a day behind him, he says, and should be here by morning."

"Very good," Horemheb said. "Give him water and some food." Turning to his officers he ordered, "Prepare the army for an attack as a precaution, and send out our advance scouts immediately."

Just before dawn, Paramessu awakened Horemheb to tell him the Mitanni had arrived. Horemheb splashed his face with water, grabbed his kilt, and left the tent to meet the leader of the allied army.

A tall, well-muscled Asiatic commander spoke in perfect Egyptian. "I am Endaruta, Lord General." He wore several layers of cloth wrapped around his body, in Bedouin fashion.

"Welcome, brother," Horemheb replied. Giving his best formal salute, he then led Endaruta and his aides into his pavilion. The Egyptians had set up temporary headquarters next to the road known to the Egyptian army as "The Way of Horus." It led north through the Negev and followed the coast on its way to the northern empires.

"We have fought battles with the Hittites before," the Mitanni said. "Control of this dry land has passed from one country to the other many times."

"True," Horemheb replied. "Egypt will need to repair the fortifications here at Tjaru if we hope to protect our northern borders."

He listened politely to General Endaruta's explanation for the delay in meeting him. When he finished, Horemheb ordered beer and wine and the four men relaxed, taking the time to get to know each other.

Finally they got down to the important matters. Horemheb asked, "What are our chances, General?"

"Not good," the warrior said. "Our scouts report their army outnumbers ours three to one. We might have had the element of surprise, but now I'm not sure."

"I agree," Horemheb said.

"With your permission, General," Paramessu said. "May I suggest we make them come to us here at Tjaru? If we repaired the walls and fortified the city, we could bear the brunt of their assault. General Endaruta's army could attack them from the rear. We'd have them in spite of their great numbers."

Horemheb nodded, pleased with the suggestion. "A good idea, Messu, but with high risk for Egypt should they come this far and we were to fail."

Endaruta said, "We'll have at least a week's advantage, maybe two. The Hittites are expecting us to come to them, remember. We will force them to come south. They will have to come on what you call Horus's Way."

"Agreed," Horemheb said. They spent the rest of the day studying maps of the surrounding land. He decided the best place to put the Mitanni army would be in the Scorpion's Tail. The curved piece of rocky land ended in a point and could easily hide all of the Mitanni archers and foot soldiers.

Scouts from both armies went out, hoping to find evidence of the enemy's movement. The elders of the walled city of Tjaru felt threatened by the army's presence, but felt more at ease when Horemheb took charge. The desert town had a population made up mostly of criminals banished from Egypt. They had little loyalty to Pharaoh, but when faced with the danger of an advancing Hittite army, they became very cooperative in helping the army fortify the town.

"It is your archers who will decide this battle, Lord Endaruta," Horemheb said at supper. "We must determine the best position for them. Any suggestions?"

"I have studied the maps carefully, General. I believe if we dig into the bank of that dry riverbed running parallel to the city, my archers could be hidden and let fly at the last moment."

"Of course," Paramessu said. "His men would be invisible." The officers continued to plan late into the night as regiment commanders from both armies contributed ideas for the battle. By the end of the first week Horemheb felt good about their preparations. At the end of the second, a scout rode into the city in the middle of the night and shouted, "They've been spotted. They'll be here in two days."

Back in the capital of Thebes, Pharaoh stood on the palace veranda overlooking the city as his father used to do. Tutankhamun liked his new name. He didn't like, however, having a wife telling him what to do, so he ignored her most of the time. Lord Ineni, the king's chamberlain, thought it typical behavior for a twelve-year old.

At the beginning of the year, Pharaoh felt very much like a king when his victorious army returned from Nubia. They brought captives and a large gold and ivory tribute from the now submissive nation. He knew his mentor, Uncle Horemheb, had won the battles, but as Pharaoh, he received the cheers of his people as he led the triumphant army through the streets of Thebes.

One afternoon Tutankhamun turned to Lord Ay, his Chief Advisor. "I miss Horemheb, Grandfather."

The old man frowned. "He's needed in the north, Majesty. We'll let him have a great victory procession when he returns."

The young ruler, now as tall as his grandfather corrected him. "I think you mean 'I will let him,' do you not?"

"Of course, Majesty, I forgot myself." Tutankhamun noticed there had been no apology. His wife had warned him about letting Ay get away with such lapses in protocol. Ankhesenamun, five years older than her husband, had a good sense of how things should be done at court.

One morning, Ay handed the king a document. "If you would sign this, Majesty." He said it more as a command than a polite request.

The young pharaoh frowned. "What is it?" He looked closely at the parchment scroll.

"It gives me permission to finish the work on my tomb, my boy, and to continue work on yours. It is never too early to take care of these matters."

"Very well," Tutankhamun said. He moved over to a small table in his apartment. Seating himself, he signed the document using his throne name, Nebkheperura. Ay poured wax on the document and pharaoh pressed his ring with the royal seal into it.

"Thank you, Great One," the elderly man said. With only the hint of a bowed head, he left the royal apartment. Before the large door closed, Tutankhamun saw his grandfather hand the document to a dark shadow of a man waiting in the hallway. At the same instant, another figure passed Ay and entered the king's front room before the door swung shut.

"What's my father doing here? Is he bothering you, Majesty," a man in his thirties asked. He quickly knelt on one knee in a soldier's salute.

"General Nakhtmin. We're delighted to see you again," the king exclaimed. "Lord Ay's son is always welcome. I hope our gifts pleased you."

The warrior grumbled. "I am content, Pharaoh, but am not happy to be stuck here in Thebes while real battles are fought in the north." He waited for pharaoh to give him permission to stand, then seated himself on one of the divans.

"It is Grandfather's orders to bring you here, General, not mine. But I'm glad for it. I'll finally be able to hear about where you've been fighting." He saw Nakhtmin's face brighten.

"Of course Pharaoh, we could join Horemheb if you wanted to." He laughed and Tutankhamun joined in.

The officer stood. "By the gods. What an idea. I would go tomorrow if my father would allow it—you know that. You are a good charioteer and it would be good for you to see battle. Our pharaohs have always led us into the fight."

"Then we will do it," the twelve-year old said, laughing again. They both knew it to be impossible. Tutankhamun clapped his hands and ordered beer and sweetbread for refreshment, taking his friend outside.

They stood at the railing of the veranda overlooking the river. Nakhtmin said, "I have a feeling that Horemheb will not come back and I'll have to take his place."

Tutankhamun made the sign against the evil eye by touching his thumb to the fourth finger, and then brushing his hand across his mouth. "What a horrible thing to say."

"But it's true, my King. Ever since your father, may his name be remembered, married Ay's daughter, he has dreamed of becoming pharaoh himself. Forgive me, Great One for saying it."

"I have known these things," Tutankhamun said. "Ankhesenamun tells me everything that is said and done in my court. This is not a surprise to me. But when we have children, may the gods provide them, Ay's dream will come to an end."

"Then may the gods bless you with many children, Majesty. That is, when you're old enough to make them." Nakhtmin said it with a knowing grin, causing the king's face to turn red.

Tutankhamun laughed nervously and changed the subject. "I shall command that you be sent north to meet with Horemheb and return with news of his battles."

"Yes, Majesty. Shall I call my father back to make it official?"

"No, I'll write out the command and give it to Ay in the morning. He is only an advisor. Remember that."

"Good," the soldier declared. "Now let's have a game of Senet."

A week later, in the northern desert, Paramessu recognized the man on horseback heading his way. Several guardsmen accompanied him. "General Nakhtmin. May the gods be praised," he shouted.

"Captain Paramessu. Where is your General?" Nakhtmin returned the officer's salute. "Is he in the pavilion?"

"No, he's in town, General. Let me get my horse." Paramessu returned quickly on his mount and they rode into the ancient settlement. At the mayor's villa, vacated to give the Egyptian army a command center, they dismounted and Paramessu hurried inside, returning with the general.

"Nakhtmin. You old hound," Horemheb shouted. "Come, join us, you and your men." He ordered his aides to bring beer, fresh bread and dates for his guests.

Over refreshments, Nakhtmin informed Horemheb that their ship had docked at Avaris two days ago and they had ridden through the night.

"Then you need rest. Sleep now, and we'll share old war stories at supper. Messu, show them where they can bed down."

"Good, we'll talk later," Nakhtim said. He yawned and followed Paramessu to one of the back rooms.

Later that day, they gathered in the dining room and shared freshly cooked partridge, quail, gazelle, and emptied dozens of jars of beer.

"First tell me about my beloved Mutnodjmet," Horemheb began.

"Ha. *Your* Mutnodjmet?" Nakhtmin bellowed. "She's my wife, Harm." They burst out laughing, enjoying an old joke. After the death of Horemheb's Amenia, both men had been attracted to the same woman, but she chose Nakhtmin. His friend knew, however, that Horemheb still loved her.

"She's well, brother," Nakhtmin said. "She sends her affection—but that's all." He grinned, and that made Horemheb smile. "Now, tell me about the Hittites, Harm."

"They were forced to retreat, my friend. Neither army could gain an upper hand. We stopped them even though we were outnumbered. General Endaruta's archers were magnificent and I think are among the best in the world, even better than the Nubians. He and his army stayed here several days to make sure the Hittites had gone for good. I've chosen a few other places in the region where more fortresses should be built, if his majesty approves."

Nakhtmin listened, nodding his head from time to time. Paramessu told him how they had been outnumbered three to one and about the hidden archer's trap at the dry riverbed. Nakhtmin's men beat their empty cups on the table in praise of the clever tactic.

"You must tell Pharaoh and Ay, brother," Horemheb insisted. "It is imperative we build the new outposts along the road." Nakhtmin didn't need convincing.

"It is you who must tell them, Horemheb. Come back with me. My father needs to hear your reports."

Forgetting his place, Paramessu said, "Yes, you should go, General. The army is secure and well dug in."

"Leave me," Horemheb said. The men stood to leave. "You stay, Nakhtmin." When the others had gone, he looked at his friend. "I will come with you, because in all seriousness, I worry about our boy-king."

Nakhtmin spoke just above a whisper. "My father is afraid of you, as you know. He believes you want the throne, but sees himself on it, not you."

Horemheb looked at him closely. "In all honesty, brother, your father is an old man and our young king is going to outlive us all."

"May the gods make it so. But I worry for the king's safety too."

"How is he? Is he well?"

"Pharaoh's taller now and is filling out. I think he'll favor his mother when he's grown—not his father, thank the gods. His tutor says he learns very quickly and is quite intelligent. He's a good charioteer and loves driving them. He's also a very good archer."

Horemheb smiled, pleased to hear such a positive report.

"He's changed everyone's names back, you know. He's now Tutankhamun and the god Aten has been removed from the names of everyone at court."

"Ah, that's a good thing. Tutankhamun," he repeated. "It has a good sound to it. May Amun be pleased. Was it his idea or your father's?"

"It was his," Nakhtmin said. "I'm convinced the boy wanted to do it when he became Pharaoh. He told me so himself."

When Horemheb left Tijaru, he placed Paramessu in charge of his officers and the army. He and Nakhtmin and their guards rode through the night under the feeble light of a quarter moon. They stopped first for water, hidden at the base of a large cluster of boulders. They encountered no other life, except for a troop of dog-headed baboons that barked at them. Their wild booming cries shattered the silence as the soldiers waited their turn.

Two days later, they could hear the crew aboard Nakhtmin's ship cheering when they saw the two generals and their men approaching. With their horses lifted on board by ropes and pulleys, and everyone on deck, the "*Wings of Horus*" set sail for home.

It took four days before Horemheb could see the first whitewashed buildings of the capital. "Beloved Thebes, beauty of the hundred gates. How we rejoice as we see thee appear before us. You adorn our holy riverbanks with thy temples and gleaming walls."

Nakhtmin laughed. "What's this, Harm? You've become a poet?"

"No, those words I remember Ramose reciting over and over when we were growing up."

As the galley docked, a messenger from the king came to meet them. He told the two generals they were to present themselves at the palace that evening.

"It is to be a feast of celebration," the courier explained. He then rode back to the palace.

That evening, members of the royal family, including Lord Ay, welcomed Horemheb warmly. Pharaoh's grandfather remained Chief Advisor, and Ramose appointed Vizier of Thebes once again.

Queen Ankhesenamun greeted Horemheb as he knelt before her.

A sudden movement behind him made him turn around. Tutankhamun walked forward to greet him. Horemheb could tell the young man had trouble restraining himself from embracing his uncle.

Moving to stand next to Lord Ay, Horemheb looked around the room. "Where is Nakhtmin? I thought he would be here before me."

"I've not seen him," Ay replied as they walked into the dining room to take their places.

"The king has sent guards to see what has delayed him," Ay added.

Horemheb nodded and went to the chair assigned to him by the king's steward. Pharaoh decided the feast should begin and the king's guests were served the best wine. For the first time in a long while, Horemheb could look closely at the young Pharaoh. It pleased him to see how much the young man had changed. His face did remind him of Nefertiti as Nakhtmin said.

Lord Ay sat at the king's right, and the two generals sat next to Ramose. Horemheb left the chair next to Ay vacant for the elderly man's son.

Conversations around the table centered on news of the city and how much had changed during Horemheb's one-year absence. After the meal, the guests went out onto the large veranda to enjoy the cool air. The king and queen sat on ebony chairs placed on a small platform to elevate their heads above those of their guests.

"Tell us about your encounters with the Asiatics," Pharaoh said.

"Your army fought bravely, Great One," Horemheb said. "The Asiatics have been expelled from your borders." The guests cheered and applauded, and he went on to praise Captain Paramessu and General Endaruta's Mittani army. When he told them about the hidden archers in the dry riverbed, they clapped again.

Lord Ay put a damper on everyone's enthusiasm by asking, "What has become of the enemy, General? Have they been crushed for good?"

Horemheb scrunched his eyebrows as he always did when displeased. "No, my Lord. Since we were outnumbered we could only fight them off and push them from Tjaru. But the enemy has returned to those foul places under the rocks from where they came." He saw his nephew smile. "Our defenses are in place, and they cannot come through again." *That should silence the sly old fox.*

Just then, the captain of the guards came out onto the veranda and motioned for Lord Ay to approach him. He whispered something in the man's ear. Ay cried out and hurried away.

"What's happened, Captain?" Tutankhamun demanded. Because Pharaoh stood up, all of his family and guests did the same.

"It's General Nakhtmin, Majesty. I'm afraid he's dead."

CHAPTER TWENTY-TWO

VICTORY IN THE SOUTH

The royal physician met Ay at the door. His chalky-white face and furrowed brow showed concern. Horemheb arrived at that moment, having followed Ay home. He listened to the physician's report.

"There's not a mark on your son's body, my Lord. Lady Mutnodjmet told me he had a very high fever when he returned home today."

The elderly man turned to Horemheb, unable to accept what he'd heard. "Was he sick on the ship?"

"No, my Lord. He's been in perfect health."

The physician continued. "Your daughter-in-law did say, however, that several of the servants have had high fevers this week. It has to be the pestilence from the northeast. It comes upon us sometimes at this time of year."

Horemheb nodded, remembering a killing fever carried by flying insects from the delta which decimated the capital five years before.

Inside the front room, the grief-stricken father paced about. "Have you found evidence of poison, Lord Heru?" He shook his head again in disbelief. "This can't be happening."

"I found no evidence of poison, my Lord. The family has consumed the same food and drink as your son."

"Come with us, Horemheb," Ay said. He led him to the tiled bathing area where his son lay on a table.

Lady Mutnodjmet sat weeping on the floor. A white linen cloth draped the body, but Ay, now filled with anger, yanked it off. He examined his son's corpse carefully from every angle before collapsing onto a small wooden bench.

When Mutnodjmet saw Horemheb, she stood and fell exhausted into his arms. He helped her to another bench, sending a servant for water.

Horemheb shouted, "By the gods. Tutankhamun will also be in danger."

Rushing outside, he climbed onto his horse and raced back to the palace. He could hear the hoof beats of the physician's horse behind him. The Captain of the Guard met him and told him the guards already surrounded the royal apartments. Permitted to pass through, Horemheb and the physician hurried into the residence. A servant ran to tell the queen he had returned.

When Ankhesenamun saw him, she rushed over. "Oh, bless Amun, Uncle. Come quickly. He's very ill." Her words sent a chill up Horemheb's spine. Together they rushed into the king's bedchamber.

Leaning over the bed, Horemheb asked, "Majesty, what's wrong?"

"I'm so hot, Uncle. I'm burning up all over. Please help me," he groaned. "My head hurts as if someone put a knife in it, and my back too."

Lord Heru moved to the bedside and bowed his head before examining the young man closely.

After a moment he shook his head. "It's the same sickness, I'm afraid. Now that we know it is the pestilence from the delta, maybe we can stop his fever." He shouted to the servants, "Bring his copper bath at once. Fill it with the coolest water."

Everyone ran to obey, but Horemheb saw the fear in his nephew's eyes, and he moved to a chair at the head of the bed.

"We thank the gods this fever is not contagious, General," Lord Heru said. "This type of fever does not spread between people."

Horemheb nodded, left the chair and sat down on the edge of the king's bed. He put one hand on Tutankhamun's shoulder, and with the other gently wiped the king's brow.

"You'll be all right," he said. "We'll fight this fever and bring your temperature down. I'll have the servants put some linen netting over and around your bed. It will keep out all of the pesky insects. Who knows what sickness they bring with them? It'll be like we are camping on the hunt, Great One."

Tutankhamun could manage only a weak smile.

After a cooling bath, the king began to tremble and shudder as if someone were shaking him. Horemheb thought at first it might be the falling sickness like his father's, but he only felt cold and the shaking soon stopped. He and the healer stayed at pharaoh's side. The queen slept on a bed she had ordered brought into her husband's room.

"He's resting now," Heru whispered. He and Horemheb walked out onto the adjacent veranda. "You know his wife told me he's had these attacks before. They always leave him weak and debilitated." The healer paused. "I know your being here will help him most of all."

"Ah, Physician," Horemheb sighed. "You now refer to the sickness of the Ka and the mind. The Ka can be a powerful thing."

Suddenly, Tutankhamun cried out in pain and they both rushed back into the bedchamber. Horemheb saw the queen weeping over her husband, and his heart stopped.

The fever claimed three-hundred and twenty-seven Thebans that year, but Tutankhamun recovered thanks to his physician's care and Horemheb's encouragement.

The next eight years passed quickly and Pharaoh celebrated his seventeenth birthday by choosing to go south with his army into Nubia. Horemheb agreed he should do so.

"A Pharaoh with no military victories to put on his tomb isn't respected in Egypt," his uncle said.

At dawn a week later, the royal flotilla sailed south from Karnak. Horemheb looked back at the lime-washed buildings of the city shining like the tangerine tints of the rising sun. "Thebes, the glorious," he whispered.

As he approached the royal cabin, Horemheb found the king standing outside. "I have heard the happy news about the Queen, Majesty, and I congratulate you. The upcoming birth of your first child will be a momentous event."

Tutankhamun smiled at him as they moved to the railing. "My queen is in her seventh month, and it has not been easy for her."

Horemheb paused a moment before responding. "I know she opposed your decision to go to war, Majesty, but such is the fate of women. Praise the gods we are men." The king nodded as they walked toward the ship's bow.

Horemheb hadn't noticed at first, but he saw the king leaning on a walking stick to keep his balance. He debated asking about it, but threw caution to the wind.

"Have you injured your leg, Majesty?"

"Yes, I twisted my knee somehow, but it will be all right."

His uncle grinned. "That's good, because I want to ride at your side when we chase the Nubians back where they belong."

The young king smiled, but became suddenly serious. "Can we not put an end to these attacks, Uncle? My father fought Nubians, as did my grandfather, and many Pharaohs before. Why can't we crush them once and for all?"

Horemheb nodded as he watched large number of crocodiles on the muddy bank slip into the water, hoping for a meal to accidentally fall from their ship. "I could have stopped these wars, my King. I have never told you about it."

"Oh?" Tutankhamun said.

"Yes, I fell in love with Queen Abar, well, she wasn't queen then, only a princess. When your grandfather defeated the King of Nubia, he and his daughter were brought to Egypt as prisoners. At his death, she became queen and we were very much in love. She wanted me to marry her and return to rule beside her as King of Nubia. My hesitation gave the rebels time to kill her and take over the throne."

Pharaoh looked incredulous. "Did Aunt Amenia know about her? I have pleasant memories of my aunt from my childhood. She always showed me great affection."

"Yes, Majesty, she did know about Queen Abar. It happened before our marriage." Horemheb grew silent and Pharaoh allowed his adopted father time with his memories. They sailed past a noisy herd of hippos who snorted their displeasure at being disturbed.

The young king said, "My Uncle Nakhtmin said the Nubians will be easy to defeat."

Horemheb shook his head. "When you get to the first whitewater rapids, my son, you'll see why it will not be easy. The canyons cut out by our sacred river make perfect defenses against invasion. I am convinced we'll have to go farther south this time."

"Grandfather Ay is pleased you are coming with me."

"Well, he would be, wouldn't he?" Horemheb said. "He's hoping something will happen to both of us, Majesty. He wants to be pharaoh."

Tutankhamun frowned. "I've known it for many years, Uncle, but I don't like to be reminded of it."

"Apologies, Great Kemet. I say it only because I have your safety in mind. That's why I'm glad I'm here with you. We can keep an eye on each other."

Paramessu moved toward them and awaited acknowledgment. "We're approaching the Island of Abu, Majesty."

"Excellent. Tell the ship's captain we may spend a day here."

Tutankhamun moved to the railing to watch the rest of his fleet of ships advancing against the current on their way south to Swentet.

"By Seth's foul breath, pull," the ship's captain shouted to his oarsmen. The men on the large rudder-oars pulled hard, turning the galley ever so slightly toward the island.

Horemheb walked over and stood beside the king to watch the docking.

"You're going to see strange trees here, Majesty," he said. "There are rope trees, whose roots stretch many cubits from branch to the ground." He saw the young man's eyes grow wider as he listened. "There is a Dragon's Blood tree whose bark, when cut, pours out a bright red sap."

"I don't believe you, Uncle." Pharaoh's eyebrows furrowed with skepticism.

"Ah, no? But there are also trees that walk, Young One. A great beast lives here whose legs are as big as the trunk of a large tree." That made Tutankhamun laugh.

The arrival of Pharaoh's ship surprised the dockworkers of Abu. One of the men shouted to the soldier on guard duty. He ran up the road to the garrison and a few moments later, an officer on horseback raced to the landing with six of his men.

When people on shore saw Pharaoh, they fell prostrate toward him, careful to turn their palms upward.

Horemheb shouted, "Greetings, Captain. Pharaoh has chosen to visit your garrison and wishes to see the great creatures of the island."

Pharaoh raised his hand, motioning for everyone to stand.

"His Majesty honors us by his presence," the officer called up to them. "Shall I bring horses, my Lord?"

"Yes, do so at once," Horemheb replied. He explained to the king. "It will take too long to raise our horses from the hold."

As they waited, Horemheb and the king walked farther along the railing so they could watch the last ships from Thebes approach Swentet and the army fortress.

"I've been wanting to tell you, my son, how much you resemble your mother, may her name be remembered."

"*Bakher*," Tutankhamun said. "I miss her every day, Father. She would not let me use my foot as an excuse for anything, and she encouraged me in so many ways. I wonder what she would think of me now, heading into battle."

"She would be proud, Majesty. Very proud. You have become one of our best charioteers and archers. She can see you from her golden afterlife, and is very proud." The young man nodded, and looked up at the azure sky.

The captain of the galley motioned to Horemheb, and the general nodded. "I think they're ready for us, Majesty. Now you're going to see how much more we old people know than you young ones."

Tutankhamun laughed and walked down the gangway. Horses awaited them and it didn't take long for them to mount up. They followed their host as he led them away from the docks. Horemheb and Pharaoh rode side by side, with the Captain of the garrison riding on the king's left.

"The Abus are currently on the far side, Majesty," the officer said. "It won't take long to get there."

"Lead on," Horemheb commanded.

After a short ride, they reached the far side of the island, named for the local word for elephant. The captain reined in his horse and raised his arm, the signal to halt. Dismounting, he crouched down and waited for the others to follow his example.

"Over there, Majesty," the soldier whispered. "In that wooded area straight ahead." Horemheb and the king squinted their eyes, trying to see.

"I don't see anything," Tutankhamun mumbled.

"Wait a moment, until they move," the officer said.

As they watched, a large gray shape moved away from the trees and turned in their direction.

"Look at that," Pharaoh said. A large bull elephant, undoubtedly the leader of the herd, flapped his huge ears and raised his trunk.

"Was I right or not, Young One?" Horemheb said.

"For an old man, your eyes seem to be relatively good."

"Uh-oh," their guide said in a normal voice. "I think he's spotted us."

"But he's not moving," Horemheb said.

"He will be. We should mount up, General."

Only two soldiers did so, the rest, including Horemheb and the king, wanted to see what the bull elephant would do.

After a loud trumpeting, the elephant started to run toward the small creatures intruding into his world.

"We must go, Majesty," Horemheb said. He and the king mounted once again and followed the captain.

"Help me," a soldier shouted. He had stayed back to watch. "My leg is caught in a hole." One of his comrades rode toward him. Jumping down, he tried to extricate the leg.

"It won't come out, Captain," the other soldier shouted. "I'll keep trying."

The loud trumpeting of the elephant and the sound of his thunderous footsteps made the horses skittish and the trapped soldier's horse ran off.

The soldier trying to help shook his head. "It's no use."

"You've got to leave him, Atum. Come on," his commander shouted.

The soldier tried one last time to help his comrade but without success. Leaping onto his horse, he spurred it away and raced toward the rest of the group.

The enraged elephant saw the man on the ground and headed for him. Stomping his feet in front of him, he reached out his trunk and pulled the man up, tearing off his leg. The soldier's cries only made the beast angrier, and he threw the man up into the air. To stop the screaming, the bull crushed him to death with his feet, before shaking his head violently back and forth at the fleeing men. Horemheb would never forget the sounds of the soldier's screams before he died.

Shocked into silence, Pharaoh's party returned to the garrison. The king motioned for the officer to approach him.

"We are sorry this happened, Captain. It is our fault. We asked to see the beasts, but did not realize how dangerous it would be. Tell your men that we will honor their comrade by embalming his body, and preparing his sarcophagus for a proper burial. We will give you a document for his family to assure them he died in an attempt to protect Pharaoh."

The Captain knelt and saluted, too overcome with emotion to say anything except, "Majesty."

"See to it Uncle," Tutankhamun said. He then turned and walked back onto his ship.

Two days later, after the army had assembled and supplies brought forward, Pharaoh Tutankhamen led the first attack against the Nubians. His warriors cheered and beat their shields as they followed him into battle. Horemheb kept on the king's right and Paramessu on the left. The Egyptians advanced through the narrow pass near the whitewater rapids and trapped the Nubians in a canyon south of the sacred waterfall. The Nubians, greatly outnumbered, fought to the last man.

When the king's army returned to camp, Horemheb reported to Tutankhamun in the royal pavilion.

"Before one of the Nubian's died, Great One, we learned that the main body of their army is camped above the second waterfall. There is a vast plain above the river, but it will be difficult to take horses up the cliffs. We'll have to go on foot." He saw his nephew rub his knee and knew it had to have been hurting him. A servant came to remove Pharaoh's blue war crown, giving the king a linen towel to wipe away the sweat from his shaved head.

"I'll be able to tell the artists how you looked as we attacked the enemy, your Majesty," Horemheb said. "You were the image of a Pharaoh, tall and proud in your war chariot. You showed great skill in balancing and firing your arrows at the same time. You did well."

Tutankhamun's face flushed with pleasure at Harm's words. Realizing his sore knee would impede him from keeping up with the army, he swore, "By Seth's great buttocks."

Shocked by the sudden outburst, his personal guards rushed to see what had happened, and then they burst out laughing.

"Leave us," Tutankhamun ordered, somewhat embarrassed. "General, you stay." When they could speak privately he said, "This leg will only slow you down, Uncle. Seth be cursed."

"May he dwell in eternal darkness," Horemheb said.

The young man sighed in exasperation and sat down on a bench outside his tent. "My father would not have been pleased with me. He did not believe in war or violence."

Horemheb took the liberty of sitting down on a bench opposite him and replied angrily, "Your father didn't approve of anything, my Lord, if you'll forgive my bluntness. Now that you're an adult, you understand these things. Without a strong army to protect Egypt, your kingdom will fall. The only way to peace is to be stronger than those who oppose you. It is Maat—a balance."

Tutankhamun nodded. "The gods blessed Akhenaten, may his name be remembered, with an insight none of us understood." He said it more to himself than to his friend. "He loved, and became obsessed with the Aten. He should have been a priest instead of Pharaoh. I see that now." He rubbed his sore knee for a few moments, trying to ease the pain. "I will go with you as far as the place where you leave your horses."

Horemheb nodded, knowing it would be pointless to argue. "Very good, Majesty. The men will be pleased, but I insist on leaving a company with you to protect the horses in case the Nubians try to attack from the rear."

Tutankhamun stood and stretched his arms over his head. "That's settled then. Now I'm going for a swim."

Horemheb laughed, because Pharaoh meant of course, that Paramessu and twenty guards would swim with him, keeping watch for wayward crocodiles and hippos.

CHAPTER TWENTY-THREE

AY'S SHADOW

Back in the capital of Thebes, Lady Benefer tossed and turned, unable to sleep. A noise startled her in the middle of the night and she went to the window.

"Something's wrong," she said to her husband. "I've just seen the royal midwives running to the palace. She'll need me."

Ramose nodded and hurried with his wife the short distance to the palace. When they arrived, they heard the Royal Wife cry out in pain. Benefer rushed into Ankhesenamun's room to help. Word quickly spread through the palace and the guards cleared the corridors. Ramose joined with members of the king's council in the garden to await news.

Ramose grumbled. "Pharaoh should be here. We knew it would be risky for Tutankhamun to be gone at such a time."

Lord Padiaset, high priest of Amun stood. "I'll offer prayers and incense for her safe delivery," and then left to carry out his promise.

As the sun was rising, Pharaoh Tutankhamun's daughter arrived stillborn and the people of Thebes went into mourning. Lady Benefer stayed at her side, holding her hand through the night. The two women embraced and wept until there were no more tears.

Later, at his friend Maya's house, Ramose became concerned. "His majesty has to be told."

"Not so, Mose," Maya said. "If Pharaoh is engaged in battle, such news will affect him and his men. If they lose heart, it could mean a defeat."

Ramose nodded. "You're right, of course. I didn't think. It is Ay who decides these things anyway. But I don't trust Ay. In fact he may have already sent a messenger pigeon hoping to cause such a defeat."

"No," Maya answered, "the Lord Chamberlain told me Ay hasn't decided when to send the message."

Just then a stranger, an elderly woman, approached Maya's villa and the servants admitted her into the foyer.

"Come along," Maya insisted, leading his friend to the front of the house. The elderly woman bowed her head slightly to the two noblemen.

"Mother Bakht," Maya began. "Come sit in the garden." He offered her refreshment, but she shook her head and sat down on a polished limestone bench. Ramose took a moment to remember where he had last seen the woman, then remembered she had been the previous queen's chief mid-wife.

"I've asked you here," Maya started, but she interrupted him.

"I know why I'm here, my Lord. You want to know if Lord Ay interfered with the birth of Pharaoh's baby. I am endangering myself by coming here." The men knew she spoke the truth, and they would need to make her visit worth her while.

"Agreed, Mother, we are grateful," Ramose said.

"Good," Bakht sighed. "I assure you Lord Ay did not pay any of my women to harm the baby. The poor infant, may the gods welcome her."

"No poison or herbal medicines were used that could have caused the stillbirth?" Ramose asked.

"None," Bakht replied somberly.

"Will she be able to have another?" Maya asked.

"Yes, of course, provided she is given enough rest and food. Even next year it would be possible."

"Then accept our thanks, dear woman," Maya said. Standing he handed her several silver coins.

She continued to hold her hand out. "I am grateful noble Lords and I will say nothing."

Maya looked at his friend and then took more coins from his purse and added them to those in her hand.

"I will be silent, my Lords," she said. Maya walked her to the door.

When he came back, Ramose asked, "Can we trust her?"

"She doesn't like Ay any more than we do, my friend. She'll not say anything. As it happens, she's a relative on my mother's side, so she'll be loyal."

Ramose thought for a moment. "It is you who must set sail at first light, brother. Ay doesn't need to know you have gone."

"All right, I'll go, but remember, messengers to the king risk their lives every time they enter his presence. Many end up dead."

In the south, at Pharaoh's camp beside the first whitewater rapids, the army divided into two regiments. Horemheb's army would advance farther south, beyond the second whitewater rapids and engage the enemy again. Tutankhamun's company would advance and encircle Horemheb's horses and supplies in a defensive position.

Horemheb's men marched two days and attacked the Nubians on the plain above the second whitewater rapids. Once again his archers were responsible for the Nubian's defeat.

Because of his leg injury, Pharaoh remained with his troops, where Horemheb's warriors left their horses before climbing up onto the African plain. His regiment engaged the Nubians who fired arrows from the tops of the canyon cliffs. His majesty's skill with the bow motivated his warriors. They shouted in triumph as they watched their attackers fall one after the other from high above.

Two days later, Tutankhamun heard cheering as Horemheb returned with his men. "We have suffered few casualties, Majesty," Horemheb reported. "We've taken so many prisoners we've run out of rope to tie them up."

"Horus has blessed us," Tutankhamun declared. The men shouted and pounded their shields with their short swords. Their jubilation continued all the way back to the fortress at Swentet.

The day after their return, a merchant vessel docked in port. A short time after, Horemheb saw his brother-in-law coming toward him. His heart sank, knowing that Maya's presence could only be a bad omen.

After greeting each other, Horemheb took Maya aside. "What news, Brother? Why have you come?"

"Pharaoh's baby is dead," Maya said. "There is no other way to say it. His daughter has been delivered stillborn. Thebes is in mourning.?"

Horemheb sat down on a makeshift stool. He felt as if he'd had the wind knocked out of him. "This will destroy him," he said. "Marriages between brothers and sisters are not accepted by the gods. Ah," he sighed. "This only proves it. Such sad news, and Pharaoh has been so excited about his victory here. I can't think of how to tell him." Paramessu came at that moment and greeted Maya. Horemheb told him the news.

The three of them sat silently until Paramessu finally made a suggestion. "You must take him somewhere away from his men, to tell him, General. That way he can express his emotions privately. In fact, brothers, I wouldn't tell the army about it until we're almost home." He saw Horemheb nodding and continued. "The men are celebrating a great victory and you must let them enjoy it."

"Well spoken," Horemheb said. "We'll do as you say. It would also be best if you returned before Pharaoh sees you, Maya. You don't want Pharaoh to associate your face with bad news. Unconsciously, every time he sees you he'd think of what happened."

"I agree," Maya replied. His voice sounded relieved now that he would not have to see the king. "My ship is returning at midday and I'll be on board. Ramose and I wanted to be the first to bring you the news. We know from Mother Bakht, the chief midwife, that Ay had nothing to do with the death of the baby."

"Thank you for that," Horemheb said. "You've given me time to prepare his majesty. It will be hard and I'm not looking forward to it."

He called for beer and for a while they spoke of other things before Maya left. When his ship sailed, Horemheb stood at the entrance of his tent and watched it heading north. He asked for his horse and rode to Pharaoh's galley.

Horemheb knew that Tutankhamun had just enjoyed the pleasures of a bath and a good meal in his cabin. All of the luxuries of Egypt were available on the great ship. He knocked at the door and was told to enter.

"Uncle," Pharaoh said, "I think I have washed away half of Nubia."

"My Son," Horemheb replied with a troubled expression. "I'm deeply concerned about something, and I thought if you would ride with me we could talk about it."

"Of course, Uncle. Let me dress while you tell the guards to bring my horse."

"Thank you, Majesty." He turned and left the cabin. He told the guards his plan, then waited beside his horse until Pharaoh came out and mounted his. Ten guards went with them for protection as Horemheb led Pharaoh a short distance into the hills.

"Wait for us here," the general ordered the guards. "We'll be up there near that outcropping of boulders." His men saluted and watched as their leaders continued up the path.

Dismounting, they sat on the edge of the largest boulder and looked down at the river and ships below.

"Now, what is it, Uncle? What is troubling you?"

Horemheb bowed his head and prayed for the strength to control his emotions.

As Tut learned the news of his baby's death, his eyes filled with tears and he cried out as loudly as he could. The sound echoed back from the walls of the deep canyon. He struck the boulder closest to him with his fist and then rubbed the pain away.

Horemheb waited until Pharaoh regained control of himself, then walked with him back to their horses.

The next year Queen Ankhesenamun awaited another child. The king would not allow her to leave the palace during her months of confinement and her midwives were with her constantly. Lord Pentu, physician and successor to his ill-fated predecessor, kept a close watch on every aspect of the queen's life.

One day, while Horemheb and Tutankhamun were out on an overnight hunt, the older man regretted what he had to say. "Once again, I cannot be here in Thebes when your baby is born, Majesty."

They were in the marshlands north of the capital. While not born a noble, Horemheb loved wildfowling, as did the royal family. By using throw sticks and bows and arrows with great skill, they brought down geese and other water birds. The king didn't respond to his comment right away, disappointed to hear his uncle's announcement.

Turning to face his mentor, he spoke in a quiet voice. "Why is that, General? Pharaoh is not sending you away."

"True enough, Great King." Sitting down on the dead trunk of a large palm tree, he continued. "The Asiatics have attacked us again in the north and I must return with the army in a few days' time." He saw the disappointment on the young man's face. "Your grandfather has known about this for some time. I thought he would have told you, my Son."

Tutankhamun sat down on the log a few feet away. "I know you have your new wife to hold you here, General. These are difficult days for Ankhesenamun and I am worried about her. Your wife is a great comfort to both of us."

He referred to Lady Mutnodjmet, widow of his friend Nakhtmin. Horemheb had loved her for several years. He still found her a very attractive woman who complemented his own ambitious personality. Women liked her, including the queen. Their marriage ceremony had been very private. Only their closest friends attended the small service and sumptuous banquet in their honor provided by their closest friends, Ramose and Benefer.

Horemheb nodded. "She's glad to help her queen, Majesty. I will pray for Horus to be with you." He discovered he suddenly felt emotional and cleared his throat. "Remember, it is you who are Pharaoh. You have the power to marry another queen who can give you a son." He saw the frown on the young man's face. "I know that sounds cruel and unfeeling, but it is the way of our pharaohs." The king nodded. His uncle sensed his reticence and quickly added, "For now you must remain strong for your queen's sake."

"And I will, Father," Tutankhamun said. He used the revered title of respect. He stood, took his bow and quiver and ordered the beaters to start up again. Moving slowly through the underbrush, he notched an arrow and followed them. Horemheb grabbed his bow and hurried to catch up.

Two months later, Egypt mourned the loss of Pharaoh's second daughter. When the days of mourning were completed, the tiny mummified stillborn girl joined her sister in the yet unfinished tomb of their father.

Early one morning, the king's steward hurried into the royal apartment. "Majesty, come and see." He led the king out onto the veranda and pointed to the river below. "Yesterday a rider arrived with the news that your victorious army is returning. You can see their ships approaching the capital."

Laughing, Tutankhamun felt like shouting. "It is Horemheb. Call the captain of the guard." The steward bowed slightly and rushed off to find him. When he appeared, the king said, "Tell General Horemheb a procession is being prepared for him tomorrow. We will honor our brave warriors with a great celebration."

The captain saluted and did as ordered.

On the fourth day of the month of Ta-b, with the sun high overhead, the city's wide avenues were prepared for the triumphal arrival of the Army of the North.

The captain of Horemheb's ship approached him. "Thousands are lining the streets, General. I can see the reviewing stand from here. We'd better get you ashore before their majesties arrive." The sounds of large kettledrums began a measured cadence as Horemheb rushed to his chariot. The procession had begun.

Queen Ankhesenamun rode on her golden palanquin, while Pharaoh drove his favorite chariot. The people coordinated their cheers, which sounded like the echoes in a deep rocky canyon. Those on one side of the boulevard shouted "Tu-tankh," while the opposite side shouted back "A-mun." They kept it up all along the street until the royals took their places.

The beat of the large drums intensified as the warriors fell into ranks and marched toward the palace. Thousands of soldiers marched past and saluted the king, their families and friends clapped for them. The officers and commanders came next, followed by hundreds of Asiatic prisoners chained together and forced to march up the avenue.

"What's that?" a man in the crowd shouted. He pointed to a cage pulled by two horses, suspended from a large wagon.

"There's a prisoner in there," another cried out. The delighted crowd jeered and threw things at the man.

Captain Paramessu came next, driving his chariot. The people applauded him and tossed flowers before him, clapping and shouting his name. General Horemheb followed, resplendent in his polished warrior's breastplate. He drove his chariot with determination, armor gleaming in the sun.

"The people like you, General," Paramessu shouted over his shoulder. "You're a hero."

Horemheb only grumbled under his breath and looked straight ahead. As they approached their majesties, he stopped the wagon with the cage.

"Open it and bring him down," Horemheb ordered. His men quickly unlocked the cage and forced the manacled prisoner to lie prostrate on the ground. Horemheb stepped down from his chariot and walked to the royal platform. When he knelt on one knee and saluted Pharaoh, the crowd roared. Tutankhamun stood and raised his hand for silence.

"Welcome, Horemheb, General of the Army of the North. Friend to Pharaoh. The gods are pleased with you this day, as are we." He walked slowly down the steps and approached his uncle with a smile.

Horemheb spoke under his breath. "You must place your foot on the prisoner's neck, Majesty. The miserable dog before you is General Manapa, the commander of the forces against your kingdom."

Tutankhamun motioned for Horemheb to stand, then turned so all could see him place his golden-sandaled foot on his enemy's neck. The crowd cheered again, louder than before.

"Follow me, Majesty," Horemheb said. He led the king toward a special company of one hundred soldiers who marched behind the general's chariot. Each warrior carried a long spike on which the severed hands of the enemy had been impaled. "There are five-thousand right hands here, Great One. Fifty on each spike."

The sight made the young king catch his breath in surprise and horror. Traditionally, the severed hands of the defeated enemy are placed at the king's feet, but never had it been done in this fashion.

Looking away, Pharaoh spoke so only Horemheb could hear. "There will be a great celebration at the palace tomorrow evening for you and your officers. A feast is also being prepared for your men at the barracks, which I hope pleases them." He paused and then caused the crowd to gasp by putting his hand on Horemheb's shoulder. "And I'm glad you're home, Respected Father."

"You honor us, Majesty," Horemheb responded. He saluted the king as the young man walked back up the steps. The drums resumed the cadence as the victory procession continued.

When the procession ended, Ramose met his friend and rode with him to Horemheb's villa. "After you and Pharaoh finished with the enemy commander, Lord Ay whispered something to the king and I heard him. He said you'd make a good Pharaoh and Tutankhamun needed to keep his eye on you."

"What did Pharaoh say?" Horemheb asked.

"He ignored his grandfather and saluted the rest of the army as they marched past."

"He's wise beyond his years," Horemheb replied. "I'm proud of him."

With the completion of Lord Ay's tomb in the Valley of the Kings, Pharaoh's grandfather felt content. As a blood relative, the elderly man believed that if anything happened to his grandson, he would become Pharaoh.

The next day after a meeting of the king's council, Lord Ay took the new chamberlain aside. "Where is His Majesty going tomorrow?"

Lord Meketre hesitated, then answered. "He is hunting with Horemheb and Paramessu, my Lord."

"Thank you, my friend. We are preparing a surprise for him."

When Ay reached his villa, he sent for the captain of the king's guards. Upon his arrival, he led the officer into the garden where someone else awaited.

Ay introduced the other man. "Mena and I have something we would like you to do for us, Captain."

He watched as the officer became nervous when introduced to old Queen Tiye's notorious servant. Many at court knew the name, but no one really knew what the man looked like. Ay liked the fact that Mena stayed in the shadows. Mena looked at Lord Ay with a twisted smile. Ay could see the fear on Captain Sefu's face.

"Before the hunt tomorrow, Captain, I want you to notice everything the king takes with him. Which of his six chariots he chooses. What bow will he use? Most important of all, where will he be hunting."

"As you wish, Lord Vizier," Captain Sefu replied. "Is there a particular reason for all this information?"

Ay didn't like the impertinent question and nearly exploded.

Mena saw Ay's reaction and spoke up. "Let's just say we want to give His Majesty a gift for his next hunt and we need this information. It is a secret, so don't breathe a word."

"Understood, my Lord. Will there be anything else?"

Ay, now under control, took his arm and said, "Let's share a jar. You can tell me more about your wonderful family." The older man had no real interest in the officer, and kept his face as blank as a desert cliff.

The Captain looked around for Mena, but he had disappeared into the shadows. Flattered that Pharaoh's Chief Advisor showed an interest in him, Sefu told him everything.

CHAPTER TWENTY-FOUR

THE HUNT

Out on the marshland not far from Thebes, Pharaoh and his uncle rested after an enjoyable day's hunt. "There must be a million stars out tonight," Tutankhamun sighed. He lay on his blanket, arms folded behind his head. "Not that I could count to a million."

"It's true," Horemheb agreed, his eyes fixed on the vast canopy of stars. The large transparent cloud called the Pool of Cow's Milk shown vividly that night, much to the delight of the two men.

"I've missed these hunts," Tutankhamun said. "I wish my father had liked to hunt. I can hardly remember him now."

Horemheb didn't respond, but simply closed his eyes for a moment. His voice filled with emotion. "I only wish the gods had given me a son like you, Majesty. You've grown into a fine man, and a good hunter."

Tutankhamun looked touched…and didn't respond.

Horemheb spoke in an officious tone. "You brought down more geese today than I, Oh Worthy Archer." His words made the king laugh. "The guards say you are an excellent marksman, and it pleases me to hear them praise you."

The king felt proud. "I had a great teacher, Father, I still want you to teach me how to use a fighting spear. You told me you used one all the time growing up."

Horemheb laughed. "I'd forgotten. It seems so long ago. But I did become good at it, I must admit."

They were silent for a longer period and marveled at a falling star streaking across the blackness of the night sky. "There's another arrow from Hathor's bow," the general observed. "Did you know that some of those rocks that fall from the sky are buried in your ancestors' tombs? They have small amounts of iron and gold in them that can be made into jewels and other precious objects. They are considered very sacred because they fall from the sky."

Tutankhamun began to yawn. "But where do they come from?"

"From the gods, Majesty."

Something had been troubling Horemheb all day, so just before they fell asleep he asked the young man about it.

"Have you noticed Captain Merkha following you around, my Son? He's been watching you very closely."

"No," Tutankhamun said. But then he sat up. "Now that you mention it, he has been acting strangely. He has examined my bow and arrows and wanted to know the name of this place. What is he doing?"

"He's reporting to someone, Majesty," Horemheb said. "After the death of your father, wasn't the Royal Guard put under your grandfather's control?"

"Of course," the young man said.

"Ay's making sure you know he's watching your every move." That silenced the king.

What is the old man doing? Horemheb thought.

Tutankhamun's voice became angry. "But if he wanted to turn the guards against me, wouldn't he have tried something by now?"

"The people love you too much, my Son," Horemheb answered. "The guards, the courtiers, no one would let him get away with such an evil act. The gods would not allow it, Majesty."

"It is kind for you to say, Father, but we both know that isn't true." He laid back down and pulled his blanket around himself against the chill in the air. "This is another reason you cannot return north, General. My family needs your protection from grandfather and anyone else who might attempt to harm us."

Horemheb shook his head, genuinely conflicted. "I must return, Majesty. The army needs me. I have to go for Egypt's sake. We must push back the Asiatics once and for all."

The king sat up again so he could see the general's face, which made it even harder for Horemheb to continue. "I will leave Paramessu here to protect you. He's my closest friend and a good soldier. I trust Messu with my life, Majesty. I know he will give his life to protect you and Ankhesenamun. Your grandfather will be told he's staying in Thebes to be near his invalid father."

Tutankhamun sighed. "I see. It is Egypt that comes first then. As the gods will. So be it." He soon drifted off to sleep as Horemheb just lay there, his mind torn between his love for Egypt and for the one he had sworn to protect. It took him a long time to finally fall asleep.

After Horemheb's departure the following week, Pharaoh gave Captain Paramessu an apartment in the palace next to the royal family. Tutankhamun liked him at once because he had many of the same personality traits as Horemheb.

Ay, on the other hand, did his best to ignore the officer's presence. At the next council meeting, he raised his voice and said to the captain, "I told you to leave."

"I obey only His Majesty," Paramessu shot back.

"Majesty," Ay said, turning toward the king. "I insist. These are matters of state."

"We will tell you one last time Lord Ay," Tutankhamun said. "Where we go, the captain goes. Do not make us tell you again."

Anxious looks passed around the table. No one spoke to Lord Ay in such a way. Pharaoh's grandfather realized he may have overstepped his authority.

"Of course, Majesty, as you will," the elderly man said. His answer surprised everyone.

Later, Horemheb's aide reminded Tutankhamun of something he had said many times, "A cobra cannot change its venom, Great One. That old man's overly polite response is an attempt to maneuver around you, Pharaoh. He'll try it again."

Tutankhamun nodded. "I grow tired of his attempts to control me."

"You must never allow yourself to be alone with him, Majesty. Promise me."

"You exceed your authority, Captain," Pharaoh said. "But we do appreciate your devotion."

Paramessu saluted and stopped talking.

A week passed and the captain received a summons to the royal apartment.

"We would like to go hunting, Captain, as Horemheb and I used to do. Organize it."

In a private workshop not far from the palace, Mena watched the chariot maker examine the royal vehicle.

A well-muscled workman admired the craftsmanship. "I can see why the king likes this one. It's lightweight and all its connections skillfully attached to the main frame. Look how well the yoke and pole have been put together. This is good work."

"I didn't bring it to you to be admired, Sudi," Mena growled. "We want you to weaken something so the wheel will come off."

"That's easy, my Lord. As you can see, the wheels have six spokes. They are connected to the rim with wet cow intestines. When they dry they can't be moved. You only have to cut through two of the connections and the wheel will disintegrate."

The disfigured man spoke in his raspy deep voice. "Not I, Sudi. It is you who will do the cutting. Do so at once."

"Have you brought what I asked for?"

"It's all here, my friend. One Deben of pure gold."

"Then, watch closely," Sudi admonished. Using a sharp blade he cut half way through the tough dried gut that connected the spoke to the wheel. He did the same to the spoke next to it as well. "From this side you can't see anything wrong, my Lord. I would suggest, however, that whoever transports it on and off the ship handle it carefully."

"Understood," Mena said. He walked toward his accomplice with the gold bar on a blue cloth.

Sudi didn't see the hidden blade until too late as Mena thrust it into his heart, killing him at once.

"Come," he called to six slaves who entered and carefully picked up the chariot and carried it away. Mena stepped over Sudi's body and hissed, "Seth will welcome you my brother for what you have done."

THE HUNT

Two days later, early in the morning, a company of guardsmen led by Captain Merkha sailed north to the marshlands. They headed for the hunting ground that Horemheb often used.

The king brought his favorite chariot—the one he felt responded best to his driving skills. It made him feel secure. He knew every part of it by touch. The large flat plain on which they would hunt supported gazelles and other game in abundance, and the king looked forward to the diversion.

At the end of the first day, Paramessu felt it had been successful. "You were very good today, Majesty. Two gazelles. That's amazing."

Tutankhamun did well, while the captain had not brought down anything. The guards joked with the officer about it that evening around the campfire, while praising the skill and success of Pharaoh.

Paramessu grinned. "Wait until tomorrow, Great One. You'll not stand a chance." The guards guffawed, making good-humored sport of the captain. Jars of beer cooled by the river were brought from the ship. Roasted venison never tasted as good as it did around a campfire.

In the morning, Paramessu awakened before his men. He saw Tutankhamun standing outside his tent watching the sky. All the world appeared washed with a somber shade of ochre. The sun rose slowly, a dull ball of orange on the horizon.

The king's groom readied Pharaoh's horses and hitched them to the chariot. By this time, Merkha's men were awake. An understanding existed between the officers to give the king a head start. They admired Pharaoh's skill in driving close enough to fleeing game, and then his ability to bring down the quarry with his bow.

"I see gazelles!" the king suddenly exclaimed, and leapt onto his chariot. Taking his bow and quiver from the groom, he urged on his horses, hoping to get well ahead of his competition. Flicking the reins, he raced away from camp. Paramessu ran to his chariot and hurried after him. Tutankhamun nocked his first arrow, took aim and brought down a large gazelle. Then, something went terribly wrong.

Time stood still as Paramessu watched in horror. The left wheel of the king's chariot struck a rock, shattering the wheel, causing the axel to dig into the dirt. The shock threw Tutankhamun forward onto the ground with a loud thud.

Instantaneously there came a sickening crunch as one of the wheels ran over him.

"By the gods!" Paramessu shouted. He pulled up and leapt to where the king lay crumpled in the dust. Tutankhamun didn't respond to the officer's shouts. Merkha arrived and Paramessu shouted, "Send for the physician! Have the men bring a stretcher." Paramessu stayed with the king and didn't like what he saw. The weight of the chariot had gone over the king's left side and it was evident some of his ribs had been crushed. His left thigh also looked broken. The soldiers arrived with the physician and a litter. Carefully, they picked up the wounded king, they rushed him back to the ship. The healer rode on Paramessu's chariot so they could arrive before the litter.

"By Seth's entrails," the healer exclaimed. "What happened?"

Paramessu told him what he had seen. They laid Pharaoh out on deck where his servants tried their best to bathe him.

"These are serious wounds, Captain," the physician said. "We must leave at once using every oar available. Time is crucial. He could die before we get to Thebes." The new royal physician had stepped into the ill-fated sandals of Lord Pentu and now sensed his own doom. No one on board spoke. Several guardsmen stayed behind with the other chariots and horses as the king's ship raced for home. The oarsmen fought the strong current, but by mid-morning they reached the capital.

"No one must know Pharaoh has been injured," Paramessu ordered. "Just say it is one of the men wounded in the hunt. We'll rush his majesty to the palace."

Tutankhamun remained unconscious as eight men placed his bloody body onto the litter and ran behind Paramessu, who led on horseback. Only a few curious onlookers watched as they passed by. At the palace, the guards and servants recognized the king. Their cries of alarm echoed through the halls.

In all the confusion, Captain Merkha managed to slip out of the palace and ride to Ay's villa. He pounded on the door until Mena let him in and took him to the Chief Advisor relaxing beside the garden pool. Rushing to his side Merkha shouted, "The king's been seriously injured, my Lord. He may not live."

"Pray the gods will save him," Ay said. His voice lacked any sincerity. He looked at the obviously shaken officer and decided the man could not be trusted.

"Take me to him."

As Merkha turned to follow Lord Ay, a sharp pain struck his back and the blade of a short sword burst through the front of his chest. Mena's evil smile looked down on him as Merkha crumpled to the floor.

Queen Ankhesenamun held her husband's head on her lap. Tutankhamun lay dying. The physician had told her his ribs were crushed and his left thighbone broken. He regained consciousness from time to time and the physician forced him to drink drugged wine for the pain.

"His left lung has collapsed from the injury, Majesty. He can barely breathe." Ankhesenamun held Tutankhamun's hand, still covered with blood.

Suddenly her husband squeezed hers and whispered three words, "Letter", "north", "prince."

The queen felt his hand go limp along with the rest of his body. "No, no, Brother," she cried out. "Stay with me." She dropped his hand. "He's gone."

"Leave him to us, my Lady," the physician said. Helping her stand, he called for the queen's servants to take her back to her bedchamber. "I'll bring her a sleeping potion as soon as I'm finished," he told them.

Ankhesenamun's maidservants brought her a basin of water. She stripped off her robe and they washed away her husband's blood. An attendant brought her a clean nightgown. Shortly after, the physician asked permission to enter. She nodded and sat down at her dressing table.

"Drink this, Majesty," the healer said. "It will help you rest. Pharaoh's body, may he be remembered, has been taken by the priests to the House of the Dead. You must leave him in their care." He placed the golden cup on her table and bowed his head.

"Leave us," the queen said. "Please leave us good physician. I know you did all you could. I pray your death will be swifter and more merciful than Pharaoh's."

"May it be so, Great Lady," the physician said. His voice cracked as he began to resign himself to his fate. He bowed his head again and left the chamber. The queen lifted the cup and drank the wine.

"Send for Captain Khui," she ordered the steward. When the officer arrived and saluted, the queen said, "Find Maya, Captain. Bring him to me first thing in the morning."

"Yes, Majesty," the captain replied, saluted, and then left.

"Leave us," Ankhesenamun told her servants. "Kebi, I want you to sleep here on the divan. I may need you in the night."

"Yes, Majesty," her lady-in-waiting and friend answered.

The queen lay across her bed exhausted. She tried to cry, but no tears came. She closed her eyes, but unfortunately all she could see were images of her husband's horrible injuries. Finally, the power of the potion eased her into a deep sleep.

She awakened in the morning to the sound of the steward's voice calling her. He stood at the door when Kebi opened it for him.

"Majesty, Lord Maya is in the foyer. You summoned him last night."

"Thank you," she replied. "You are excused." The servant bowed and withdrew.

The queen's attendants prepared her bath and helped her dress. Before she ate her morning meal she went to the foyer. Captain Khui waited with Maya and the latter fell prostrate as she approached them.

"Captain, I need you to bring Pharaoh's scribe at once." The officer saluted and left to carry out her instructions.

"Lord Maya," she said turning to him. "I need to write a letter. If you could wait out on the veranda I will not be long."

"Of course, Majesty," Maya said.

When the scribe arrived, she dictated a letter and he showed her how to put the royal seal upon it. She dismissed him with a warning not to disclose the subject of the letter on pain of death. Carrying the document, she went out on the veranda and gestured for Maya to come closer.

"Good friend," she began. "I have here an important letter you will take for me to Washukanni in the north. It is so urgent you must leave at once. Captain Khui has chartered a ship for you. This is a matter of life and death. Will you go?"

"Of course, my Queen." Maya bowed. He accepted the letter and asked to whom it should be delivered.

Calling him even closer she whispered the name. "I entrust the future of Egypt to you, Maya. May the gods go with you."

CHAPTER TWENTY-FIVE

THE MASK

During the seventy days of mourning for Tutankhamun, Lord Ay had plans of his own; plans the queen and royal family knew nothing about. He called for his trusted aide Mena to meet him the day after Pharaoh's death.

"I will go to the Valley of Kings," Ay said. "Bring your men."

"Yes, my Lord, or should I say your Majesty'?"

"Quiet, you fool. Bring your men and we will go across together."

It took them the rest of the morning to hire two feluccas and sail across to the west side. When they docked, Ay's slaves brought his carrying chair ashore. They took Pharaoh's Chief Advisor up the dusty path to the location of two new tombs.

When they arrived, Ay said, "Bring the construction foreman to me."

When he came, the workman prostrated himself before the nobleman.

Ay gave him permission to stand. "There has been a change of plans. Mena and his men must move some of Pharaoh's sacred objects. They will do all the work. Here are some coins for you and your workmen. Take the day off." The foreman grinned and hurried off to tell his crew.

"This is what you will do, Mena," Ay said. "Follow me." Stepping down from his chair he entered the new tomb. Artists were hurriedly trying to finish it for Tutankhamun's burial.

"The sarcophagi of his two daughters are to be taken to the other tomb. I'll show you where. I want your men to stay here to see that all my orders are carried out."

"I understand, Majesty." Mena's quiet response made Ay smile.

In the days that followed, Lord Ay removed the furniture from the four rooms. The sacred objects for Tutankhamun's afterlife, were placed in the rooms of the smaller tomb built for himself. Ay also supervised removal of paintings and bas-reliefs from ceilings and walls. Plaster would have to be prepared for the new artwork. He made sure the young pharaoh's four chariots were placed inside as well, as were his walking sticks, bows and arrows. One of the new paintings in the smaller tomb portrayed Tutankhamun leading the battle against the Nubians. Another depicted him receiving tribute from the defeated Asiatics.

One morning several days later, Ay and Mena met to share a meal on Ay's veranda. Mena cleared his throat, and then ran his tongue over his front teeth. "My Lord, the priests have finished Pharaoh's innermost sarcophagus and they want your permission to use the golden mask they've prepared."

"Golden mask?" Ay said.

"Yes, my Lord. They need your approval. It cost a considerable sum."

"Where is it?"

"In the temple of Amun awaiting the arrival of Pharaoh's body."

"Very well. Today you will oversee the finishing touches of the tombs and I will go to the temple." Mena nodded and the two men agreed to meet the next morning.

With the sun at its zenith, Ay's bearers carried him quickly to the temple. Dozens of priests came out to greet him. They surrounded him as he stepped out of his carrying chair and walked up the steps to where the high priest waited.

Inside, Lord Kahma led the elderly man down several steps into the crypt where the final three coffins of the nineteen-year old pharaoh's body would rest temporarily. The six golden shrines to protect the coffins awaited in the nearly finished tomb. The many-layered golden coffins now rested behind the altar in the sanctuary upstairs. Their size and weight would require a wooden sled to move them, pulled by eight oxen.

"Where is the mask?" Ay asked. "What is wrong with it?"

"Nothing my Lord," the high priest answered. "We are asking your approval to use it."

"Well, let me see it." His voice demonstrated his impatience. Two priests carried the beautiful golden mask for him to see. Inlaid with blue lapis lazuli and pure gold on the Nemes head covering, it took Ay's breath away.

"By the gods," he exclaimed. He stared into the face of his departed daughter Nefertiti. "What is this?"

"This mask, my Lord," the priest began, "had been prepared for Tutankhamun's mother, but another had been chosen instead. Because it resembles Tutankhamun so much, we felt it could be incorporated into the final mask covering his divine face."

Ay looked closer. "It does look like my grandson, I agree. The boy resembled Nefertiti a great deal." His feet were growing tired, and the smell of the mildew in the crypt displeased him. Turning, he said, "Use the mask. Mother and Son will be pleased. Now get me out of here."

As the high priest led him up the steps, Ay glanced back at the golden mask. He shivered as Tutankhamun's quartz and obsidian eyes followed him up the stairs.

In the desert near the Great Sea, the Army of the North had been fighting the Hittites for more than two months. Their allies, the Mitanni, proved to be strong fighters and expert marksmen, but their combined assault of Kadesh did not succeed. The allies were repeatedly pushed back. With supplies depleted and morale gone, Horemheb and his aide, Mitry, decided to retreat through the desert. They were heading for the sea and their ships.

"Mitry, this has been a difficult campaign," Horemheb said. They had marched all night to avoid the heat of the sun, and were preparing for sleep. "We'll head for Sidon and pray our ships are still there."

"It should take us two weeks to get there, General," Captain Mitry told him. His prediction proved correct. The army cheered when they climbed the last hill and saw their ships anchored in port. A few days later, after all the ships had sailed for home, Horemheb relaxed on deck of the last ship to remain.

Captain Mitry rushed across the deck and blurted out, "May the gods help us, General. May his name be remembered." Mitry made the sign against the evil eye.

"Wait. What did you say?" Horemheb said.

"Tutankhamun died in a hunting accident, General. He fell from his chariot and succumbed to his wounds. Lord Ay is Pharaoh now."

Horemheb shook his head in disbelief. "How do we know this?"

"The ship's captain told me. An Egyptian ship brought the news two months ago."

"Ay is Pharaoh? Gods no." Horemheb shouted. Grabbing his sword he stormed down the gangway. He stopped in front of a large sycamore tree near shore. With all his strength he began to chop it down.

"Damn him," he cried out. "That foul-smelling jackal," he yelled, striking the tree again and again. "Spawn of Seth." His men watched him but kept their distance. "I should have been there," he cried out, before falling exhausted to the ground. Mitry brought him water and ordered the men to return to the ship.

Once his heartbeat returned to normal, Horemheb plunged into the sea. Washing away the sweat with the cool water helped calm his spirit. Seated on deck once more he let the sun dry him off.

"I'm afraid for Paramessu," he said to his aide. "He would not have permitted this to happen. He too may already be dead—murdered perhaps by those trying to kill the king."

Mitry nodded. "If it was murder, then my Lord, there's nothing he or anyone could have done."

Horemheb shook his head. "They may say it was an accident. I'm not so sure."

Horemheb watched in surprise as another Egyptian ship docked the next day. One of its passengers walked over to speak with the crew of Horemheb's ship.

"Our ship has a damaged steering-oar," he told the ship's captain. "We've put in for repairs." At that moment he looked toward the bow of the vessel and saw a familiar face. "Hey, Old Man of the Spear," he yelled. "May the blessings of Horus rest upon you, General."

"Maya? How is this possible?" Horemheb said. As the two rushed to greet each other they laughed and embraced as brothers.

"This has to be an act of the gods, Brother," Maya marveled. "The odds of us both meeting in Sidon are too great for it to have been chance."

"I agree, and this is the last of our ships to sail for home. You see," he said pointing below, "Our oars are ready for departure." Looking for Mitry he shouted, "Captain, bring two jars at once." His aide nodded and went to pull up the beer that had been cooling over the side.

Choosing a shaded spot outside his cabin where they could sit and drink, they enjoyed the beer in silence. Finally Horemheb couldn't wait any longer. With bitter anger in his voice he asked, "What really happened to the boy?"

"Paramessu can tell you more than I," Maya said. He went on to share with him all he knew about the accident. When he finished, Horemheb got up and started pacing the deck.

"Such a waste," Horemheb growled. "To die at nineteen. So young. I know Messu did everything he could to protect him." He paused, remembering something and smiled. "That boy did love his chariot." Maya nodded. Returning to his seat Horemheb asked, "Now why have you come so far north, Brother? Surely it is not to see me."

Maya's attitude changed, becoming even more serious. "I have just completed a mission for the queen, Harm. I sailed under a flag of truce and carried an important letter overland to the city of Washukanni. It took many weeks for me to reach the Hittite king."

"Hittites?" Horemheb exploded. "Are we sending letters to the enemy now? What does Ankhesenamun want?"

"You know such letters are sealed, Brother," Maya reminded him. But when he saw Horemheb's face he quickly added, "She did tell me what the letter said in case something happened to it. The Hittites sent me back to tell her an answer would be coming at once."

"Go on," Horemheb insisted. "What did she write?"

"She told the Hittite king that she had no husband, nor any sons to ascend to the throne. She asks their king to send one of his sons to marry her and become Pharaoh."

"By Seth's foul breath," Horemheb swore so loudly the ship's crew turned to see what had happened. "After all we've been though. No, by the gods, never again. No son of the Hyksos will sit on the throne of Egypt again while I'm alive. Gods, Maya. You carried the destruction of Egypt in your hands."

Maya gulped down the last of his beer. "Don't blame the messenger, General. I carried the Queen's words. She told me they came from Tutankhamun himself before he died."

"I can't believe that," Horemheb shot back. Both men became silent. Suddenly inspired, Horemheb knew what he had to do. "I'll walk you back to your ship, Brother," he said. They talked about family and friends on the way. When they reached the ship they found the repairs to Maya's vessel completed. After farewells, Horemheb watched as Maya's ship raised anchor.

"Tell my wife I'm coming home," he shouted. Maya nodded and waved back.

Returning to his men, Horemheb called for Mitry to join him. "Captain, I have an important mission for you. I can entrust it to no one else. You and a company of men of your choosing will remain here until the task I give you has been completed."

"As you command, General."

"I have been told that a Hittite prince is on his way to Thebes. He must be stopped, Mitry, at all costs. He cannot be allowed to reach Egypt." The captain nodded and Horemheb continued. "Whatever you do it must not be done by Egyptian hands." He saw Mitry's look of confusion and explained further.

"The Hittite prince's escort will be coming under a flag of truce. You'll convince his guards that his marriage with Egypt is ill-advised and forbidden by the gods of both our countries." He waited for his words to sink in before adding, "We'll pay his guards, of course. I'll leave enough gold coins to divide among them. That should please them."

"Yes General. Gold speaks the loudest."

"The prince's death must be made to look like an accident. His body is to be treated with respect and returned to his father."

"I understand, General. We'll not let him pass. I'll keep thirty men behind. You can count on us."

"I do, Mitry," Horemheb said. "I'll send a ship back for you and your men when we get home." The captain saluted and left to begin choosing his men.

Standing at the ship's stern, Horemheb looked up at the sky. "I don't know what you were thinking, Tutankhamun. Bringing back the Hittites is not the way to save Egypt. May you look down from your golden life with approval on what I must do."

THE MASK

The journey back to Thebes gave Horemheb plenty of time to reflect on the young pharaoh's death. His men had been demoralized when told of it. For them, the young Pharaoh became a symbol of a new Egypt, ready to lead the world once more. Horemheb, however, became more upset over the fact that Lord Ay had exceeded his authority and taken the throne.

"Seth's buttocks," Horemheb swore. "He's forced Ankhesenamun to marry him. Of course. As his wife, she validates his claim to power." He stood and walked to the railing. As if speaking to the hippos floating past he said, "The poor woman will have been wife to three Pharaohs. First, as wife to Akhenaten, her father. Then, to Tutankhamun, her brother, and now to her grandfather." He shuddered at the horror of it all. Turning his face into the wind he added with a grin, "It also means it is too late for her to wed any Hittite prince."

Four days later, when the ship docked at the capital, there were no crowds to greet them this time. The troops from the other ships had reported their standoff in the north. Only Paramessu and Ramose were there to welcome him home.

"You are as welcome as the annual flooding of the river," Ramose said. His words made Horemheb laugh. The yearly inundation being the happiest time of the year. "Our wives are preparing a feast for you as we speak." Horemheb embraced his oldest friend and held him an instant longer than usual.

Paramessu stood some distance away, not able to look at his commanding officer. When Horemheb greeted him he could only say "I failed you my Lord." His emotions welled up and he turned away. The general took him by the shoulders and turned him around.

"I know you did all you could. Maya told me what he knew about the accident, but said you could tell me more. There'll be time for that later." He jumped into Ramose's chariot and his friend drove them back to town. Paramessu followed on horseback.

Lady Munodjmet greeted her husband at the door and he embraced her. As he inhaled the fragrance of her hair and jasmine perfume, he felt he could hold her forever. Suddenly, he found himself surrounded by children.

"Wait," he shouted, pretending to be afraid. "Who are these little monkeys?" Ramose's children circled the great general and pulled him into the garden.

"Tell us a story," the youngest boy asked. Horemheb fascinated them with tall tales of battles in the desert and voyages on the great river.

At a supper of wild quail cooked in honey and goat's milk, the old friends laughed and reminisced about happier days. The music of a lute and sistrum lent a pleasant atmosphere to their evening. Tutankhamun's name never came up, nor that of his successor. When the women excused themselves, the men moved onto the veranda and watched the sun setting over the Nile. It dipped below the horizon, coloring the sky a dazzling yellow in the far west.

Horemheb sighed and decided to ask for the news he had been dreading. "Tell me what happened that day, Messu. Tell me everything you can remember—everything."

Paramessu did so in great detail. "I relive the accident every night, General. When I try to sleep, I even see it my dreams. I've waited for you to come back to tell you what was going on that day. Tutankhamun told me that Captain Merkha was making him nervous. He said the man was watching his every move and asking all kinds of questions about the hunting ground and the royal chariot. We both thought it was unusual, but I foolishly failed to do anything about it. I see now that Merkha knew something was wrong with Pharaoh's chariot."

"Did you examine it after the accident?"

"No, General. The guards were so angry it had caused Pharaoh's death they took it to the barracks and were going to burn it the next day. No one could find it in the morning. In fact, no one could find Captain Merkha either."

CHAPTER TWENTY-SIX

MAN OF THE SPEAR

"Seth's rotting entrails," Horemheb shouted. "The chariot had to have been tampered with. Now we'll never know." He looked around at his friends. "None of this is to be repeated on pain of death." They nodded and remained silent.

Ramose was quiet a long time, but then said, "Ay is wrong for forcing his granddaughter to marry him. It's not natural. But then of course, she did marry her own brother."

"I agree," Horemheb said. "It goes against Maat. The throne of Egypt needs new blood. The old is weak and impure." His friends nodded and their conversation now turned to family and life in the city.

Horemheb said, "Well, I don't know about you, but I long for my bed."

The couples and Paramessu bid each other good night and left Ramose's villa. After a short ride, Horemheb smiled, pleased to see the familiar outline of his house in the moonlight. His wife arrived shortly after, carried in her chair by their servants.

After sending everyone to their quarters, a blissful silence filled the house. Mutnodjmet undressed and sat at her dressing table brushing her hair. Horemheb lay on the bed watching her as he loved to do.

"I worried about you and prayed to Horus for you, Beloved," she told him in a quiet voice. "All those months in the north without a word."

He got off the bed and sat down on an ebony chair behind her. Taking the brush from her hand, he gently ran it through her hair as she closed her eyes. The lamplight reflecting in her copper mirror lit up the reflection of the beautiful woman he'd married.

He said, "A lamp placed inside an alabaster jar will shine through its translucent sides, my Love. Tonight you seem to be glowing."

"Do I?" she said. "What a nice thing to say." After removing her eye shadow, they went to bed and she lay beside him, holding his hand for a long time.

"I miss him, Djmet," he whispered. "He could have been my son."

"Hush," she whispered. "I know, and he loved you like a father. He told me so many times."

They were silent again, enjoying holding each other. "I must remove that evil man, Djmet," he continued. "When that happens, I will become Pharaoh and my mother's prophecy will have come true. You, Beautiful One, will be queen of Egypt and worshipped by our people." Mutnodjmet could feel his pulse quicken as he talked, making her smile. He spoke now about his real love—his Kemet, the Black Land. His Egypt.

"If Horus wills it," she answered. He turned to her and they made love slowly and with great affection as if they had all the time in the world.

The sound of someone pounding on their front door awakened them the next morning. "My Lord," the steward pushed the door ajar and called to his master. "A messenger from Pharaoh is waiting in the foyer."

Horemheb pulled a sheet around himself and walked slowly toward the front door. He bellowed, "Who dares disturb Pharaoh's general so early in the morning?"

"Pharaoh commands your presence at the palace, my Lord General," the trembling guardsman managed to say.

Horemheb shouted, "Go back and tell the old man I'll be there when I've paid my respects to his grandson. Do you understand?" The man saluted and rushed out.

After a leisurely bath and his morning meal, Horemheb kissed his wife and headed for the military barracks. Paramessu came out to greet him.

"Take me to Tutankhamun's tomb, Messu," he said.

Ten armed men from his regiment joined them. After commandeering a felucca at the river, they sailed across to the Valley of the Kings. Paying the owner several copper coins, they ordered him to wait for their return.

As Horemheb walked up the dusty road toward the tomb, he felt the eerie timelessness of the place. Ancient Pharaohs lay at rest here, in this place where the sun slips below the horizon for the night. Each had left his body here in exchange for a new golden one in the life to come.

"Here it is, General," Paramessu said, pointing to a new tomb sealed with Tutankhamun's name on it.

"Well, look at that. That's not right is it?" Horemheb said. He pointed to the tomb's entrance. "The door should bear the seal of the Pharaoh who succeeds him." He looked at the tomb next to it and said, "This too, is all wrong. Before I left for the war in the north, I saw them working on these tombs. The one on the left had been chosen for Ay's burial. What has this cursed son of Seth done?"

Young boys were in place to hold polished copper mirrors that directed the sunlight into the inner recesses of the burial chamber. Horemheb entered the larger tomb and walked through the four rooms.

Suddenly the general shouted, "Look at this, Messu. These are not Tutankhamun's things. Ay's switched them." He walked angrily around the chamber, knocking objects to the floor. "May the god of darkness swallow his Ka whole."

Outside again, Horemheb said, "I want to see if my nephew is really buried in the other one. Call the priests to open it."

"But it's sealed, General," his aide protested.

"The priests can reseal it when I'm done." It took a good deal of patience, and a few gold coins, but Horemheb felt satisfied that Tutankhamun lay surrounded by the earthly objects he loved. With his body encased in six golden shrines and three sarcophagi, he couldn't see the funeral mask. Looking at the newly painted walls he smiled at the images of Tutankhamun in his chariot fighting the Nubians.

He smiled because the artists painted it exactly as Horemheb had described it. Paramessu and the guardsmen stood beside him.

"Now there is a pharaoh," Horemheb declared.

The priests resealed Tutankamun's tomb and put Ay's name on it according to sacred tradition. Behind Horemheb's back, Paramessu and the guards made the sign against the evil eye because of the sacrilege their general had done.

"Give the priests more coins," Horemheb said. "We'll wait for you at the felucca."

By the time they reached Thebes, night had fallen. The moon hung halfway up the sky, the yellow of its rising turning into a brilliant silver disc. The general and Paramessu agreed to meet in the morning at Horemheb's villa.

The next day, Horemheb and the captain rode in the general's chariot to the palace. They were made to stand in the throne room with other petitioners awaiting the king's pleasure. Some in the room recognized the general and became nervous. Intimated by his presence, they moved as far away from him as they could.

The chamberlain entered and scowled, shaking his staff as he approached the two soldiers. "His majesty commands you to come to his apartment at once, General." The two soldiers followed him down the corridor to the royal residence, but only Horemheb would be admitted. Once inside, he found Pharaoh Ay sitting on the veranda in the shade.

Ay's face was turning red. "You ignored my order, General. That's a dangerous mistake to make and one not taken lightly by your Pharaoh."

Horemheb didn't kneel or bow his head politely. Instead he walked up to Ay's chair and folded his arms—a sign of disrespect. "I obey only the one you've buried in a tomb not his own. You shoved him in a corner and have taken his wife." His voice grew louder as he continued. "I don't take orders from a law-breaking commoner who claims to be Pharaoh." Pleased by the fear he saw in Ay's eyes, he continued, his voice more strident.

"Hear me, old man. I, Horemheb, son of Kheroef, Brother of Pharaoh, now declare myself Vizier of all Egypt. I give you until the end of the Festival of Amun in two months, at which time you will proclaim me Pharaoh."

He saw Ay's eyes rapidly moving, first one way, and then another as if seeking some way to escape. Suddenly, the hair on the back of Horemheb's neck stood up and his warrior's reflexes took over. Stepping quickly aside, he turned just as the blade of Mena's short sword brushed past him. Because of it, the man of shadows lost his balance and started to fall. Horemheb pulled his dagger from his belt and plunged it deep into the assassin's neck.

"Thank Horus," Horemheb exclaimed. He kicked the bloodied body aside and walked closer to the now trembling Ay. "One serpent dead, and another soon to be. Do you think for a moment the army will be behind you—you cursed son of Seth? They will not. Do as I say and you might live. If not, your reign ends here and now."

Ay fell onto his knees, then lay face down before the stonemason's son. "As you command, my Lord," he mumbled in defeat. Without another glance at the self-proclaimed usurper, Horemheb spat on the floor and returned to his friend waiting in the foyer.

"Call the guards," he ordered Paramessu. "There's some filth that needs to be removed from the veranda."

Queen Ankhesenamun hurried out to meet the general. The men knelt before her, but she made them stand.

"I could hear from my window what you said to him, General. I am grateful and relieved you are ending his rule. We cannot prove it, but we are convinced he is responsible for my husband's death—may his name be remembered."

"Let it be so," the men responded.

The Queen reached out and put her hand on Horemheb's arm. "Tutankhamun's Ka will be pleased to see his uncle and adopted father succeed him."

"I would like to think so, dear Lady." Bowing his head again, he and his aide left the palace.

A week later, Captain Mitry and his men arrived from Sidon in the north. He went directly to Horemheb's villa. When he had been received and invited to seat himself, Horemheb came into the front room.

Mitry jumped up and saluted. "It has been done as you ordered, General. Prince Zannanza has unfortunately met with an accident on his way to Thebes.

His horse threw him and he broke his neck. His men are returning his body to the king."

"A sad bit of news, Mitry," Horemheb said. Then he smiled. "Especially for the Hittites."

Two months later, when the Festival of Amun came to an end, Pharaoh Ay raised his hand for silence. The large crowd of revelers became quiet.

"Dear subjects. We have been ill these last days," he said. "On the advice of our physicians we can no longer carry out our duties as your Great House. I have chosen General Horemheb, Brother of Pharaoh Amenhotep and Beloved Uncle of Tutankhamun, may their names be remembered, to be my successor."

A great roar of approval filled the temple and courtyard. Its polished walls echoed the applause out into the streets. The city of Thebes celebrated all night long.

No one regretted Ay's departure and allegiances shifted quickly to the popular General of the Army. A week later, Ay died mysteriously in his sleep. An official report stated that a cobra had been seen in his garden that day.

No declaration of mourning would be proclaimed. The new Pharaoh did allow the body to be embalmed respectfully under the ministrations of the priests of Amun. He also permitted the burial in the larger tomb Ay had so desired. Even though most of the courtiers told Horemheb they were convinced Ay had been responsible for his grandson's death.

When the burial ceremonies ended, Paramessu took his general aside. "Why didn't you move Tutankhamun to the right tomb, General?"

"He is in the right tomb, Messu. I cannot undo what the gods have done."

On the day of their coronation, Horemheb and his queen sat on their thrones in the Great Hall marveling at the beneficence of the gods. The double crown of Upper and Lower Egypt sat on his head as if it had been made for him. Standing in the front row of courtiers facing them, were their friends, Ramose, Maya, Paramessu and their wives.

MAN OF THE SPEAR

Former Queen Ankhesenamun sat on a throne next to Queen Mutnodjmet. It was Horemheb's way of honoring his adopted son's widow.

When the ceremony concluded, the royal couple remained to receive guests invited to the ceremony. As the various ambassadors and officials came forward to present themselves and their gifts to Pharaoh Horemheb, the king motioned for Ramose to approach and stand at his side. Between the presentation of the Ambassadors from Cyprus and Phoenicia, the new king leaned over to speak to his friend. "Do you remember long ago when you visited my village?"

"Yes, Majesty," Ramose replied. It pleased him to use the title for his friend. "You said, 'Let's follow the river to the Great Sea and see what the world is like.' I remember."

"And I said a man without a dream is as dead and as lifeless as a stone. Do you remember that too?"

"How could I not remember, Harm. Look at you. Your dreams have come true. I am honored to be your friend. And only for this once will I admit that your mother has been right all along."

Other guests interrupted them, and Horemheb waited for another interval between ambassadors before speaking again. "Only Horus could have done this, Mose."

Trying to sound pompous, Ramose responded. "Pharaoh speaks the truth." He only succeeded in making the Ruler of the World laugh. "May I have permission to bring my gift?" he asked.

Horemheb nodded and his friend walked over to Captain Khui who handed him something long wrapped in blue linen—the color of Pharaoh's war crown. Climbing back up the steps he handed it to the king.

Horemheb smiled as he removed the cloth. He held in his hand a golden spear—as long as the old spear he had carried as a young warrior.

"Aha," Pharaoh shouted. Everyone in the hall turned to look at him. He held the spear high above his head as he had done as a prisoner in a Nubian village many years ago.

"Man of the Spear," Horemheb shouted. The courtiers smiled and applauded him. "I am proud of the name. I am grateful for the memories this brings to my heart and mind, old friend."

The next morning on his first official day as Pharaoh, Horemheb stood on the sandy shore of the Nile. The sun would soon rise to announce a new day. He loved the feel of the sand under his bare feet and he scrunched his toes into it. He stared down at his reflection in the water and saw a well-muscled warrior, with a touch of gray at his temples. The passing years had been kind to him.

His guardsmen remained at a distance, ready should a stray crocodile see the king as an easy meal. Horemheb turned and motioned to his friend to join him. "We're much older than we were that morning back in Nen-nesu, Mose," he said.

"It's true," Ramose said. "You look ever so much older than me."

Horemheb chuckled. He balanced himself on one leg while wrapping the other around the golden spear in the Nubian way. "I count on you to be at my side, my old friend, now Lord Vizier of all Egypt."

"I am here, Majesty. I am honored to serve you and your queen."

They stopped talking and watched as the golden solar orb pushed up from behind the distant hills. The god Ra had awakened from his nighttime journey and had begun his flight toward the west. The two friends moved away from the river and walked back to their chariots. Shu the god of the wind, blew away the morning mist, and the sky became a clear blue. High above, sailing on the wind, a flash of white caught Pharaoh's eye. At first, he thought it to be one bird, but he discovered there were two. As they flew closer, he could see they were falcons. One of them screeched and dove down toward him. At the last moment one falcon dropped something at Pharaoh's feet, then flew back to join the other.

Horemheb bent down and picked it up, looking closely at what he held in his hand. There were some dried twigs and he looked puzzled for a moment, then burst out laughing.

"Look, Mose, they're building their nest." He raised his spear above his head and shouted to them. "Thank you, Wings of Horus. You have made a builder's son Pharaoh. Help me do just that and raise your Egypt to a new glory that will never be forgotten."

Ramose and the guardsmen shouted, "*Bah-ker.* May it be so."

Above them, the wind carried the pair of falcons higher and higher until they vanished into the light of the golden sun.

AFTERWORD

HOREMHEB WITH THE FALCON GOD HORUS

Pharaoh Horemheb also died childless, leaving his throne to a fellow army commander named Pa**rames**su. The new pharaoh changed his name and became Rameses I. With him begins another dynasty—one which, under the rule of his grandson Rameses the Great, would see Egypt rise to new heights of imperial power.

Even though Tutankhamun's ten-year reign was not significant, it is because of the greatness of his tomb that he is remembered. Lord Ay did his rival a great favor in trying to ignore the importance of the boy king and burying him in obscurity. Over the years other tombs were built above it, and it was forgotten. Ay's act assured it would remain undiscovered until that day on November 4th

1922 when Howard Carter walked down some dusty steps and found the burial place of a little known ruler whose name is more famous than any other.

It is perplexing however, to try and understand why Horemheb would take it upon himself the task of removing from Egyptian records the existence of Akhenaten and his son. The City of the Sun's Horizon was dismantled and its stones were used to fill many of the pylons and monuments in Thebes and elsewhere. It is puzzling because the brilliant general served both kings admirably but now tries to erase every trace of them.

Horemheb proved to be a good ruler, and Egypt became stronger and a power to be reckoned with. He appointed judges and regional tribunes—reintroducing local religious authorities and divided legal power between Upper and Lower Egypt between the Viziers of Thebes and Memphis respectively. These deeds are recorded in a stela which the king erected at the foot of his Tenth Pylon at Karnak. Occasionally called the Great Edict of Horemheb it is a copy of the actual text of the king's decree to reestablish order to the Two Lands and curb abuses of state authority. The stela's creation and prominent location emphasizes the great importance which Horemheb placed upon domestic reform.

It is pleasant as a writer to think that perhaps on the day his tomb was discovered, the boy king might have heard Carter's answer to Lord Carnarvon's question: "What do you see?"
Carter replied "Wonderful things!"

I like to think underneath that golden mask, Tut was smiling.

"You waken gladly every day,
all afflictions are expelled.
You traverse eternity in joy."

Tomb inscription

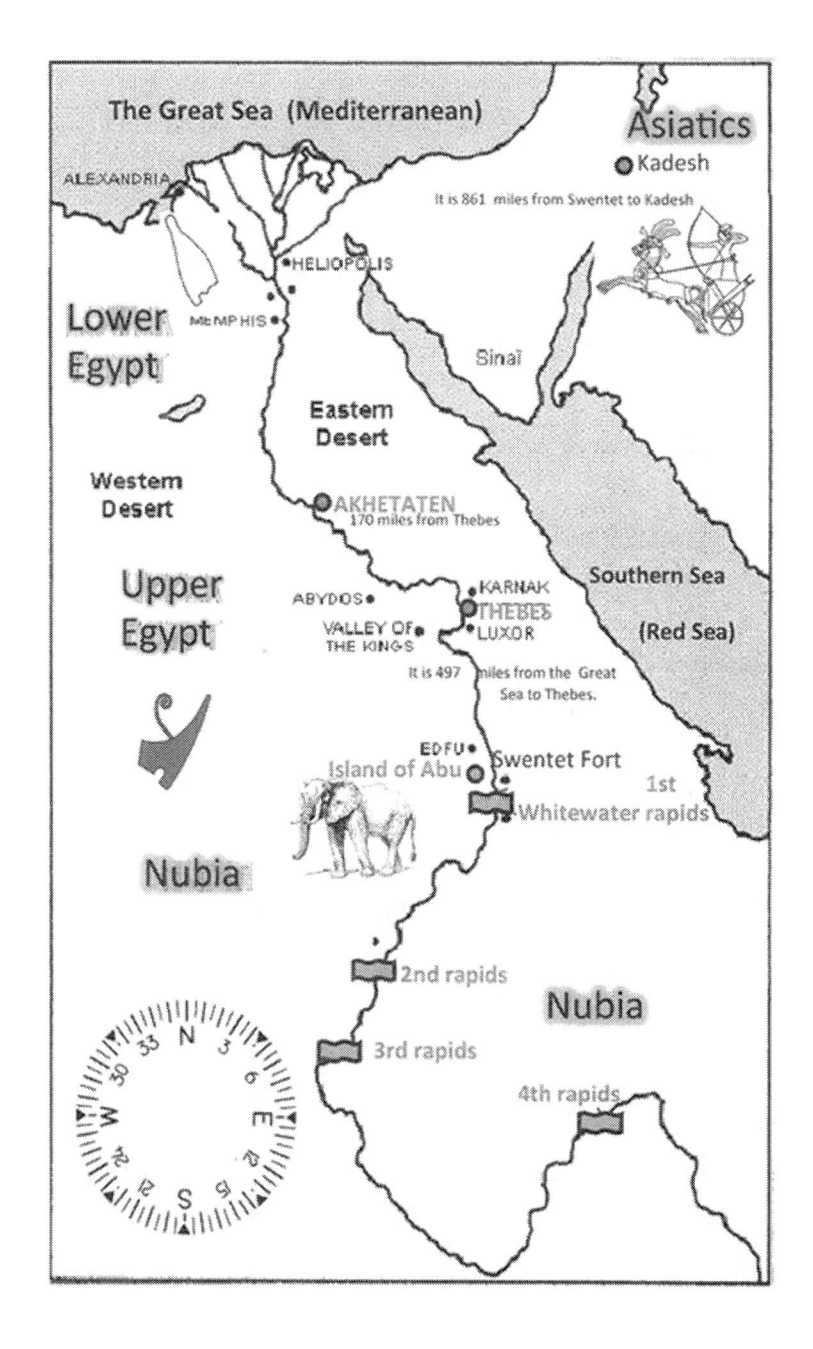

Behind the Golden Mask   Map 1

The Great Sea (Mediterranean)

Asiatics
- Kadesh

ALEXANDRIA

It is 861 miles from Swentet to Kadesh

• HELIOPOLIS

Lower Egypt

• MEMPHIS

Sinai

Eastern Desert

Western Desert

○ AKHETATEN
170 miles from Thebes

Upper Egypt

ABYDOS •

• KARNAK
○ THEBES
• LUXOR

VALLEY OF THE KINGS

Southern Sea (Red Sea)

It is 497 miles from the Great Sea to Thebes.

EDFU •
Island of Abu ○ Swentet Fort

1st Whitewater rapids

Nubia

2nd rapids

Nubia

3rd rapids

4th rapids

Printed in Great Britain
by Amazon